André Caroff's
MADAME ATOMOS

The Resurrection of
Madame Atomos

André Caroff's
MADAME ATOMOS

The Resurrection of
Madame Atomos

Translated by
Michael Shreve

A Black Coat Press Book

Acknowledgements: Thanks to Françoise Carpouzis & Catherine Losserand.

Madame Atomos Change de Peau and *Madame Atomos Fait Du Charme* Copyright © 1968 & 1969 by The Estate of André Caroff; English adaptation Copyright © 2013 by Michael Shreve.
Introduction, Copyright © 2013 by Jean-Marc Lofficier.
Au Vent Mauvais... Copyright © 2008 by François Darnaudet & Jean-Marc Lofficier and The Estate of André Caroff; English adaptation Copyright © 2008 by Jean-Marc & Randy Lofficier.
Cover illustration Copyright © 2013 by Jean-Michel Ponzio.

Visit our website at www.blackcoatpress.com

Table of Contents

Introduction

This volume collects the thirteenth and fourteenth installments of the saga of Madame Atomos, a series of 18 novels published between 1964 and 1970 in the *Angoisse* horror imprint of French publisher Fleuve Noir. Our introduction to Volume 1 contains a biography of its author, André Carpouzis, a.k.a. André Caroff (1924-2009). More information about Fleuve Noir and its popular brands of science fiction and horror can be found in the introductions to the other volumes translated from their imprints and published by Black Coat Press: Richard Bessière's *The Gardens of the Apocalypse*, Gérard Klein's *The More in Time's Eye* and Kurt Steiner's *Ortog*.

The saga of Madame Atomos (her real name is Kanoto Yoshimuta) is about a brilliant but twisted middle-aged female Japanese scientist who is out for revenge against the United States for the bombings of Hiroshima and Nagasaki—where she was born, and where her family died in the nuclear holocaust.

Madame Atomos seeks to repay the United States by unleashing deadly new threats, such as radioactive zombies, giant spiders, a madness-inducing ray, flaming tornadoes, etc. The heroes opposing her are Smith Beffort of the FBI and Yosho Akamatsu of the Japanese Secret Police.

Volume 2 introduced the character of Mie Azusa, a.k.a. Miss Atomos, a younger version of Madame

Atomos, groomed to continue the fight in the event of her death.

In Volume 3, after Mie fell in love with Smith Beffort, she joined the fight against the deadly Madame Atomos who, in the meantime, had returned from the dead.

In Volume 4, Madame Atomos overreaches and the US Army finally destroys her powerful flying fortress. With her organization in shambles, she is forced to re-group, while increasingly devoting all her energies to achieve revenge on Smith Beffort and Mie.

In Volume 5 Madame Atomos continues waging war on the United States, first by turning the hapless residents of Baltimore into blood-thirsty monsters, then by unleashing uncontrollable wild fires over Nevada.

In Volume 6, Madame Atomos exacts a terrible revenge upon her enemies by killing both Dr. Soblen and Bob Beffort, the baby son of Smith Beffort and Mie Azusa. The latter swears revenge upon her once-mistress, while the deadly Japanese mastermind attempts to re-build her evil empire...

Now read on...

Jean-Marc Lofficier

André Caroff

Mme ATOMOS CHANGE DE PEAU

ANGOISSE

FLEUVE NOIR

THE RESURRECTION OF MADAME ATOMOS

Chapter 1

Smith Beffort tore the page off the calendar and

The armored truck drove down Quebec Road, turned onto Queens City Avenue and then turned again to avoid the traffic jams. The route was always the same. The driver and his two guards were completely relaxed. This particular cash transport was actually one of the safest in Cincinnati, maybe in all of Ohio. In fifteen years of service, no incidents, not even the most minor, occurred on this route.

This probably had to do with the fact that truck 504 had only a very short trip. From the general depot to main post office was barely three miles. A perfect drive along big, usually empty streets, going by six permanent checkpoints. No alleyways or bottlenecks. Almost no sharp turns that might hide an ambush. Armored body, puncture-proof tires, bulletproof windows and wind-shield. All the doors of 504 were locked from the outside at departure and could not be opened until arrival. Furthermore, in case of an emergency, the guards could contact police headquarters directly by radio and lock down the gun slots while waiting for help.

In short, the 504 truck seemed impregnable and the experts of the insurance company, during their trials of resistance and maneuverability, had declared that this vehicle answered exactly to the norms of security demanded by the contract signed by Lloyds with the US Post Office.

Today was the first Saturday of the month of May 1968 and the 504 was transporting only 200,000 dollars in used bills. The sky was blue, the temperature relatively mild, and the weather forecast a beautiful weekend throughout Ohio, but with a chance of showers in the evening if the low front moved in from the northwest, etc.

This did not keep the inhabitants of Cincinnati from escaping to the country, although the real exodus did not start until noon when the school children had shaken off the week's fatigue with a typical late morning. Still, no one was working in Cincinnati this morning except for the cabbies, deliverymen, and the occupants of truck 504, who accepted it stoically.

At the corner of Montana Avenue and Harrison Avenue, right after checkpoint 4 and before the building under construction, a gust of wind shook the bended antenna on the roof and the driver said that the weather was probably going to change for the worse. His partner answered that it was all the same to him because he was planning to go to the movies. Afterward the two men began the usual conversation about the movies they had seen lately and the 504 went calmly on its way. The two guards behind them were keeping half an eye on the back of the truck and a limp finger on the triggers of their machine guns. Everything was quiet, normal, routine...

Light traffic; almost no pedestrians; only a little, bottle-green delivery van coming up fast behind the 504. Routine...

The van turned on its blinker, started to pass and disappeared from the guards' sight only show up in the side view mirror. The driver conscientiously squeezed the truck over to the right and glanced in the rear view mirror, thinking that the green van was passing a little too close and then strangely slowing down.

At that very moment, out of sight of the guards and driver of the 504, a man was sliding open a window built into the roof of the van. Then he pressed a button that automatically deployed a telescopic pole that was wired to a powerful battery and it reached out toward the base of the bent antenna on top of the 504. When contact was made, there was a flash and the antenna snapped, flew off its base, broke its second point of contact and curved through the air without even grazing the armored truck's roof.

Then the delivery van finished passing in front of the truck and slowed down again. The two vehicles reached the building under construction. The worksite looked deserted, enclosed by a 15-foot high fence over which you could steel girders sticking up and the arm of a huge crane whose enormous claws were unusually lowered. From this side of the fence no one could tell what was going on at ground level.

All of a sudden the green van moved to the left and turned on its blinker again. The driver of the 504 veered to the right to pass between the sidewalk and vehicle, but hit a pothole and swore as he slammed on the brakes when the van went the wrong way. The collision took place under the crane. The 504 had hit the right side of the van and spun it around, although the truck itself stayed straight, without too much damage, but the engine died.

When an incident like this happens, there are always a few seconds of surprise on both sides.

The green van was stalled across the road and the driver sat still. The truck got its engine started and one of the guards picked up the radio to warn the Central Office as regulations required. No need to sound an alert. With one glance they would say that it could not be an attack!

Meanwhile, the claws of the crane sliced silently through the air, stopped above the truck and dropped, gripping the vehicle up in its four stiff fingers. The "snatch" made a noise that sounded like an explosion as the 504 rose off the ground like a butterfly, over the fence, swinging in the air, while the guard tried in vain to get the antennaless radio working.

In the worksite, hidden from the street, a huge tanker truck was parked. Its tank was open like the door of a cargo plane but open to the sky, and it contained enough water to engulf two vehicles like the 504.

The crane came to a stop over the tank and let down its load, loosening its grip only when the roof was underwater. At the same time, the tanker closed up its jaws and left the worksite while the crane operator and van driver ran off before the eyes of a few petrified witnesses.

Ten minutes later the 504 contained only four corpses and 200,000 dollars, a little wet. It had become a kind of safe that a blowtorch could inevitably break into.

Three months earlier, in February, in Billings, Montana, Madame Atomos had once again escaped from Smith Beffort and in the height of irony had made an appointment to meet again in Cincinnati in May[1]. They knew that the formidable woman was trying to rebuild her criminal organization and that she had some support, for example that incredible A.O.F.M.A.[2], and that she needed vast sums of cash to build her super-laboratory. This, of course, was what Beffort and his team were hoping to stop.

Stripped bare Madame Atomos was dangerous. At the head of a gang she was very dangerous. In control of a laboratory that could provide her with a disintegrating ray again, she would become dreadfully dangerous. The woman's only ambition in life was to destroy and murder. Hiroshima and Nagasaki had been the original pretext for Madame Atomos' hatred for the United States, but what remained of that now?

Moreover, who could swear that the terrible woman was still of sound mind? Who could say that she was working toward a specific goal, according to a determined plan, and not just playing it by ear?

Kill, kill, kill… Little Bob Beffort, Doctor Soblen and Lucky Simms were her last victims[3]. Who would be eliminated in her next operation?

"We're four days into the month of May," Smith Beffort said, "and she hasn't shown herself yet. I wonder if she's not going to strike somewhere else while we're waiting here in Cincinnati?"

Mie and Yosho Akamatsu did not even look up. They kept playing chess as if it were nothing. Little by little as the days passed Smith was becoming more and

---

[1] See *The Evil of Madame Atomos* in *The Revenge of Madame Atomos*.
[2] American Organization of the Friends of Madame Atomos.
[3] See *The Revenge of Madame Atomos*, q.v.

more nervous and irritable. Several times over the course of the past few years Madame Atomos had been at his mercy, but the diabolical Japanese woman had always found a way to escape the final punishment.

Smith was beginning to feel an inferiority complex after this series of failures. In the end he wondered whether he was really capable of thwarting the projects of his archenemy. Of course, Atomos City, Atomos Island and her criminal organization had been destroyed, but all that might count for nothing if Madame Atomos became rich again.

Well, that was exactly what she was trying to do.

At 10:30 the telephone rang in the living room of the bungalow that Beffort had rented for his stay in Cincinnati. The G-man got his long legs moving, crossed the room and picked it up.

"Smith Beffort?"

"That's me..."

"Samuel Tiger here. I have some news for you." Tiger was the director of the regional FBI office.

"Madame Atomos?" Beffort asked, full of hope.

"To tell you the truth, I don't know. I just called because you asked me to inform you of any incidents..."

"Exactly," Beffort agreed. "What's it about?"

"Something pretty weird," Tiger started haltingly. "Fifteen minutes ago two calls notified the west side police station that an armored truck was lifted off the road by a crane and stuck in a construction site..."

"Lifted?" Beffort asked. "What does that mean?"

"Whatever you think it means," Tiger was forced to say. "In fact, the truck was literally picked up off the ground and since then nobody has seen it. Personally I think it's a little too much."

"A hoax?"

Tiger hesitated again before saying, "I'd bet on a hoax if the truck wasn't carrying 200,000 dollars."

Beffort whistled softly and asked, "Don't beat around the bush, would you? When such an amount has disappeared, it's usually not…"

"I know!" Tiger interjected. "But there's something kooky in this affair. The truck had a radio but didn't use it. Moreover, when they went to look on the other side of the fence, they didn't find it and they couldn't find its tire tracks in the mud."

Beffort snickered to himself. He was already convinced that only Madame Atomos could pull off such a stunt.

"And," Tiger continued, "I forgot to tell you that before getting grappled by the crane the truck had an accident with another vehicle whose driver took off."

"And the crane operator?"

"Also took off."

"Who called the west side station?"

"Two witnesses who don't know each other. They both live across the street from the worksite. One is a civil servant and the other's a shopkeeper."

"Give me their addresses. I guess you're going to go looking for the armored truck?"

"Of course. And at the same time we'll try to find out who was driving the vehicle that caused the accident. Here's the names and addresses of the witnesses…"

Smith Beffort and Akamatsu crossed Harrison Avenue and entered the construction site.

"Strange story," Akamatsu commented after listening to the two witnesses being questioned by Beffort. "They agree on all points, but only the shopkeeper mentioned a man in a leather jacket."

That was the man with the telescopic rod who had cut off the 504's antenna. According to the witness, the man had jumped out of the little green van right after the truck had crossed over the fence and he walked calmly toward a black Buick with a case that looked like it contained a fishing rod.

"I'm not so interested in the details," Beffort said dryly. "Looking at the result of the operation, my mental adding machine tells me that Madame Atomos just made off with 200,000 dollars, all the while proving once again how clever she is! The 504 was impregnable, had a radio and some firepower. Madame Atomos managed to silence the radio and stop the truck under the crane. So, with no target the guards didn't have any reason at all to use their weapons. Nice work!"

Akamatsu nodded half-heartedly and leaned with Beffort over the countless tire tracks that criss-crossed the site's muddy ground. Nothing but heavy loads, some zigzagging grooves from a wheelbarrow, a couple of intersecting lines from a motorcycle...

"The truck didn't drive by here," Beffort declared as he lit a cigarette. "Since it didn't just vanish, we have to figure that they loaded it on a platform. Hold on! Look at these tracks, Yosho."

Twenty inches wide and ten deep. S-shaped in profile and W from above. The trench still wet and thus relatively fresh. The two men followed them, ended up at the exit and saw the muddy tracks head toward Bridge-town. Farther down the road, the tracks faded into nothingness.

"No need to go on," Beffort said. "Better get back to headquarters and order the patrol cars to stop any rigs over 15 tons. Still, I wonder what could have kept the guards from opening fire?"

Akamatsu shrugged his shoulders, buried his hands in his pockets, but said nothing. He knew that the question was only the first of an endless series.

At noon Samuel Tiger arrived home. It was not usual for him, but a telephone call from his wife had made him jump into his car.

"Come, quick, Sam! Come, quick! I can't move... just enough strength to drag myself to the telephone... I think I'm going to die!" Then, inexplicably, she hung up. Tiger's two return calls remained unanswered, so he ran out of his office as worried as a man could be in such a situation.

Now he had just left the elevator and stood petrified before the astonishing note pinned to the door of his apartment:

Samuel Tiger, you will die like all the important people in Cincinnati will die within the next eight days. In your apartment you will find your wife's corpse and a lethal trap prepared specially for you. I am telling you because I am following the rules of the game for Operation Ohio that henceforth pits me against Smith Beffort, the federal agents and the Green Dragon Force. From now on, Madame Atomos will strike only after a warning! My intelligence against yours. What is the ordinary object that you should not touch if you want to stay alive? Good death, Samuel Tiger! Hiroshima! Nagasaki! Compliments of Madame Atomos!

It was crazy, unbelievable, and terrifying all at the same time.

Without his wife's phone call and without the dreadful signature of Madame Atomos, Tiger would have thought it was a bad joke. He tried, in fact, to believe this for a few seconds, but how can a man think calmly when he knows that a corpse is waiting for him at home?

Tiger put his key in the lock, opened the door and ran toward the living room. From the entrance he was sure that Helen was dead. Immobile in an armchair, eyes wide open, dilated by horror, she could not have looked more like a corpse.

Tiger bit his lip to keep from screaming, remembering Madame Atomos' warning in time, and walked slowly over to the armchair. He had a son boarding at College Hill High School and wanted to stay alive long enough to see him become a man.

His hand touched his wife's arm, felt it warm and also a certain tensing of the skin. Tiger suddenly realized that, in spite of all appearances, Helen was still alive. She had no visible wounds. They probably injected her with a slow-acting poison and could only be saved by a quick intervention.

Tiger swung around, reached for the nearest telephone and picked it up.

Ordinary object!

The explosion almost tore off his head... and at the same time killed Helen, who had only fainted.

Chapter II

At the same time, in a small rundown factory in Covedale, Scarlett and Keating, Madame Atomos' two top killers, opened the 504 truck like a cheap can of beans and brought out the four corpses and 200,000 dollars.

Since the affair in Billings, that is to say for three months ago, Madame Atomos' team and wealth had grown tremendously. By a curious irony of fate, the sinister Japanese woman found herself forced to imitate Smith Beffort and hire on a whole bunch of criminals of all kinds.

Her gang was becoming the spitting image of the Green Dragon Force with the sole exception that Beffort's men were working for Society. Pulled out of prison by Beffort, Owen Bernitz and his boys were working for the United States with as much zeal as a man on death row sawing through the bars of his cell. Because, in fact, the members of the Green Dragon were saving their hides, if not their souls, since getting rid of Madame Atomos would bring about their complete rehabilitation.

In the other camp, the zeal was no less fierce and the motives pretty much the same. Scarlett, Keating and their buddies had enough crimes on their conscience to fill the archives of the FBI. They were all wanted and would go directly to the electric chair or gas chamber if they fell into the hands of the law.

When all was said and done, one side was lucky enough to be chosen by Smith Beffort and the other side was unlucky enough to be selected by the A.O.F.M.A., Madame Atomos' recruiting office.

However, the Green Dragon Force always knew where to find Beffort, Mie Azusa or Akamatsu. In the Atomos gang only Scarlett and Keating could say what their boss looked like and were able to reach her by radio or telephone using a predetermined code. The others had to be satisfied with following orders and receiving their monthly payments from Scarlett. Madame Atomos was just a shadow, a character that changed all the time, almost a myth to some.

Seclusion, mystery, security.

Thefts, armed robberies, murder.

Scarlett pulled out the walkie-talkie antenna, put the earphones in and pressed the call button. A few seconds passed and the Madame Atomos' voice came over, "A.S. here! Talk S.T.!"

"Operation Harrison wrapped up, Madame," the killer said curtly.

"Perfect. Send the paper to account 679 and burn the sardines in their can. You've done what's needed for the Judge?"

"Everything's ready, Madame."

"Good," Madame Atomos sounded satisfied. "You can talk to me on channel 300 after he's dead. Vacation for 19 hours."

"Got it. Over and out?"

"Over and out," Madame Atomos confirmed.

Scarlett turned off the device, got rid of the earphones and said to Keating, "Lob in the gas. We're going to burn the shack, the truck and the corpses. Everything's set for the Judge?"

Keating gave the thumb's up. "A-Okay. He'll being eating his birth certificate as easy as Tiger and his wife. Ah, the boss has got some smarts, eh?"

Scarlett nodded, silently, gravely. Madame Atomos was beginning to scare him...

Smith Beffort unfolded the anonymous letter that had been put in Judge Stark's mailbox. It read:

You will be dead, Your Honor, before tonight because you fit perfectly within the framework of my Operation Ohio. Just as I warned Samuel Tiger, in order to respect the rules of the game, so I am telling you: Watch out for round objects. Good death, Judge! Hiroshima! Nagasaki! Compliments of Madame Atomos!

Beffort let out a little sigh. He had seen the warning pinned to Tiger's door and knew that this letter was no joke.

Stark, a cold, austere, clean-shaven man verging on sixty, snickered and said, "This damn woman is so sure of herself, isn't she? If she thinks she impresses me, she's wrong. I'm going to do exactly what I've planned to do without being bothered by this ridiculous warning."

His house was surrounded by FBI agents. Akamatsu and Beffort were in his office. He could brag as much as he wanted, Beffort understood it perfectly well. He asked, "What were you planning to do, Judge?"

"Every Saturday I play gold at Gold Manor and I have no intention of breaking my habit."

Beffort furrowed his brow. Mrs. Stark stood up, very pale. Her voice was shaky when she said, "That's crazy, John!"

"I simply refuse to be intimidated!" the Judge replied coldly. "To back down is to encourage crime!"

Very dignified, quite courageous, but completely idiotic when it comes to Madame Atomos, Beffort thought. He said, "Your wife is right, Judge. Madame

Atomos is threatening you with death and she generally keeps this kind of promise. You're going to stay nice and quiet here at home…"

"Don't count on it! You can protect me just as easily at Golf Manor."

"Not if the round object she mentioned is a bullet! We can watch the course and close the roads there, but we can't keep a sharpshooter from bringing you down with a scope on his rifle."

The Judge shook his head. "I'm going to Gold Manor with or without you. I wouldn't want to read in the papers on Monday that Madame Atomos forced Judge Stark to hide out at home all afternoon!"

"It's better than being killed."

"Not when you're a candidate in the upcoming elections. I don't want to play into the hands of my adversaries by covering myself with ridicule."

"You'd rather play into the hands of Madame Atomos?"

"Not particularly, but I'm in no position to sacrifice my popularity for my security."

He did not say it, but he was still figuring that it was a magnificent godsend to put him in the limelight like this. Monday's papers would play up his courage and the readers would be looking at a photograph of the Judge with some caption like, "In spite of all Madame Atomos' threats, Judge Stark played his usual round of golf without a worry…"

Beffort very quickly understood that he would never break the Judge's stubbornness. Moreover, he had no legal means to keep him locked up at home. So, he gave in.

"Okay, we'll go with you to Golf Manor. Just give me one hour. That's how long it will take us to set up our security system. Of course you won't drive. You won't touch anything between your house and the course and you'll play with the balls that we give you. Follow our instructions to the letter, Judge, otherwise it's out of our hands."

"It's a promise, Mr. Beffort. At my age you have no death wish."

Judge Stark arrived at Gold Manor at 3:30 p.m. Beffort and Silver, Tiger's replacement, had done everything in their power to avoid a disaster. The roads had been closed for an hour and specialized teams had gone over the course with a fine-toothed comb, as well as the woods around it. Lookouts were posted at all strategic points that a sniper might use. The clubhouse was not closed, but the golfers had to undergo identity checks, just like the caddies and employees of the bar and locker room.

Since they had to wait, a group of journalists and photographers were standing around near the building. When the Judge got out of the police car, the flashes popped and a murmur arose among the crowd of regulars. Stark was popular in Cincinnati and would undoubtedly be even more so in less than 48 hours. It was a done deal. Dead or alive, they would be talking about him.

"Look at the old dog," Silver grumbled spitefully. "He's making us work like it was President Johnson suddenly landing at the airport! If he gets himself killed, we're going to look ridiculous."

Beffort shot him a worried look and whispered, "I don't know how it'll happen, but you might as well consider Stark a dead man already."

"Because he came here?"

"No. It doesn't matter where he goes, Madame Atomos has anticipated everything, including our reactions and the unexpected. The Judge doesn't have a chance in a million to get out alive."

Silver turned pale. "Don't you think you're exaggerating, Beffort?"

"Tiger had been warned, right? Now we know that he answered a call from his wife, who was acting under duress, and that he knew all the risks he was running by entering his home. He shouldn't have touched the telephone, but Madame Atomos had kind of forced him to do it by making him think that he could save his wife. Right now we are sure that Stark is under fantastic protection. We're sure we've thought of everything."

Silver stiffened up. "As far as the round objects, that's true!"

Beffort bent down and picked up a little rock. "This is round, it's here and you haven't examined it. On the course that Stark will have to follow, there are hundreds of rocks like this. What will we do if one of them contains a bomb powerful enough to blow Stark to smithereens when he walks past it?"

"That only happens in the movies."

"The movies are often a reflection of life and Madame Atomos is a very good director. She was sure that Stark would never give up his round of golf and she fixed it so that we'd be concentrating on the balls that the Judge will use. See, Silver, think about it. What round or cylindrical object might the judge touch during his round?"

"His clubs, of course. We took them apart. They're in good shape and haven't been tampered with."

At that instant, Yosho Akamatsu came out of the locker room and said, "Everything's okay, Smith. The Judge can go in and change."

Stark smiled nervously and entered between two federal agents who would not leave him alone during the whole day. "Honestly," he said, "I think that Madame Atomos is going to fail."

Beffort glowered at him before going first into the building decorated with pennants and club trophies. A central aisle, clubs and balls on the right, a row of lockers on the left. The showers were in the back next to a row of dressing rooms in a narrow corridor that led to the bar and restaurant.

Stark brought out the key to his locker and put it in the lock.

"Wait a minute," Beffort demanded. "Remember that you can't touch anything before it's examined." He moved the Judge aside rather roughly, opened the metal door and said, "Tell me what you need and I'll give them to you."

"Do you really think…"

"No objections, please. You're not authorized to play except under certain conditions that you promised to respect. I'm listening!"

Embarrassed, Stark looked around but saw only expressionless, watchful, wary faces. This made him nervous and at the same time suddenly understand that he was really playing a dangerous game. So far he had felt like he was living an incredible adventure that did not directly concern him. Now, with his back against the wall, he felt his legs go wobbly. Then he saw that he was making Beffort and his men wait and very gentleman-like said, "Excuse me for being distracted, I was thinking about something else…"

Smith Beffort shrugged his shoulders. "Take your time, Judge. As long as you're here, you have nothing to fear and I'm in no hurry to see you die. Scared?"

Stark did not answer. He took off his coat.

Beffort said, "You can still decide not to play."

The Judge's hands were trembling over his shoelaces.

Beffort added, "Sit down here and let's just talk calmly for the afternoon. That'll give your wife the pleasure of seeing you come back alive. What do you say?"

The Judge stood up and glanced at the door. "You know very well that I can't back down. Outside the journalists and my friends are waiting for me... If you would be so kind as to hand me those shoes and that jacket..."

Unflinching, Beffort inspected the shoes and searched the jacket pockets before finally handing them to Stark. The Judge sat down, tied his laces, stood up and put on his jacket.

"Cap and tie, please?"

They were the club colors: green, orange and red with a wavy white band that looked a little ludicrous. Thus disguised, the Judge felt like a student. The tie around his collar would be floating in the wind on the course... Between the two discreetly placed federal agents, Stark looked more like a good old clown. He looked at himself in the mirror and with an unexpected smile on his face said, "Don't you play golf?"

Beffort shifted feet and leaned against the locker. "Not when Madame Atomos is in the game. Do you need anything else?"

"No."

Beffort closed the locker and slipped the flat key into his pocket. The Judge scrambled through his jacket pockets, brought out a pack of cigarettes, a lighter, a handkerchief and a box of pills—he suffered from congestive heart failure. All these things came directly from his house, but Beffort and Akamatsu examined the cigarettes and lighter and sifted through the pills.

"Ridiculous," Stark murmured, annoyed by all the precautions. "I've already used all these things since noon."

"Round objects, Judge."

"Still! I opened that pack of cigarettes and the box of pills this morning! As for the lighter, it hasn't left my pocket."

Beffort gave everything back and Stark swallowed a pill right away, lit a cigarette and struck the lighter. Just to be contrary.

Beffort and Akamatsu glanced at each other, but did not say a word. The Judge's life was hanging by a thread, by handling just once too often a round object that could be electrified, poisoned or booby-trapped. Unless it was something that did not come from his home... A bunch of possibilities.

"Whenever you're ready," Stark said.

Akamatsu walked to the door and called out, which brought the caddie running up to grab the clubs and plastic bag of white balls. The boy must have been under 16, freckled faced with crafty, cocky eyes. All this show of force made him laugh to himself. To him Madame Atomos was just an old bag, completely crazy, who could not really be taken seriously. True that at that age you believe in nothing and no one.

"Hello, Mac!" Stark said. "Doing well?"

"Doing fine, Judge, doing fine." Mack said, chewing his gum.

They left and the folks waiting outside quietly applauded the Judge, who smiled when the flashes went off again, but his face froze right afterward. As far as the eye could see, there were men with rifles, silhouettes on the horizon like tin soldiers, or standing on car roofs with binoculars like they were watching an opera...

Then Mrs. Stark sped up in a taxi escorted by two motorcycles and Beffort felt like something completely unexpected was about to happen. He stopped the Judge in his tracks and waved to the wife not to move. All around them the federal agents and Akamatsu had their hands on the butts of their paralyzing pistols.

"What's going on, Mrs. Stark?" Beffort asked.

The woman looked baffled, scared by the state of alert that she had just unleashed. "But... nothing," she blushed. "I just wanted to be here in case..."

She could not finish. She walked up timidly, clasping her handbag. The Judge swallowed his anger and buttoned his jacket, the middle button, the only one that a man usually uses...

"Well, Judge," Mac asked, "shall we go?"

Stark nodded, took one step and collapsed to the ground, struck down by the powerful poison that a tiny needle in his jacket button had just injected into him. Beffort swore and leaned over him.

That made two for Madame Atomos.

"I know! We were waiting for something astounding because it was Madame Atomos and she killed the Judge in a ridiculously simple way. That's part of her psychology. In fact, we really had thought of everything, except that button." Beffort stopped talking and went to pour himself a glass of water.

Akamatsu said, "I understand your regrets, Smith, because I have the same feeling of guilt. We should have known that Madame Atomos had prepared her trap before warning Stark. Anybody could have slipped into the locker room this morning and put the poisoned needle..."

Mie Azusa-Beffort left the window where he had been standing and curled up on the sofa. She was in a weird slump, feeling a physical and mental lethargy that was almost neurasthenia. A weakening of the nerves, sadness, lack of will power, difficulty thinking...

After the death of her son, Mie had lived off her hatred for Madame Atomos. For months her desire for vengeance had been her drug and then time and the lack of results came together to bury her slowly in a kind of morbid resignation that bordered on neurosis. Now she was like a vegetable, with no purpose and no desire because deep down inside she was convinced that Madame Atomos was invincible.

Neither Beffort nor the doctors could do anything for her. They had to wait patiently for nature to take its course, for some event to give her back her battle lust and by consequence a lust for life.

Smith Beffort put down his empty glass, sat down and lit a cigarette. "After the disappearance of the 504 truck, the death of the Tigers and now Judge Stark, we still haven't found the slightest trace of Madame Atomos or any members of her organization. In a city like Cincinnati, that's unthinkable!"

Akamatsu smiled and with soothing calmness said, "On the contrary, I find it quite natural. We're only at the beginning of this famous Operation Ohio and Madame Atomos hasn't exactly accomplished a masterstroke by hitting targets who were forewarned, certainly, but who weren't ready for the fight. From now on everything's going to get harder for our enemy's underlings. Every famous person in Cincinnati is under surveillance, expecting to be the next victim, and they're on their toes. Another death sentence must have been passed already. I bet it won't take long for us to hear about it."

Beffort looked at his watch and frowned. "It's 8 p.m. Do you think that Madame Atomos never sleeps?"

"She promised to eliminate the VIPs of the city in eight days," Akamatsu reminded him. "We've counted a hundred or so. That would mean around 12 executions every 24 hours. That's some serious work!"

"One death every two hours," Mie commented dreamily. "Madame Atomos must already be behind in her planning. But we're a long way from the massacres of the past, aren't we?" She paused and stared at her husband. "In fact, Smith, are we on the list of victims for Operation Ohio? I don't think that Madame Atomos has set up this meeting just so that we can admire her performance. You don't answer? Well, that means we're on the list!"

"Don't get all worked up, Mie," Akamatsu pleaded.

"I'm calm, Yosho. I'm just trying to figure out where we fit into Madame Atomos' plan of destruction. In my opinion, we're pretty important and have only two or three days. First a regional director of the FBI, then a judge... on the social scale, I put us just above the Mayor. Right?"

Beffort waved it off and jumped in. "What's the use of beating our brains out about it if Madame Atomos is going to warn us?"

"That's right," Mie recognized. "In that sense, at least, there's been some progress. As long as we haven't received an invitation to death, we can sleep soundly."

Her voice stayed flat, apathetic, and it was impossible to tell what she was really thinking. At any rate she was not scared.

At that moment Silver checked in over the telephone and said that the firemen had been called over to Coverdale that morning to put out a fire that was devastating an abandoned warehouse. Unfortunately, everything from the basement up to the roof had gone up in flames and the investigators could not examine the site of the tragedy until evening.

"Okay," Beffort cut him off. irritated by all the explanations. "Get to point!"

"In the ruins," Silver said, "they found the 504 truck, cut open by a blowtorch, and the barely identifiable remains of the four men inside. I was just trying to explain the delay in..."

"I understand, pal," Beffort said less severely, "but you've got to realize that I don't care much about all that. Tell me where the 200,000 dollars went. Give me something about the guys who set the place on fire and I'll take it."

"For the moment," Silver considered, "that's beyond me. However, I can tell you that Max Powell, the Deputy Mayor, just received a note from Madame Atomos."

"Damn!" Beffort exploded, "why didn't you say so!"

"All in good time," Tiger's replacement articulated sententiously—which was, incidentally, one of Dr. Soblen's favorite things to say.

"How's he supposed to die?" Beffort asked.

"The note didn't say," Silver complained. "Madame Atomos advised Powell to be very careful of the void..."

"The void?"

"Nothing else."

"Does Powell live at the top of a building?"

"No, he has a private home on Galbraith Road in Deer Park and couldn't fall farther than the first floor."

"That's plenty enough to die," Beffort said.

"Yes, but it's almost 8:30 and Max Powell will go to sleep in two or three hours. Once he's in bed, I don't see how Madame Atomos could push him out a window before 8 a.m."

"Hold on, did she give a time limit?"

"Even better," Silver grumbled. "She said that if Powell was still alive after 8 a.m., she would consider him the winner and leave him alone. It's a funny play in a funny game. This woman is completely off her rocker. Do you want to come and watch?"

"I'm coming," Beffort confirmed. "What number on Galbraith?"

"62, behind the privet hedge."

A relatively modern house, a few fruit trees, almost a full square mile of land surrounded by the hedge Silver mentioned. A quiet neighborhood, dark, a little troubling...

"It's 9 p.m.," Beffort said as he pulled up to the curb.

Mie Azusa Beffort giggled oddly and said, "This poor Powell only has a few hours to live."

"He might escape," Akamatsu remarked calmly.

"How's that? Bob and Soblen are dead, aren't they?"

Beffort turned to her. "Be quiet, Mie! You're obnoxious when you keep reminding the rest of the world about the fate our son and our old friend. Pull yourself together and look things in the face. We have to fight Madame Atomos! Not give in to her!"

That was the first time that Smith had spoken so hard to his wife since Bob's death. He continued, "You forget that Heaven has been kind to us. As Miss Atomos, with a motor brain implanted in your skull and being the loyal servant of an incredible machine, you should not have survived the destruction of Atomos City or Atomia Island. Providence provided for your operation and gave you a husband and child. You are a normal woman although you should have been dead a long time ago, almost against all logic, and you don't have the courage to live anymore!"

"Smith!"

"You know I'm right! If you don't have any more strength to fight to avenge Bob, at least make an effort to help save others. For example, force yourself to save Max Powell. He's 40 years old, has a wife and four kids. If he dies, his wife and children will lose their only means of support... You know, Mie, sometimes the death of a parent is far more tragic than that of a child. So stop crying over your life, take a gander at others and you'll see that there are people a lot worse off than you!"

He knew he was being hard, but he also knew that his wife was Japanese and so a fatalist and that she

35

would have reacted differently if she had not been more or less softened up by American society.

Mie was just about to reply, but Beffort cut her short by opening the car door and saying to Akamatsu, "This house actually has only one floor. I wonder what kind of void Max Powell should be wary of?"

Yosho furrowed his brow. "What kind of void? I see only one."

"Sure, we know that a void is space that contains no material body, but since the threat is coming from Madame Atomos, let's use our imagination. Powell is supposed to die by a void, okay. Now, could it be an artificial void?" He glanced at his wife, who was pouting.

Akamatsu said, "How can you create an artificial void in a house? Don't forget that Madame Atomos doesn't have the same power as in the past."

At that moment a form came out of the shadows. It was Silver, weapon in hand, alert as a desert fox. "Good evening," he whispered.

"Why are you whispering?" Beffort was interested.

Silver smiled. "No reason at all, really. It's kind of a joke, isn't it? I guess the hidden presence of Madame Atomos is the reason…"

"That's not surprising," Beffort admitted. "Where's Max Powell?"

"In his living room. He sent his wife and kids to his sister's and swore that he wouldn't move from his armchair until tomorrow morning. It's a simple defense, but I think it's a fine way to avoid the void."

The small group crossed the yard, climbed the few steps and entered almost directly into a huge room where a man was watching television. He was wearing only his pajamas and slippers and was obviously prepared to spend a sleepless night as comfortably as possible.

"No need to tell you," Silver explained, "that G-men are stationed all around the house. Then more loudly he said, "Mr. Powell, this is Smith Beffort, his wife and Yosho Akamatsu."

The Deputy Mayor turned around and laughed. "Hello! How're you doing?"

He did not seem shaken up. Beffort said so. Powell took his cigar out of his mouth, blew a big cloud of smoke toward the ceiling and explained, "Truthfully, tell me how this Japanese gal's going to kill me by a void? I'm a fan of crosswords, charades, all kinds of puzzles. I've thought long and hard about the problem and have concluded that nothing can touch me if I don't move from this seat. And you can see that I'm not moving! Even if I'm being impolite to my guests. Do you want to have a drink and watch the Sinatra Show?"

"Thanks," Beffort refused, "but I'd rather check out the basement of your house."

Silver was a little startled and Powell's face darkened. "My basement?"

"Well," Beffort spoke calmly, "maybe you're aware that Madame Atomos loves to attack from the bottom up, literally, and when least expected. While I'm talking to you, someone is probably setting a trap in which you'll fall."

Powell shrugged. "I'm sitting in this armchair and I'm going to stay here no matter what happens. Can you tell me how Madame Atomos will manage to saw through the floor without me noticing? And of course my cellar is made of cement. To cut a hole without waking up the entire neighborhood would be downright amazing!"

"Madame Atomos is downright amazing," Akamatsu said politely.

Max Powell put his feet up on the low table in front of the armchair and said calmly, "I'm not scared and don't try to make me lose my cool just to make your-selves look useful."

"Hey!" Silver barked. "I don't…"

"Be quiet!" Powell shot back. "You're in my house and I forbid you to scream! I said and I repeat that you're trying to make yourselves look useful. What's more, you have no idea what to do! You were all at Gold Manor, right? That didn't keep Madame Atomos from killing Judge Stark right under your noses!"

"You're pushing it," Beffort reproached him gently.

Powell narrowed his eyes. "By God, you come on pretty strong, G-man! Who's supposed to die before 8 a.m. tomorrow morning, you or me?"

"That's exactly why I'm here… to help."

"Since you got here," Powell said ironically, "all we've done is talk. You're making my mouth dry. You're no help at all. So just sit down, be quiet and watch the Sinatra Show with me."

Beffort waved his team out of the living room. He closed the sliding door and said, "This Powell is a hard-head. But he's right when he says that his armchair is his best bet. If Madame Atomos doesn't find a way to get him out of there, I'll wager that he'll be alive at 8 a.m. Come on, we're at least going to check out the base-ment."

They went down the cellar stairs and stood there under the living room.

"The cement is in good shape," Akamatsu noticed. "If there's a trap, it's not going to be here."

The light bulb in the basement was very bright. Sil-ver blinked and said, "I already came down here and I can guarantee you that nothing's changed. Plus, how can

Powell fall into a void when he's pretty much sitting on the ground?"

Beffort looked stumped. "I don't know, but even if it seems impossible, we have to expect the worst..."

Mie jumped in, "Unless we haven't understood the word *void* correctly."

"There's no other meaning," Akamatsu said.

Mie corrected herself, "That's not what I meant. I mean that Max Powell should be watching out for a void that doesn't have the word *fall* attached to it. We just have to find out how a void can kill"

Beffort shook his head and said, "Don't forget that Tiger and Stark were murdered after some preparation. For Tiger, Madame Atomos had rigged the telephone to explode when he picked it up. As for the judge, it was one of the buttons on his coat. In short, I think that it's logical enough to presume that Madame Atomos has also made preparations for Powell's death."

He examined the basement, which, to tell the truth, was a waste of time, and concluded, "Note that just like for judge Stark, we're going around in circles even though we know about the threat looming over Powell. That's what is so frustrating!"

Silver sat on an empty crate. "Logically, nothing can happen. Powell doesn't have any desire or any reason to get up from his armchair. If he does, it would to go to the bathroom. Now, we've carefully inspected the toilet. There's nothing wrong with it and one of my men is posted at the door."

"Okay," Beffort said, "let's go back up and look somewhere else."

The group went back to the ground floor. Akamatsu glanced into the living room. Max Powell was still slumped in his chair watching the Sinatra Show. He sensed Akamatsu looking at him, turned around and shouted through the glass door, "Well, any news?"

Akamatsu gave him the thumb's down and was about to leave when the phone rang. It was placed in a corner of the living room, right behind the television. Max Powell put down his cigar in the ashtray, got up, adjusted his slippers and went to answer. He listened and furrowed his brow. Sinatra's voice drowned out all other sounds so that it looked like it was difficult for Powell to hear.

Beffort opened the door. Powell smiled, covered the phone with his hand, leaned forward a little and said, "Don't worry, G-man. It's your friends at police head-quarters who are worried about my health."

At that very second Beffort saw that the TV screen had gone blurry. Then it flashed and quickly imploded, sounding like a bomb. Max Powell opened his mouth, dropped the telephone and fell to the ground, his head riddled with shards of glass. At the same time, the televi-sion started smoking and all the lights in the house were short-circuited , blacking out simultaneously.

Beffort and Akamatsu ran to Powell, lifted him up and carried him into the entrance hall.

"Quickly!" Beffort ordered, "Call an ambulance!"

Silver ran to the door. In his opinion, Powell would not hold out for long.

The living room had suffered little damage in the television explosion, but there were traces of the fire extinguisher that Beffort had used to put out the fire.

The forensic specialist stood up holding the remains of a square device with a short, twisted antenna. "The accident was caused by a radio signal," he said straightaway.

Beffort stuck out his chin. "What's the void have to do with all this?"

"Without it none of it could have happened. The TV screen is made up of a big, glass bulb that is a total vacuum. If for any reason the glass breaks, either from faulty manufacturing that went undetected in spite of all the checks or from overheating if you forget to turn it off or even if there's a quick change in temperature, there would be, not an explosion, but an implosion. Pieces of the glass tube under the atmospheric pressure would fly inside, but naturally continue their path and could kill someone standing behind the TV In this case, the implosion was caused by a radio signal at the exact moment when Max Powell was in the wrong place."

Beffort and Akamatsu knew precisely how it all unfolded. It was obvious that Madame Atomos had telephoned Powell in order to be sure that his head would be only a few inches from the television at the right time. But this was only possible because someone had been able to slip the square box inside the TV.

If Powell had not leaned slightly forward to answer Beffort's silent question, he would inevitably have been killed on the spot.

Beffort, Mie and Akamatsu let Silver lead the pre-liminary investigation and went to the hospital where Powell was fighting for his life. In the waiting room, they found Mrs. Powell. The woman was falling apart but trying desperately to keep her dignity.

"Mrs. Powell," Beffort said, "can you tell us if you had your television repaired recently?"

The woman nodded and explained, "Last night it suddenly stopped working. There was a little wind and Max knew right away that the antenna had just snapped. We went to bed and this morning after Max left a re-pairman came. He said that he had been told by my hus-band…"

"Was it true?"

"Now I know it wasn't, but at the moment I had no reason to be suspicious. Since the set was fixed, it didn't really matter who did the work."

"Who did the work?" Beffort asked.

"I don't know. The bill was supposed to be put in the mail. The man simply asked me to sign a paper after making sure that the TV was working properly, then he left."

"Did you watch him repair it?"

"No, I was in the kitchen." She wiped her eyes with a wet handkerchief that was balled up and then contin-ued with difficulty. "I should have spoken to Max about that man! I'm responsible for…"

"You're not responsible for anything, Mrs. Powell," Beffort interrupted. "By the way, would you recognize this mysterious repairman?"

"Of course! I…" She stopped and slowly straight-ened up when she saw a doctor standing in the doorway. "My husband?" she whispered.

The doctor spread his arms and said gently, "Be brave, Madam..."

In spite of her grief, and maybe urged by a vague need to do something, she wanted to go to FBI headquarters immediately. Now she was sitting in front of a board on which an identikit specialist was putting face parts according to her description.

An incredible puzzle that gradually took form as the minutes ticked off. The man had brown hair, very slim, was around 5 foot 8 inches tall; black eyes, close set to the bridge of his nose with straight, bushy eyebrows; jutting cheekbones, hollow cheeks, thin, barely visible lips, etc.

"How are you going to find him?" Mrs. Powell asked.

"We're going to wire this portrait to Washington," Beffort informed her. "There they will select some photographs that will be sent back by plane. Tomorrow morning, probably before noon, you will be able to identify your husband's murderer with certainty. When that's done, we'll send out the description and the guy will be nabbed as soon as he steps outside."

He threw away his cigarette and with less enthusiasm added, "Then if this guy talks, maybe we can capture Madame Atomos... with a whole lot of luck!"

The night passed without Madame Atomos or her team of killers sending any other invitations to death. In Cincinnati, the police force had been ready for war since the successful attack against the Tigers. This reassured the population, but certainly meant nothing as far as the Atomos gang was concerned.

At 8 a.m. a car came to get Mrs. Powell and bring her to headquarters where Beffort, Mie and Akamatsu were waiting. Beffort asked the lady to sit down before they turned off the lights in the projection room and the operator threw the slides from Washington onto the screen. The sinister heads started filing by before Mrs. Powell's eyes. They all looked more or less like her portrait, but on the sixth image she stiffened up.

"That's him!"

They turned on the lights and Beffort grabbed the corresponding file. "Doug Egerton," he read, "32 years old, two-time murderer, on the run and sentenced to death in absentia. Has nothing to lose and I doubt that we'll take him alive."

"Dead will do us no good," Akamatsu said.

Beffort said nothing for a few seconds. Finally he spoke again, "When he thinks he's cornered, he'll fight it out and no doubt rather die than end up in the chair. Instead of putting the official police force on his trail, we'd better give him to the Green Dragon Force, even if we lose a little time. Do you want to call Owen Bernitz, Mie?"

The young lady hurried to the telephone. It looked like Mrs. Powell's grief had given her a spurt of energy.

At nine o'clock Silver called Beffort. "The game's starting up again," he said in a nasty voice. "This time Madame Atomos is upping the stakes. Seven people have to die before noon by electrocution! But the letter was put on my desk and Madame Atomos didn't give any names of the future victims!"

"She's starting to cheat. You had to see it coming."

"She said that we should be able to save all the people she's sworn to kill. To "help" us, she's given a list of 90 names. I'm number 55! The Mayor is 87. And then, in order, there's Yosho Akamatsu, your wife and yourself. Charming, isn't it?"

"Forewarned is forearmed," Beffort cited.

"Sure, but only if goes in the order on the damn list! Now, Max Powell only came in 54th and he's already dead. And finally, we can't base it on their social standing either. The list isn't even in alphabetical order!"

Silver was outraged and his outrage would have been laughable under any other circumstances.

Beffort said, "Okay, but we know that seven of us have to die by electrocution. That's important information. Warn everyone and make sure that they all watch out for themselves. I take it that most of them are already under protection?"

"Almost all. We belong to the category of those who have to defend ourselves. Now I have to sound the alarm. Will we see each other before noon?"

"I'll be there pretty soon," Beffort answered.

Silver hung up. Beffort did the same and turned around to face Mie and Akamatsu. "Did you get the gist of our conversation?"

Mie nodded. Without showing any emotion she said, "The real battle is starting and we'll inevitably die if Owen Bernitz doesn't find this Doug Egerton."

Akamatsu laughed a little. "You have no faith, Mie! We escaped Madame Atomos when she was demonically powerful and you think that we're going to die now when she's no more powerful than you or I?"

"She's already murdered eight people."

"Exactly," he replied, "but she had particularly favorable circumstances on her side. Plus, her traps were in place before the victims were warned. If you want to know what I really think, I'll tell you that all these crimes are working as a huge diversion."

Beffort nodded. "You're thinking of the laboratory, aren't you, Yosho?"

"Of course! Madame Atomos did what she had to in order to focus all our attention on Cincinnati. She is even sacrificing one of her men, Doug Egerton, so that the Green Dragon Force will be busy looking for him. Meanwhile, somewhere we don't know, a laboratory is taking shape... That's where the real danger lies! Madame Atomos without her fantastic weapons is no longer Madame Atomos. Believe me, Smith, we have to leave Cincinnati and its unfortunate future victims and throw ourselves full force on the trail of Madame Atomos. We're just extras on the set here!"

Suddenly and logically Akamatsu had just put things in perspective and torn apart the myth of an Atomos resigned to become an ordinary criminal. The terrible Japanese woman could not sink into banality or be content killing a few Americans at a time. She needed devastation and slaughter!

Smith Beffort stuck his hands in his pocket. "I really do want to jump on the trail of Madame Atomos, Yosho. That's all I ask for. You shook up the bottle, now give me the instructions as well. Because if I understand you, this Doug Egerton is a dead end?"

Akamatsu said nothing. Beffort continued, "The only good way to find out anything is to capture a member of the Atomos gang or of the A.O.F.M.A. Now except for Doug Egerton we know nothing substantial and very little insubstantial. How can we get ahead of events when we're not the ones causing them?"

Akamatsu looked exhausted. "You're right, Smith. I got up on my warhorse too quickly. Do you have any ideas?"

"There's only one," Beffort said simply. "We have to capture a gang member alive. That's all."

Then he turned to the door that had just opened. When he saw big Bernitz, he said, "Hello! What's new, Owen?"

"A corpse, boss. Your Doug Egerton didn't get far after rigging Powell's TV the cops just found him on some vacant lot in Norwood with a 9 mm slug in his neck."

"Execution?"

"And how! The guy didn't even have a 25 automatic on him! His arms and legs weren't bound but traces on his wrists and ankles proved that he'd been tied up for a long time before being taken out."

Beffort offered him a cigarette and asked, "Of course there's no clue to follow up on?"

Owen took a half-hearted drag off the cigarette that he had accepted out of politeness. He far preferred cigars, especially unlit and smoked down to a juicy stub... "Doug Egerton had sawdust in his hair," he said. "As far as whether it can kick start a trail, gotta see the boys in the lab."

Just then Silver showed up and from the doorway said, "Bad news, Beffort! Egerton just..."

"I know all about it," the G-man cut him off. "But tell me about this sawdust."

Silver looked truly surprised. "Damn! You know more than I do! I just got off the phone with them."

Beffort pointed to Owen and said, "Say hello to Mr. Bernitz, the chief of the Green Dragon Force. He was looking for Egerton and found him at the same time as the cops. He said that the dead man's hair contained some sawdust that the lab was dealing with. No need to tell you that this small detail is of the utmost importance. Can you speed things up?"

Silver nodded. "I'll get the guys in the lab to send a report as soon as possible." Then, completely switching gears, he asked, "Are you coming to make a tour of the potential victims?"

Beffort shook his head. "Sorry, but this sawdust changed all my plans."

"Oh? How's that?"

"It's a product that you won't find just anywhere. If Doug Egerton stayed almost 24 hours on the ground of a lumberyard before being killed, it's a good bet that the place is one of the Atomos gang's hideouts. Well, I know that the specialists can give me a bunch of information about it. I need to find out what kind of wood made the sawdust, what type of machine made it, if it's old or new... if Egerton's clothes were stained with dirt or dust different from the vacant lot in Norwood, a good analysis can show with relative precision the area of Cincinnati where it came from. So, be kind, Silver, and before worrying about the potential victims, as you say, call the laboratory."

Silver did not mess around. He picked up the phone, dialed a number and waited five seconds before getting through.

Beffort went over to Owen Bernitz. "Your 300 men are under the gun."

"Good and ready. Paralyzing arms, radio cars driving around with the mobile number 555-6289, a real dispatch center on wheels managed by Ralph Stutton. And your car is ready."

"Code name?"

"Yellow Mask."

Beffort jotted it down and asked, "Where is this Yellow Mask?"

"In front of the house. It's a black Chevy Chevelle Malibu..."

"What? Don't tell me that the department dished out!"

Owen laughed to hide his confusion. "The department has nothing to do with it, boss. It's a gift from the Green Dragon Force, which prefers seeing you live as long as possible. The car is armored, soundproof, air conditioned so that it can park for two hours in a cloud of mustard gas or any other toxic gas. Its tires can drive over a swami's bed without any damage and .45 caps will bounce off the windows. You've got a radio on board, a telephone, four machine guns—two in front and two in back—and a movable paralyzing cannon installed under the chassis. The bumpers are strong enough to plow through a 15-inch thick wall. All wheel drive. They can be all cockeyed and still carry the bucket to the right or left at almost 40 miles an hour. There you go."

Beffort was stunned. "Who laid this golden egg?"

"Sammy, Stutton, Baxter and almost all the guys and me," Owen answered modestly. "We've been working on it for two years, but I think it's ready. Just to be in fashion we dropped on the Malibu body. But it's more serious under the hood. Doesn't matter if you floor it over 150... It's no bicycle!"

Beffort gulped. "I believe you, Owen. Can I ask you how much this monster cost the Green Dragon Force?"

Owen looked down, blushed, and admitted, "Not a cent, boss. Just our savings and..." He took a deep breath before finishing, "three years without whiskey for the whole team!"

Chapter V

Even up close the Chevrolet Chevelle Malibu drew no special attention. It had a few extra embellishments to camouflage the machine gun barrels, two antennas coming right out of the panoramic side view mirrors, but it was impossible to tell that the body was armored under the shiny black paint or to spot the paralyzing cannon stuck under the chassis.

"Nice work," Beffort was sincerely in awe.

Big Owen grinned and said, "You can get up to 100 in 18 seconds! Under the hood there's 400 hp with three Holley double pumper carbs and a special camshaft. Look, boss, here's the key. The red button fires the cannon; the green controls the machine guns in front; the white, the guns in back. Apart from that, it's a car like any other. Except it weighs two and a half tons!"

Silver looked at his Ford parked next to it and complained "After this, I'm going to feel like I'm driving an old soapbox! I guess you're going straight to the lab?"

"By the shortest route possible," Beffort confirmed.

"If you find anything, let me know," Silver beseeched, obviously regretting that he could not participate in the expedition. "At headquarters they'll always know where to reach me."

"It's a promise," Beffort assured him.

Silver got into his car and headed downtown.

Beffort climbed behind the wheel and Bernitz sat next to him while Mie and Akamatsu took the back seat. The radio and telephone were under the dashboard. Owen pointed out where the buttons were to fire the weapons.

"Be careful not to put your finger too high or you'll wipe out everything that moves within a one mile radius."

Beffort frowned. "There's no kill switch?"

"Sure, under your left foot," Owen reassured him. "Press... there, the network's blocked. Now you can start the engine."

Beffort turned the ignition and a blue light indicated that the engine was running. Owen flipped a switch and two screens lit up on either side of the light. One gave a sketchy representation of the street in front of the car and the other outlined the courtyard of the buildings behind the Malibu. But on each of the screens there were blinking marks moving around.

"The dots are pedestrians," Owen explained. "The dashes are cars. By moving the arrow you can aim the machine guns or paralyzing cannon on the target of your choice. Respective distance: about one mile for the automatic weapons and 500 yards for the cannon. The precision depends on the speed you're driving, but in our trials I hit a bull's eye at 800 yards going 90 miles an hour. Then the gunfire sprays and you have to shoot the ray. If you use the whole shebang at the same time, the target obviously gets the full effect. In seven minutes of continuous firing, which would be a downright massacre, you'll empty the ammo reserves and the cannon as well. If they're still giving you trouble, you can always just charge through them with the bumpers before calling 555-6289 for a refill, whose location you can know by a simple radio call. In fact, the only way of stopping the Yellow Mask is to make it fall in a ditch or snatch it from the ground with a crane."

"Like the 504 truck," Akamatsu commented.

"Exactly," Owen calmly agreed, "The only difference being that the Yellow Mask is totally waterproof and it would do no good to dump it in a tanker truck. If that happens, you'll have help on the way after giving your location to 555-6289."

"Let's say," Beffort argued, "that the antennas are knocked out?"

"Doesn't matter. They don't do anything. The real radio setup is under the chassis. The antennas are decoys. Any other questions?"

Beffort smiled. "No questions, Owen," he said good-humoredly.

Since the death of Soblen and their son, this was maybe the first time that Mie saw him look unworried. Before this, she had lived with a serious man, wound tight as a spring, with his finger always on the trigger of a weapon, and who talked about Madame Atomos even during his short nights of sleep. Mie did not understand how the simple fact of having the Yellow Mask could transform Smith, but Akamatsu and Owen knew very well that this new, terribly destructive toy gave Beffort some mad hope of seeing Madame Atomos at his mercy soon.

The Malibu rolled smoothly and obediently. Beffort had the pleasure of appreciating it between headquarters and the laboratory. Once there, an assistant informed by Silver took the group up to the fifth floor where the chief gave Beffort the typed report of Doug Egerton's analysis after making him sign for it, out of pure formality. An administrative exchange without human contact.

The lab delivered the results of an analysis and its work stopped there. A little disappointed by the bureaucracy, Beffort read through the report and recovered some of his enthusiasm. In short, it said that the sawdust came from a fir tree and was at least two years old. Still, it contained enough moisture to lead them to believe that it was kept somewhere humid.

Beffort skipped the rest of the details that could tell him nothing and went on to the analysis of Doug Egerton's clothes. The dirt from the soles of his shoes: vegetable soil mixed with humus and oily products probably meant for lubricating engines; metal fragments almost reduced to dust; very hard steel; carbon level 80%... As for the dust taken from his pants and jacket, it was a strange mix of dry paint, gas, antifreeze, acid and 50% of it contained all the different kinds of wood that can be found in the United States.

The report made no conclusions. It was an analysis and that was all.

Beffort gave the paper to Akamatsu who scanned it before passing it on to Mie. After reading it in turn, she gave it to Bernitz.

"Well?" Beffort asked, asking each of them for their opinion.

"Complete and partial at the same time," Akamatsu frowned. "Instead of all this mumbo jumbo, the lab should have told us where in the area we could find this vegetal soil." Then, getting a hold of himself, he added, "But if it didn't do so, it's obviously because it wouldn't give us much to go on. Wherever there are woods, the soil is vegetal."

"Anyway," Mie said, "this soil didn't come from the empty lot in Norwood. That's for sure."

"Well," Owen Bernitz said, "I can tell you that Doug Egerton came directly from an abandoned sawmill."

Everyone looked at him. Beffort asked, "Why?"

"Abandoned," Owen stated, "because humid. Sawmill because they found all kinds of different wood. Then the soil contains oily products to lubricate machines and metal fragments from hard steel. The oil was used for the machines. The steel dust came from sharpening the saws. The dry paint certainly fell off the walls or ceiling. As for the gas, antifreeze and acid, they absolutely prove that one or more cars came there this winter, maybe right near the end of February, precisely when Madame Atomos got herself out of Billings."

Beffort whistled softly. "Wow! Owen, you're full of surprises!"

"Not at all. I worked in a sawmill when I was a kid. I sharpened those buzz saws of Swedish steel with a file, tooth by tooth, for hours, and I was up to my ankles in steel dust. You don't forget a thing like that. Hey, now that I think about it, I also remember Doug smelled like sawdust. Gotta have worked in the field to recognize the odor of freshly cut wood."

"Freshly cut? Then the place wasn't abandoned?"

"Wood, even after two years, always smells like wood," Owen smirked. "Especially when it's piled up in planks along the wall of the sawmill when the ground is humid. Believe me, boss, I know what I'm talking about."

"It's very likely," Akamatsu admitted.

"I also think that Owen's right on target," Mie said.

"Okay," Beffort concluded. "We're going to get a list of all the sawmills in the region, chose the ones that have been closed for 24 months and then sort those by the most isolated. If Madame Atomos has a base near Cincinnati, it's sure to be somewhere away from the crowds."

While Beffort's team initiated its first action against the Atomos gang, an extraordinary meeting was taking place in City Hall. It had been called because of the death of Max Powell, the Deputy Mayor, to make funeral arrangements. Later, they would have to elect one of the members of the city council to replace him, but for now a handful of men could take care of the items on the agenda. As if by chance, with the Mayor being absent because of the flu, and with three other local officials showing up, there were seven of them there. This was the exact number given by Madame Atomos. Silver had noticed it. Policemen were stationed in the corridors and since the weather was sunny they had just cut the electricity.

A simple but very efficient measure to avoid a massacre by electrocution…

In the boardroom, the seven men agreed on the route that the funeral would follow, smoothed out the details of the ceremony at the church and the cemetery, and appointed who would give the eulogy.

Sitting in rather uncomfortable leather armchairs, they did their best to run through the session so that at 10:40 it was all over. Nevertheless, they had no desire to leave the building where they knew they were safe. Outside, the Atomos threat was looming over them for an hour yet, until 12 o'clock sharp, and it was a risk that they preferred not to take.

"Let's go to the bar," Stillwell proposed, being an important member at the heart of the council. "Like that we can stay in the part of the building forbidden to the public. What do you say?"

Lowe agreed right away, but Ackermann objected, "No way. You know the bar is closed. Jack doesn't get here until 11:30. If we wait that long, it'll look like we've been hiding."

A firm argument that left the others meditating.

"Annoying," Stillwell admitted. Then, glancing at one of the policeman standing by the doorway, he whispered, "They know that the session is over. If we stay, they'll say we're all yellow-bellied."

Lowe shrugged and said, "I'd rather be taken for a coward than make my wife a widow. Personally, I'm telling you, even if you go, I'm staying. I've already proven how brave I am by coming here this morning when everyone else on the list is locked up at home."

"Well said, Lowe!" Briant approved.

Stillwell scowled, then spoke persuasively, "We can't please everyone. The hard thing is simply not to leave but make them believe that we're not really scared to do so. Why the hell didn't we drag out the session?"

That was the question that all of them were asking themselves. In fact, each of them had carefully hidden their fears, thinking that the others did not have any and now it was too late to turn back.

Landers coughed and stammered, "Uh... I think I know where Jack keeps the key to the bar."

There was silence. Finally, Stillwell asked, "Where's he put them?"

"On the back of the little closet door there's a shelf. On this shelf is a box of cigars. The key should be inside. After all, we have every right to open the bar and drink whatever we want, don't we?"

"Why not?" Lowe said. "As long as Jack doesn't keep the key on him. When he comes, we'll pay for our drinks and that's that..."

Stillwell grabbed his handkerchief, put on his hat and decided, "Let's go, my friends!"

They all felt a little ridiculous making such a big deal out of such a small thing, but it was certainly due to their nervousness. After all, their lives were at stake.

The police sergeant in charge asked from the doorway, "Are you leaving, gentlemen?"

Stillwell said gravely, "Not right now, my friend. We still have a few questions to address... in the bar."

The sergeant smiled. Stillwell did the same and led the way. The small group went single file down the corridor, turned before the stairwell and entered a soberly decorated room. The bar was in the back, past the tables and chairs that they used for the receptions organized by the city. Daylight poured in through a huge window that directly faced the front of the building.

In spite of this, it was gloomy. Briant said so. Akermann said that it was probably due to the fact that Jack was not there. Lowe went farther and gave a speech to prove that a drinker went to a bar as much for what was put in his glass as for the way it was served... It was long, boring and useless.

"Be quiet," Stillwell ordered. "We have to find the key for the drink shelf before Jack comes, otherwise we'll look ridiculous. You know where it is, Landers, so go get it."

Landers opened the small closet (small since it was never used, the one in the corridor being preferred because even though it was the same size, it was called big) and quickly found himself in the dark.

"Does anyone have matches?" he asked.

"I've got a lighter," Baines responded.

He tried in vain to make it work. Salter pushed him aside to enter the closet and struck a match. He burned his fingers just when Landers got the key from the cigar box. He yelled and bumped into Landers, who dropped the key on the ground. After that it took five of them to look for it on hands and knees—which put them in a bad mood—before realizing that the key had slipped under the door and was now in the bar.

Solemnly, Stillwell picked it up and opened the drink shelf. He took off his hat, leaned on the tap and asked, "What's your pleasure, gentlemen?"

At that moment, Salter became vaguely aware that the situation and the behavior of his colleagues was weird, almost ludicrous, and that it should not have been so given the gravity of the situation. He tried to analyze his own state and figured that he was not feeling especially euphoric. It was more like a kind of daze. Salter felt like he was walking in a cloud, like sometimes happens in dreams, and that he had lost all contact with reality. Of course, he knew that he was in City Hall, but could not remember what he was doing there. He looked at his friends sitting at the bar and sniffed. The air smelled like nuts, sulfur and two or three other odors that Salter could not identify.

"Everything all right?" a voice asked.

The seven of them turned around and saw the sergeant in the doorway. He had not entered the room, just stuck his head in through the half-open door.

Stillwell answered, "Everything's fine, my friend, you can go."

The sergeant furrowed his brow, hesitated, then finally closed the door and disappeared.

Stillwell giggled, "If he comes back, we'll jump him." He passed out glasses, took a bottle of whiskey and served them enough to kill a horse. Then he said, "To your health!"

Salter lifted his glass. All of a sudden, he felt very cheerful and was even lucid enough to see that his colleagues had also changed their state of mind. They drank, lit cigarettes, started talking all at the same time without listening to what the others were saying. It lasted more than ten minutes. The alcohol was not responsible, but they were obviously three sheets to the wind and the strangest thing was that they were completely unaware of it.

After 15 minutes, a man barged into the room through the closet door. No one paid any attention to him. He hooked an electric wire to the chrome bar along the counter and stepped back before asking politely, "Would you hold onto the bar, gentlemen? The repair won't take but a few minutes..."

No one asked him what he was repairing. Everyone grabbed the bar and kept babbling away. The man went back into the closet, left through another door and entered the utility room where he flipped a switch...

Chapter VI

Within 90 minutes Smith Beffort had a complete list of the sawmills in the region. There were a good hundred of them, but 60 were crossed out right away because they were located in populated areas. Out the 40 that were left, Beffort eliminated another 20 because they were too big.

After that it was impossible for him to make a choice. The 20 remaining establishments were mid-sized or small businesses, mostly situated in the country or a forest. All of them could be used as a refuge by the Atomos gang. Visiting all of them, however, would take far too much time.

"There's only one solution," Mie proposed. "The telephone."

"Good idea," Akamatsu approved, "but how are we going to know if the place is really working or not?"

"Place an order," Owen said. "A real headache, custom work."

"For example?" Beffort asked.

Bernitz lit a cigar, furrowed his brow and said, "I'm thinking of boards cut to weird dimensions, both in width and height. That would require two different machines and a bunch of work. We won't argue price or delivery time."

"I don't see what clue that'll give us," Beffort said, though intrigued by the idea.

"Logically," Owen explained, "no shop'll refuse an order under such conditions. Anyone that refuses will be immediately under suspicion, unless, of course, they're really backed up. Either way, it'll be another short list. Even if there's still a dozen left."

"That would be something gained," Beffort decided. "Okay, Owen, grab the phone! Here's the numbers of the 20 competitors."

Bernitz picked up and called the first sawmill.

The twelfth rang and rang and rang. Up to now, they had answered right away and Bernitz had no problem getting the job done subject to confirmation in due form. Every time, the conversations were difficult to follow over the background of noisy engines and saws screaming through wood—there was no question of the sawmills' activity. This time, a full minute passed before someone answered the phone. Then there were a few seconds of silence. Finally a wary voice asked, "Who is this?"

Owen and Beffort (who was listening on another line) exchanged glances. Owen said, "Is this the Garrani sawmill?"

"That's it, yeah."

"I represent Schwartz in Cincinnati," Owen spoke like a guy tired of always having to repeat the same thing. "I would like to place an order with you. It's about a…"

"We're not taking any work," the other cut him off. "The boss is sick and the shop's been closed for three months. I don't think it'll be opening any time soon. Call someone else!"

He hung up and Bernitz did the same.

"Where is this Garrani sawmill?" Beffort asked.

"Over by Addyston," Akamatsu responded, "and it must be pretty isolated because its address is just a name. On the map you can see that Addyston is on Highway 50. The Garrani sawmill should be around there in the middle of the country in a place called *Dead Man's Gulch*."

"A whole host of possibilities!" Beffort commented. Then, leaning over the map, he exclaimed, "Hey, Yosho, you didn't tell me that Dead Man's Gulch is sitting between Highway 50 and the Ohio River? That's Madame Atomos' favorite position. Call the Chamber of Commerce, Owen. I want to know if this Garrani has officially closed up business and if so, since when!"

As Bernitz was looking for the number, the other phone started ringing. Beffort picked up and heard Silver's voice right away, "Bad news! Madame Atomos has just hit her seven inside City Hall!"

"Does that surprise you, Silver?"

"Yes. I took special care to protect the city councilmen. They were practically locked up inside rooms off limits to the public and we had gone so far as the cut the electricity. Well, someone got these seven guys to inhale a gas while they were drinking at the bar…"

"What kind of gas?" Beffort was curious.

"We know nothing about it and we never will," Silver moaned. "The sergeant in charge opened a window when he entered the bar. It was his second time down there and he thought the men had suffocated. He only saw the wire a little later."

"Electrical wire, obviously?"

"Obviously," Silver grumbled bitterly. "It had been hooked up to the bar and it looks like the seven of them just calmly got ready to be electrocuted. Maybe you don't find that surprising, either? Me, I'm stunned!"

"You will be stunned again," Beffort replied coldly, "so you'd better get used to it. After Madame Atomos leaves your region, you'll have no desire to watch any more horror movies."

"Nice prospect," Silver murmured. He was discouraged, doomed from the start.

"Any other invitations to death?" Beffort asked.

"Not for the moment, but it won't take long, right?"

"Without a doubt. Keep on your toes and try to keep the damages to a minimum. I'm onto something..."

"Thanks to the sawdust?"

"Yes. I can't tell you anymore. When I'm sure were on the right track, I'll let you know. Try to stay alive until then. Goodbye, Silver."

Beffort put the phone down and turned to Owen Bernitz who had also just finished his phone call to the Chamber of Commerce.

"So, Owen, this Garrani?"

Bernitz puffed his cigar and said, "Dead for two years. The sawmill was bought by Arthur Trigg out of San Francisco."

Akamatsu and Mie were startled. Beffort did not move, but there was a little, troubling glimmer dancing in his eyes.

Bernitz went on, "Since then, the sawmill is actually closed. Arthur Trigg hasn't done any work on it and apparently hasn't decided to start up the business again. As for the IRS, he's all paid up and nobody's got anything to complain about." Then he concluded, "Nobody at the Chamber knows him, but if he lives in San Francisco, I'm sure he's in cahoots with Mama Atomos!"

Beffort, Mie and Akamatsu were thinking that the headquarters of the A.O.F.M.A. just happened to be located in that city. It made perfect sense, in a way, since San Francisco had kicked off several movements in support of Madame Atomos' actions against the USA.

"Get our office in San Francisco on the line," Beffort ordered.

Bernitz jumped on the phone again as Akamatsu asked, "What do we do with the Garrani sawmill?"

"Nothing for now," Beffort decided. "Before jumping in feet first, I want to know who this Arthur Trigg is. The guy lives on the other side of the country, almost 2,500 miles away, and he buys a sawmill here to leave it empty. Either he's nuts or he's part of the A.O.F.M.A."

"He works for Madame Atomos," Mie declared. She was obviously getting back in the saddle, slowly measuring up to Smith again. Three months earlier, in Billings, on a bed in the Enright clinic, she had nearly caused Madame Atomos' downfall. Mie was very effective when she wanted to be. Right now it took almost nothing to get her bite—and her spite—back.

"San Francisco!" Owen Bernitz shouted.

Beffort grabbed the telephone. "Smith Beffort here. Is that you, Ritter?"

"In flesh and blood," the big man answered cheerfully. "What can I do for you, Smith?"

"A lot, but we have to act fast. I need to know who Arthur Trigg is right away. Can do?"

"Sure, one second! Trigg is loaded and on the coast they know him as…"

"The guy behind the Trigg Hotels?" Beffort sounded surprised.

"Yes, Sir," Ritter joked, "I see you travel a lot. What do you have against this fat cat?"

"Tell me about him," Beffort avoided the question.

"Bah… 30 years old, spoiled rich kid, skirt-chaser, gambler and probably a little homosexual. Personally I think he swings both ways. Besides that he also gets into drugs, beatniks, Nazis, whatever's in at the moment."

"Is it in to work for Madame Atomos?"

Max Ritter was speechless for a few seconds. Finally, he said, "You're joking, right?"

"No," Beffort assured him in all seriousness. "Your Trigg bought a sawmill in Cincinnati. The purchase dates back two years. Today we're almost positive that the Atomos gang is using the mill as a base. So, we can deduce from this that Arthur was already a fan of Madame Atomos during the height of her power. What do you say?"

"Nothing," Ritter said, "I'm thinking."

"Okay, Max, think about it, but stick some of your men on Trigg's tail. Go through his bank accounts, watch his friends and see if he's not chairing the A.O.F.M.A. And make sure that he's not hiding Madame Atomos in his bathroom! After that, call me at the headquarters here in Cincinnati. Got it?"

"Got it."

Beffort hung up and said, "Let's hit the road. We're going straight to the Garrani sawmill."

Mie hooked his arm and walked beside him, Akamatsu followed and big Owen took up the rear. What a team!

Smith watched the sawmill from a little hill. Through his binoculars, the workshop and the little house looked empty, almost deserted. When he was alive, old Garrani (in fact, what did he die of?) must not have been rolling in dough and the buildings probably looked exactly the same: roof tiles blown off by the wind, colorless, cracked walls, the surrounding fence falling down…

"It's isolated," Owen said soberly, "it's weird."

Beffort was wondering how to get closer without being spotted because from a strategic point of view, the two buildings were perfectly situated. There not a tree or a bush within 150 yards. Beyond that was a triple row of fir trees planted like sentinels on the shore of the river separating Ohio and Kentucky. To the right, a thick curtain of trees hiding Highway 50. To the left, some rolling hills that blocked off Addyston.

A dead end road led from the highway to the sawmill's yard. There was no other way in because a car could not drive on the surrounding land. Or you had to go from hump to hole on foot, like infantrymen…

"We can't do anything before nightfall." Akamatsu said.

Owen stared at him. "So the Yellow Mask counts for nothing?"

Akamatsu smiled. "All depends on what you intend to do, Owen" he said quietly. "To knockout whoever's in the sawmill, I'm sure the car will fit the bill. But to get a lead on Madame Atomos, we have to be crafty, not be seen…"

"We don't have time," Beffort cut in. "We're going to attack head on. If Madame Atomos is here, we'll take her by surprise. If she isn't, let's hope that the guy who answered the telephone will lead us to her."

Mie asked candidly, "Attack head on means what, Smith?"

Beffort stood up, went down the hill that was hiding the Malibu, opened the car door and said, "Get in, Mie, I'll show you."

Mie climbed in the back with Akamatsu while Owen sat next to Beffort who started the engine and asked, "Is your car sturdy, Owen?"

"Sturdy as a bull."

"I can go straight on."

Owen pointed his cigar ahead, settled back and waited confidently. Beffort let the car take off and then sped up. The speedometer needle jumped up and hovered around 75 as the fence came hurtling forward. Then the rotten boards exploded into splinters... The Malibu slowed down, crashed through the door of the workshop and barreled into the building. Dusty machines, piled up boards, heaps of sawdust, a glass box for an office where a panicking man came running out with his finger on the trigger of a machine gun.

The gunfire scattered without even scratching the armor. Owen rolled down his window and neutralized the man with one shot from his paralyzing pistol. While Beffort swung around, he went to pick the guy up and throw him in the back at the feet of Mie and Akamatsu.

"There's one who'll be squealing in an hour."

"Let's see if there are any others. Mie, you watch the car."

The young lady put her weapon on her knees. The three men searched the building, crossed the yard and went through the rooms of the little house, but found nothing. Everything was empty, desolate. Old dust and cobwebs... They went back to the workshop, searched the office again, but except for the telephone, nothing had been used for a long time. Behind a file cabinet, Akamatsu found an inflatable mattress, a sleeping bag, two blankets and a gas lamp.

In one of the drawers Bernitz found some canned food, bottles of beer and cigarette cartons. Under the desk were several clips for the machine gun, all full. Not a single sheet of paper and no office supplies.

Beffort went back to the car and searched the man's pockets. They were empty.

Mie, who was not looking kindly at him, said, "If he dies, we'll never know his identity, Smith."

Beffort shook his head. "Probably bound for the gallows. His fingerprints are certainly in the FBI archives. I think..." His words were interrupted by the shrill of a telephone ringing somewhere in the workshop.

In the office, Owen Bernitz was staring at the phone, unsure of what to do. Akamatsu looked for Beffort's approval, got it, and picked up. He heard, "Mr. Beffort?"

Akamatsu felt shocked. He had heard this voice only three of four times, but he would recognize it among a thousand. "Who's this?"

Madame Atomos' laughter drilled into his ears. "My fellow countryman! They didn't tell me that you, too, were part of the expedition! But I know that Beffort and Mie are there as well as the fat, disgusting head of the Green Dragon Force. Tell me, Akamatsu, why do you want to die so stupidly?"

From the car Beffort turned a finger in circles, thus telling his colleague to stretch out the conversation then he got on the radio. Akamatsu felt feverish all of a sudden. If he managed to keep her talking long enough, the FBI headquarters in Cincinnati would be able to trace the call. He felt stupid.

"Sorry, I don't understand what you mean, Shirley. You're not too hung over, sweetie?" On the phone, the silence was like death. Sweating bullets, the Japanese special agent continued, "You were sleeping so soundly that I didn't have the heart to wake you up this morning. Is it a queasy stomach that makes you think Bernitz is disgusting?" Not knowing what it was all about, Owen's eyes were popping out of his head.

Madame Atomos spoke slowly and coldly. "Don't play me for a fool, Akamatsu. You know perfectly well who I am because I'm the only one who can telephone you. You had to follow up on the Doug Egerton lead and you had to end up in the Garrani sawmill. It's done. Now, you're going to die."

"How?" Akamatsu asked flatly.

"The building is mined."

"I thought you gave you future victims a warning?"

"When it comes to simple mortals, yes. For you, I made an exception. You escaped me so often that I can't take the risk of…"

Akamatsu had already laid down the telephone and was no longer listening. He dragged Bernitz with him and rushed to the car. He dove in, yelling, "Step on it, Smith! It's going to blow any second!"

Already behind the wheel, Beffort started the engine and peeled out even though Bernitz still had one foot on the ground. With surprising agility, he big man danced inside and slammed the car door as the Malibu headed for the fence.

Chapter VII

Beffort heard four explosions and everything in his rear view mirror disintegrated. The blast roared past, twisting around the car in a hail of debris: broken boards, crooked beams, shattered tiles, windows and walls. Dirt rained down and obstructed the visibility. Beffort slammed on the brakes, swearing. On all sides the rubble was flying, a whirlwind of gray dust riddled with red-hot missiles. A little hell flying by and tearing apart everything in a 50-yard radius. Even with its armor, the Malibu would have been reduced to scrap iron if it had not escaped the epicenter of the insane tornado.

It lasted five seconds and then all of a sudden there was a strange silence. Strange because abrupt. A feeling of emptiness, humming ears, and then a voice: "6289 calling Yellow Mask... 6289 calling Yellow Mask..."

Beffort flipped the switch and picked up the radio. "Yellow Mask here. Did you pinpoint the call?"

"Not enough time," Stutton grumbled. "You in a scrape?"

"Nothing serious. Did the call come from Cincinnati?"

"Yes and certainly from a public phone booth. Headquarters had just barely got on it when it cut off. Impossible in less than five minutes."

Around the Yellow Mask, the visibility was clearing up. Through the last whirls of dust Beffort saw a red spot. A huge thing, moving fast, with a kind of elephantine agility.

"Damn!" Bernitz swore. "What the hell is that?"

The ambient silence was broken by a rumbling engine, a powerful roar mixed with dull, choppy thuds.

"Okay," Beffort spoke quickly into the microphone, "let loose the 300 men of the Green Dragon Force. I'll call back later. Over and out."

He switched off and looked around. To the right and left, though still hard to see, two other huge red things were knocking about. Farther away, way back, Beffort caught a brief sight of lights between two curtains of dust.

"Three bulldozers and six sedans," Mie, who had the eyes of a cat, murmured.

A gust of wind blew the dust away and the sun sparkled on the bulldozers' blades and revealed the six cars lined up on the mound across the road. Stuck between the river and the armada of the Atomos gang, the Malibu had no way out.

Bernitz grinned wildly and thumbed the switch for the control screens. "Let's go, boss!"

Beffort looked down and moved the arrow. One bulldozer showed up on the first screen and the radar automatically put the cab in the line of fire. Beffort pressed the button and sent a short burst of gunfire. Inside, the man doubled over and fell onto the tracks, which dragged down his body before crushing it.

"Watch out!" Akamatsu shouted.

To the right, the second machine was coming in with its blade raised. Beffort floored it, grazed the first bulldozer, which was still moving blindly, and was forced to swerve off the road to avoid the charge of the third attacker. As the Malibu bounced over the potholes, it faced the six cars, which it swept with a few rounds from the machine gun. Beffort flipped a u-turn and hit them with his rear guns.

"Two down!" Owen said cheerfully. "I'll take care of the targets, you just drive!"

Beffort got the Malibu back on the road. The car was fast and incredibly easy to handle. He was off again while the two bulldozers were barely starting to turn around.

Bernitz worked the arrow and zeroed in. "Fire!" he yelled.

Beffort glanced at both front and rear screens at the same time and pressed the two buttons. At 20 yards, the driver of the second jumped and jerked on impact and then crashed into the shattered windshield. In the rear, the double burst of gunfire turned a face and chest into a bloody pulp. The air smelled like gunpowder and echoed with the rumble of engines and the hysterical staccato of automatic weapons.

The battle lasted only 40 seconds. Madame Atomos' men had not yet realized that they were being slaughter, so they kept firing at the Malibu, which brushed off the bullets...

"Fire!" Bernitz raged.

On instinct, without seeing anything, Beffort pressed the buttons. He heard the gunfire and saw the bulldozer veer off and then wobble on the edge of a hole created by the mines. The machine seemed to hesitate and then just dropped.

Beffort spun the wheel and slammed on the accelerator. The Malibu sped toward the three cars left on the road. It barely vibrated under the impact of the bullets before opening fire itself. The first car drifted off, engulfed in flames. A burning man jumped out and stared dancing wildly and screaming. Mie hid her face in her hands. She was horrified and got sick on the floor. A gas tank exploded, spreading fire to the other driverless vehicles.

The man stopped screaming and dancing. He dropped to the ground and rolled around, still burning. The Malibu could not swerve around. It ran over him to chase after the two cars still intact, unleashing a new round from the machine guns.

Hit head on, tires blown, gas tank drilled, the back car drove off the road, jumped over a mound and rolled down the slope until it finally crashed into a tree. The other car shot off, swerved and skid onto Highway 50, picked up speed and swerved again.

"He's going to do it all by himself," Owen Bernitz prophesized.

The car was all over the road, shaking and wobbling. The panicked driver tried to straighten it out to avoid a big semi heading full speed down the highway. He swerved off, miraculously missed a tree, turned sharply to the left and came right back to end up jammed under the big rig.

"Well, I'll be," Bernitz said to no one in particular. His excitement had just vanished. He felt vacant.

Beffort pulled the Malibu gently over to the side of the road. Then he called 555-6289.

Around the same time, but in San Francisco, Max Ritter was personally taking charge of the Arthur Trigg matter. The accusation was serious. Trigg, as head of the A.O.F.M.A., had huge sums of money, almost astronomical, liable at any time to end up in Madame Atomos' pockets. Moreover, it meant the infiltration of a certain faction of society. A corrupt but unfortunately powerful faction.

If the peaks are rotten, the roots are already sick. Therefore, Trigg could have been part of a contagious sickness. A beggar chanting slogans has no effect. A billionaire whispering the Atomos doctrine, mixing up politico-intellectual pretexts like: Racial Equality! Stop the War in Vietnam! Brotherhood! And so on—it could have some serious consequences.

The United States was crawling with associations, both official and secret. From the Ku Klux Klan to the Nazis, from the commie reds to the commie pinks, from black panthers to white supremacists, the A.O.F.M.A. could take its pick. Money, the sinews of war, would give Madame Atomos the means to rebuild everything that they had taken so much trouble to destroy.

Thinking about this, Ritter broke out in a cold sweat.

He turned at the coast and stopped in the parking lot of the Trigg Palace Hotel. When he saw the police car and ambulance, he rushed over and flashed his identification as he made his way through the crowd. He grabbed Lieutenant Powers by the sleeve and asked, "Accident?"

The lieutenant shrugged his shoulders. "Crime. Trigg's just got his throat slashed in the bathroom. Sex scandal."

Ritter nodded unconsciously, turned around and went back to his car. He could have checked the bank accounts, but to prove that Trigg belonged to the A.O.F.M.A. was another kettle of fish.

In Cincinnati, the Green Dragon Force had been on the go since Madame Atomos' telephone call to the Garrani sawmill. They thought that the terrible women had called from a phone booth in the city. It was vague, but the Green Dragons were used to searching for nothing. In other times, Beffort would have taken drastic measures: arresting all Asian women, roadblocks everywhere, surveillance of the train stations, airports, etc. At the moment all this seemed pointless. Madame Atomos was obviously not trying to run away since she had not finished the job that put her in Cincinnati.

Apparently, this job consisted in executing nine people, including Beffort, Mie and Akamatsu, but this was certainly a cover, a smokescreen, a pretty shoddy masquerade. The formidable Japanese woman was preparing some top secret plan in the wings that only she knew about and that would kick off a new attack against the USA.

While the 300 men of the Green Dragon Force were hunting through the city for the slightest clue, Beffort, Akamatsu and Bernitz were waiting for their prisoner to wake up. They were in an empty room at headquarters and the hands of the clock read 1 p.m.

Since the battle of Dead Man's Gulch, they had taken the guy's fingerprints and now knew that his name was Hank Seurer. An ex-con, having done six years in Omaha and ten in Sing Sing and then released on parole, which he skipped out on right away. Currently awaiting a life sentence after six holds in Alabama, one of which ended in the death of the head teller.

"He's moving," Akamatsu whispered.

Seurer was, in fact, coming around. He opened his eyes, shook his head like a dazed boxer, and looked around him in confusion. First of all he saw Beffort and Akamatsu, then he recognized Owen Bernitz and closed his eyes, grinning.

"So, Hank," Owen spoke with ominous good-humor, "up to bat for Madame Atomos or just chasing after the ball?"

Seurer would have preferred to stay unconscious for a few hours longer. He knew Bernitz by reputation. The reputation that he had before working for Smith Beffort at the time when he laid down the law for organized crime. To fall into his hands would never be a picnic.

Owen sat down and took the cigar stub out of his mouth. "Listen, man," instinctively changing his manner of speech, "we're just here to have a little chat. If you cough up, Mr. Beffort here is ready to help you out. Meaning you won't die in the pen."

Seurer did not move. Bernitz continued, "If you zip it, you'll be in the hot seat before the end of the week and they'll stick a cross on your belly."

Seurer opened one eye and said, "If I gab, it's Madame Atomos who'll stick a cross on my belly."

"That's right, man! Only, it's not Mama Atomos who's holding the cards right now!"

"She'll get 'em back sooner or later," Seurer stated simply. "Then I'll be nothing but a patsy. Just like Doug Egerton. See what I mean? The guy who makes a mistake is offed, that's all."

Beffort took a step forward. "If you cooperate, Hank, I'm offering you a place in the Green Dragon Force. If you refuse, I'll let you walk out right now."

Seurer was not stupid. He knew that if he walked down to the corner a free man, he would be taken out. On the other side of the balance was the Green Dragon Force and its promise of amnesty at the end of the game.

He did not even have to think about it. He said, "Okay, I'll play ball. Except, I'm warning you that you're going to be disappointed. What I know about Madame Atomos and her plans can fit on a postage stamp."

With a nod from Beffort, Owen took control of the interrogation. Psychologically the old killer had more weight with the crooks. Plus, being in charge of the

Green Dragon Force he was also the boss of the new recruit.

"Hank," he started in, "don't start by ducking out. Now who brought you into the Atomos gang?"

"Scarlett. That was two months ago when I was hiding out in Frisco. The cops were after me and I couldn't go out except at night. I'd burned through all my dough and the guy stashing me was threatening to kick me out. So, you see, things were getting hot. And when it got worse, Egerton turned up in my pad. I knew him in Omaha, in the pen, which smoothed things out for us. He told me that times were over for solo jobs, that he had to join this powerful organization to survive and that if I wanted, he could put me in touch with the guy who did the recruiting."

"Did you know it had to do with Madame Atomos?"

"No! If I knew, I really think I would've hit the road. Don't think that the guys working for her were all in on it from the start. Most of 'em were scammed like me and…"

"Got it," Owen interrupted. "So, Egerton introduced you to Scarlett?"

"That's right. Scarlett didn't tell me what I'd be doing in his team, but he slipped me 500 dollars to pay my debts and clean me up. Then they dragged me around in an air-tight trailer with no windows for 15 days and I ended up on a farm…"

"Whereabouts?"

Seurer shrugged. "I told you I didn't know much! After 15 days on the road without seeing the sun, I could've been in Florida or Pennsylvania!"

"Why not Ohio?" Beffort asked.

Seurer shook his head. No, it was too far from Cincinnati. I knew that after I made another trip for 10 days to become the guard at the Garrani sawmill."

"Let's get back to this farm," Owen said. "What did you do there?"

"Paint! Better still, I painted the walls and ceiling a cream…"

"Were there people on the farm?" Owen was surprised.

Seurer sighed, pinched his nose and said, "Give me a cigarette. It's a funny story."

Beffort threw him his pack and looked at his watch. Time was passing quickly and was on the side of Madame Atomos who must have been preparing fresh attacks against the survivors on the list. But it was not possible to cut corners and put off Seurer's interrogation. The man thought he knew nothing because he had no idea what kind of problem he was dealing with. For Beffort, Akamatsu and Bernitz, one detail, however minor, could reveal the whole framework of Operation Ohio.

Seurer lit his cigarette, took a long drag and said, "The farm was used as a dorm for sleeping. The worksite wasn't there. For you to get it, I gotta tell you that the place was totally deserted. Imagine an old building stuck in the middle of the plains with a hill to the north and a gorge to the south. In fact, the farm was closer to the hill since that's where the worksite was…"

"What were they building?" Bernitz asked.

"You won't believe me."

"Try me… ten to one says it was a concrete building underground."

"Not underground but in the hill," Seurer corrected as he was starting to feel a little respect for Bernitz.

"Same thing," Owen responded. "What do you think, boss?"

Beffort was thinking, so he did not answer right away. He was thinking that the Atomos laboratory would very soon become a reality if no action were taken to hinder the progress of the work.

"How many men on the worksite?" he asked.

"About 50," Seurer answered.

"Did you talk with them?"

"I tried, but they only opened their mouths to give me orders. And they spoke every other language but mine."

Bernitz frowned. "How did you understand their orders, Hank?"

Seurer shrugged. "Even if the guy's yapping in Chinese, you always know it when you gotta wake up, go to eat or smear another coat on the wall. I thought I was gonna blue collar it 'til the whole time when Egerton came back. He threw me in that damn trailer again and we got back on the road. Egerton brought me food at night, locked the door and lay down on the other cot. After ten days, we got to the sawmill. Egerton told me to guard the shack for two weeks. Scarlett called me a few times every day to see if everything was all right. It was just great! Finally after one call, two guys from the gang turned up with Egerton all tied up like a sausage. That's when he told me we were working for Madame Atomos. The next day, one of the guys killed Egerton right in front of me, then his buddy and him carried the corpse... After that nothing happened 'til you showed up."

"Except," Bernitz said, "someone tried to place an order. It was me, remember?"

"Right! And Scarlett was interested in that!"

"Come on! The sawmill was mined and you were supposed to blow up with it. No doubt about it, Hank, you had a cushy job! Since San Francisco you were a pigeon! They hired you special to answer the phone before being turned into sausage meat. While waiting for the plan to ripen, they dragged you all over the country so you'd think the farm was in the boondocks…"

"Well, it's very far from San Francisco," Beffort interrupted, "but not 15 days of driving. Look, Seurer, when were you at the worksite?"

"I got to the farm on March 20 and I stayed until April 22."

"What was the weather like?"

"Cold but nice."

"So, you couldn't have been in Florida."

"I just threw that out there," Seurer objected. "Really I felt like I was somewhere in the north. Sorry but that's the best I can do."

Akamatsu gave Seurer another cigarette and said, "We already know that the farm wasn't in the mountains or on the coast or near a lake. Say, Hank, how do you know that you were still in the United States?"

"What a question!" Seurer was alarmed.

"I was thinking of Canada."

"No! When Egerton got gas, the attendants… Damn! Now I remember that one of them mentioned some strange place during the second trip. Egerton must have asked a question and the guy said that Chardon was only an hour away!"

Beffort took a deep breath. Seurer's subconscious was finally waking up. "That was after you left the farm," he said. "How many days after?"

"The same day! Yeah, that's right, we left at noon and Egerton got gas at around 7 p.m. Chardon! That's a name you remember, isn't it?"

Chapter VIII

There were a lot of Chardons in the United States, but only one caught the eye of Beffort and Akamatsu. It was in northern Ohio about a dozen miles from Lake Erie, not far from Cleveland and a short distance from the Pennsylvania border.

Seurer was the most surprised to see that his information, offered off the top of his head, turned out to be real.

"Do you know Pennsylvania?" Akamatsu asked.

"No," Seurer was astonished. He could not get over it.

Bernitz slapped him on the shoulder. "Until now you've had bad breaks, but starting this morning the luck's on your side. Maybe that's because you've hopped the fence..."

"Yeah," Seurer agreed passively.

Beffort turned to him. "You left the farm at noon. Around 7 p.m. you were still only an hour away from Chardon. We won't get anywhere if you can't give us the approximate speed the trailer was traveling."

"Egerton wasn't driving fast," Seurer said. "I don't think he ever went over 50. But he couldn't because he only took side roads that were in bad condition."

"Good observation," Akamatsu complimented. "Chardon is actually on Highway 6."

"The problem," Beffort said, "is that it's impossible to drive for seven hours from Cincinnati straight to Chardon without hitting Pennsylvania. So we could end up in any direction at all. Unless..." He paused, looked at the map more carefully and resumed, "Unless Egerton just took Seurer for a drive, since it doesn't take ten days to cross Ohio! In that case, we could put this farm any-where around Chardon, but within a range of 400 miles. Real drudge work to locate it. Say, Hank, you're sure you don't remember anything else?"

"No," the man answered wearily. "I can't remember what I didn't see. Don't forget that I was locked up in the trailer... All I can say is that Egerton stopped an hour after we left the farm to buy something. You see, it's nothing!"

"What kind of something?"

"A hat."

Beffort was startled. "Why didn't you say so!"

"We didn't talk about it," Seurer defended.

Beffort took off his fedora and turned it over to look inside. "Look! I bought this hat in Washington at Trad-er's and it's written right here. Where's Egerton's hat? When we found him on the vacant lot in Norwood, he wasn't wearing..."

"That's no surprise," Seurer grumbled. "The guys from the gang took it off him before capping him in the head. The last time I saw that hat it was in the sawmill!"

"Ah hell," Bernitz swore, "that's all we need!"

Beffort was already thinking of the tons of debris that they would have to sift through to find Egerton's lid...

Paradoxically, for Beffort and his men, Doug Egerton's hat had become the most important piece in the new Atomos puzzle.

Hank Seurer was put in the good hands of Sammy and a detachment of the Green Dragon Force went to Dead Man's Gulch. After the fabulous show put on by the Malibu, the police had cleared the land. They had taken away the carcasses of the vehicles and pried out the car from under the semi, but nothing, fortunately, had been done to the ruins of the sawmill.

Through Silver's intervention, Beffort got two bulldozers, shovels, pickaxes and a search team to help out. Silver looked at the crater created by the mines and scowled. "Without a stroke of luck, you might still be here in a month."

"Do you have any better ideas?" Beffort asked rather harshly.

"No," Silver admitted. "Since the deaths of the seven councilmen, we haven't heard from Madame Atomos and I can't even give you someone special to protect. It's like our victory over her commando team has discouraged her."

Beffort barely smiled. "You don't know her. When you think she's down and out, she's right in the middle of hatching a counter-attack. You'll get news from her before nightfall."

The bulldozers were heaving up huge mounds of dirt and debris onto the road where a team of men was sifting through the rubble. Father along, in the crater, other men were hammering away with pickaxes at the lunar landscape. Nothing was left of the sawmill or the small house and the vanished machines seemed to have melted in the extraordinary heat. But they were obviously buried under the six cubic feet of pulverized wreckage, which was not encouraging for finding the hat.

"You weren't supposed to get out of here alive," Silver said.

He had already said this, but was repeating himself because the sight before him was really impressive. Beffort nodded unconsciously as he watched a man holding up a round object that turned out to be just a pot that looked like a sieve.

"Mrs. Beffort must have nerves of steel," Silver spoke aloud to himself. "In fact, she's not here, is she?"

"She's taking a rest at the Mount Royal Hotel," Beffort said. In which he was seriously mistaken...

It was purely by chance. When Mie left Smith after the battle of Dead Man's Gulch, she took a taxi to the Mount Royal Hotel. She was exhausted, her nerves depleted, and she wanted nothing more than to lie down for an hour or two. Then, around Crosley Field, the taxi pulled up to a red light next to a brand new Oldsmobile Vista Cruiser station wagon. Mie only noticed it because it was pink and white. Her eyes wandered over the shiny body and stopped at the driver, who was just behind her.

Something clicked in her head and as she turned to get a better look, she was flabbergasted. She recognized the man; it was Yuri Belof; and she was flooded with memories from almost three years ago[4].

The light turned green and the station wagon shot off. Mie shook herself, leaned forward and in a tense voice said to the driver, "We're not going to the Mount Royal anymore. Follow that car!"

"The station wagon?"

"Yes. Try not to be seen. I want to know where it's going, that's all."

Yuri Belof in Cincinnati! It was amazing, unbelievable! Five years earlier this man had been an interpreter in a travel agency in Moscow. One day, he had accompanied a client name Mikonosuke Watanabe on a tour, was drugged and then woke up in Atomos City, a fully fledged member of the Organization, with a motor brain that transformed him into a robot under total control of the Greta Brain!

---

[4] See *The Return of Madame Atomos.*

This Mikonosuke Watanabe was one of Madame Atomos' damned souls and also the architect of Mie's kidnapping, who then became Miss Atomos. During the famous neutralization hour, Mie, Belof, Igor Serabian, Jean Marchand and Catherine Lomakine spoke about their past. From this small group only Mie, Belof and Marchand had survived thanks to the surgeons at the clinic in Atlanta.

Since then, Beffort and Mie thought that Yuri Belof had gone home to Moscow where his wife and three children were waiting for him. And now all of sudden he is back, a symbol of the years gone by, of the extraordinary moments that Mie had lived inside the Atomos Organization. It was overwhelming!

Mie wanted to believe that it was just a look alike, but Belof had a very particular face, very Slavic, and with that buzz cut on top of his head you could see the unmistakable sign of the two brain operations. Mie had the same marks and managed to hide them with a clever hairdo, but there was no mistaking the sinister half-moon scar.

While the taxi was following the pink and white station wagon with no problem, she became more and more certain that for some mysterious reason Yuri Belof had stayed in the United States after escaping Madame Atomos. Maybe he had been living in Cincinnati for the past three years, had tried to forget about his tragic adventure, and by some crazy stroke of fate found himself suddenly on the front lines again. With the newspapers, radio and television, he must have known that Madame Atomos was running wild in the city. And this must have unleashed a dreadful wave of terror inside him.

"The station wagon's stopping," the taxi driver said. "What do I do?"

Mie came back to reality. "Drop me here," she held out a bill.

When the taxi pulled to the curb, she jumped out and followed Belof. He crossed the street and went down the other sidewalk. He looked in good health, was walking briskly and had absolutely nothing in common with the man Mie had known. He entered a building and waited for the elevator to come down to the first floor.

Mie made up her mind and hurried forward. Up close, the scar was clearly visible. "Hello, Mr. Belof."

The man turned around, his face suddenly drained of blood.

Mie smiled and added, "Don't tell me that you don't recognize me."

He shook his head, slowly. "You're mistaken. My name's Strong." The same voice, the same eyes. Mie was petrified. "And I don't know who you are," he concluded.

He turned around, opened the elevator door and got in. "Are you taking the elevator, Miss?"

Mie shook her head. Strong let the door close, pressed a button and disappeared. Mie went back outside. She was sure that the man was Yuri Belof and that he had recognized her at first sight. She took no time to find a phone booth and called 555-6289 because she did not know how to reach her husband. Ralph Stutton answered right away.

"Can you send me a car?" Mie asked.

"On the double, Mrs. Beffort. Where are you?"

Mie looked up and gave the name of the street, specifying, "I'll be around the phone booth in front of number 65. Make it quick."

"One second," Stutton requested. He got on the radio and instantly found the position of the closest car. He announced to Mie, "Ben Brady is in your sector and will pick you up in three minutes. Stay in the booth so he can spot you more easily. Anything serious?"

"No, but if you can contact my husband, tell him that I just ran into Yuri Belof..."

"Belof!" Stutton shouted. "That's the guy who..."

"That's him," Mie confirmed. "But he acted strangely. He pretended not to know me and that his name was Strong. I think he's going to get back in his car. I plan to follow him. I'll keep you up to date on my location. What's my husband doing?"

"He's looking for a hat that belonged to Doug Egerton that might give us a clue where to find the Atomos laboratory. Last I heard, the hat couldn't be found. Say, is Mr. Beffort going to be happy when he finds out you're out there all alone..."

"I'm not alone anymore," Mie interrupted him. "Here's Brady's. Talk to you later, Ralph."

She hung up and left the booth when the Chevrolet pulled up to the curb. She got in next to Brady just in time to hear him answer Stutton who was already anxious to find out if the "boss lady" was actually in the phone booth. Mie took the microphone and told him that everything was all right.

"Stay in touch," Stutton requested, probably worried sick.

"Promise," Mie assured him.

"Hey, Ben, be careful, okay?" Stutton repeated.

Brady said he would be careful and Stutton finally went silent.

"Where to, Mrs. Beffort?" Brady asked.

"For now, we're not moving. We're going to follow a man when he gets back in that station wagon you can see over there. Keep your distance and don't get spotted. If he thinks I'm on his tail, he'll try to shake us."

Brady said he understood and lit a cigarette. In the next five minutes Ralph Stutton called twice from dispatch and Mie ended up putting him in his place rather harshly in order to be left alone.

After five minutes, Yuri Belof made his cautious appearance in the doorway. He looked right, then left, did not see Mie, who was hidden by Brady's impressive bulk, and finally went to get into his station wagon.

"Funny looking guy," Brady remarked with his usual frankness.

"Don't say anything bad about him. He saved my life when Madame Atomos was holding me prisoner."

Brady fell in behind the station wagon on Beechmont Avenue. Tailing him was easy because of the heavy traffic. Moreover, it was obvious that Belof did not think that he was being followed. After Forestville, the wagon took Highway 125, passed Cherry Grove, went a few miles more and entered Tobasco. Belof slowed down there, got on the beltway and then turned onto a side road heading north.

Just then Ralph Stutton came through again. "6289 to Gourmet. Come in."

Mie picked up the microphone. "Everything's okay, Ralph!"

"Maybe , but Mr. Beffort doesn't think so! He said you should come back."

"Out of the question! I want to know why Yuri Belof didn't recognize me and what he's doing in Cincinnati and…"

"Mr. Beffort advises you to go back to the hotel," Stutton said bluntly. "He thinks it could be dangerous, that this Belof isn't acting normal and Madame Atomos could very well be behind the whole thing."

Mie pursed her lips. "Tell my husband that I'm not a little girl and I know how to take care of myself! Now, don't bother me for no reason, Ralph. When I have news, I'll call you. Over and out!"

She turned off the radio in the middle of Stutton's protest. Ben Brady flipped it back on. "Sorry, Mrs. Beffort, but we have instructions to stay in contact with 6289. If Ralph is bothering you, plug your ears. Me, I'm on duty."

Mie clenched her fists. This Green Dragon Force was starting to get on her nerves. Then, right away, she forgot all about her little grudge because less than 100 yards ahead the station wagon had just driven through the gate of a fenced in property.

Chapter IX

Beffort felt his bad mood getting worse as the hours passed. Dead Man's Gulch was nothing but a huge worksite that the bulldozers plowed through relentlessly. The men were working with less enthusiasm and to make matters worse it had been drizzling for a while, slowly soaking into the ground to turn it into sticky mud.

"Well, 6289, answer! Where is it, this Gourmet car of yours?"

"Outside Tobasco," Stutton answered, seeing himself caught between a rock and a hard place. "Mrs. Beffort doesn't want to listen."

"Order her to drop it!"

"I already did."

"Who's with her?"

"Ben Brady. An old-timer."

"Yeah!" Furrowing his brow, Smith knew that he could not change Mie's mind, that he would be better off giving in, but he did not like it. What was Yuri Belof doing in the United States? Since the affair on the Coconino Plateau in Arizona, nobody had heard a word about him or Jean Marchand, the other escapee from Atomos City. The presence of the Russian suddenly created an unexpected suspense, a troubling uncertainty, that famous twist that the investigators in classic stories fear so much. All good or all bad, depending; the arrival of a new character in a tight scenario...

"Okay, Ralph," Beffort said, "let her go."

"That's better for me."

"But don't forget to contact the Gourmet every 15 minutes! Belof might just be the bait. Keep me informed."

"Got it."

Beffort got out of the Malibu and joined Akamatsu, who was stooped over in the gusty wind. "Still nothing, Yosho?"

The Japanese special agent shook his head and spread his hand over the worksite. "It's an impossible task, Smith. Doug's hat was obviously blown up in the explosion. We're wasting precious time on nothing."

Beffort was starting to think the same thing, but was still holding off the order to abandon the search. This hat was of the utmost importance and could quickly give them a way to nip the Atomos threat in the bud.

"In my opinion," Akamatsu continued, "we'd be better off starting our research around Chardon without delay."

Beffort turned up his coat collar and slipped his hands into his pockets. "I don't think so. Madame Atomos knew that Hank Seurer would be taken alive and did what was necessary to keep him in the dark. Plus, Egerton's execution proves that whoever knows the location of the future laboratory won't be getting any older."

"Okay, but Hank Seurer heard the gas station attendant say that Chardon was only an hour away."

With his stomach turning, Beffort lit a cigarette and said, "We figured out that it was Chardon, Ohio because it worked for us and seemed logical, but everyone knows that Madame Atomos toys with logic. Let's take a different look at it and say that the trailer traveled for ten days in a straight line. At 300 miles a day, which isn't much if you drive from dawn to dusk, it could have gone 3,000 miles. You see where that puts us?"

"Yes," Akamatsu responded. "That puts us in the south where the weather was nice at the time. Now,

Seurer said that it was cold. Why are you trying to complicate everything, Smith?"

All of a sudden a man started jumping up and down and shouting, waving something muddy and shapeless in the air. Beffort and Akamatsu ran over, slipping and sliding over the soggy ground. They were soon joined by Bernitz and Silver, out of breath and covered with fresh mud from the waist down.

Beffort grabbed the gray fedora, turned it over and swore: on the leather band all he could read was *Tibet Hat made and sold by C. Hauser*. There had been an address with the name of the city, but it had been scratched out so carefully that not a letter was visible. Speechless, Beffort and Akamatsu looked at each other. Madame Atomos had once again planned things down to the smallest detail.

Mie Azusa grabbed the handle and opened the car door. "Stay here, Ben, I'm going to see what's on the other side of the wall."

Brady opened his door. "No way, Mrs. Beffort. I'm here to protect you and I'm going to follow you wherever you go. But first I have to tell dispatch. You okay with that?"

He was gently authoritative, already picking up the radio as he was talking. Mie took a few steps on the road. The property was not really isolated. Nearby were bungalows and a garage, but it all looked very rural, or very suburban. No movement or traffic during the day. In the evening it would be different when the people came back from work. The place would wake up for an hour or two and then everyone would sit in front of the TV and the dead-end roads off the highway would become deserted again.

Silence and solitude.

Without really listening, Mie heard Brady talking with Stutton, who sounded resigned. There was no shouting. Brady signed out, closed the door and joined Mie. "You really want to go in there, Mrs. Beffort?"

"Why? Ralph isn't crazy about the idea?"

"He thinks it's reckless."

"You think so too?"

Brady opened his overcoat to reveal a machine gun and a paralyzing pistol. He declared, "Personally, I have no opinion, Mrs. Beffort. I was part of the team that was protecting you when your son and Soblen were killed... Well, I feel guilty and if I can do anything to fix it, maybe that would do me some good."

Inside the Green Dragon Force, they all felt the same. The disappearance of Bob and Soblen had given them a rude shock. A blow to the heart and to their self-esteem.

Mie waved him thanks, but kept silent. After a few seconds she said, "You know, Ben, in all sincerity, I don't think there's anything to fear from Yuri Belof. My husband and Ralph are making a big deal about it because they're horribly suspicious and they don't trust anyone or anything, but I have the feeling that Belof is just a victim."

Brady nodded politely, but was keeping an eye on the truck that had just appeared at the other end of the road. No one was more suspicious or vigilant than he when circumstances called for it. He slipped his hands into his false pockets and put his finger lightly on the trigger of the machine gun.

Mie continued, "Yuri Belof wouldn't have denied knowing me without good reason. I want to force him to talk, to confess if need be. You understand that, don't you, Ben?"

"Naturally," Ben responded. Then he relaxed. The truck turned down a little road and stopped in front of a bungalow. False alarm.

"That's why I want to see what Belof's doing here," Mie continued anxiously.

"How are we going to talk to him if we're hiding from him?" Brady asked out of common sense.

To tell the truth, Mie had not yet thought of that. First and foremost she wanted to follow Belof to see where he was living and now that she believed she knew, it seemed normal to keep on going.

"I have no intention of hiding," she decided. "We're going to knock on his door, just like that."

She opened her handbag and automatically readied the paralyzing pistol that she always carried with her. This gesture reassured Brady. The "boss lady" was not born yesterday.

"Okay," he accepted, "let's go."

They walked along the wall and reached the double gate. The black paint was chipped and the metal rusted in spots. No bell and no calling device. A sandy driveway that turned at a row of trees hiding the house. All they could see was a square chimney rising above the wind-swept treetops. With the rain continuing to drizzle over everything, it all seemed terribly melancholic.

"I don't like this place," Brady said.

"Why?"

"It's got classic Atomos hideout written all over it. High walls, invisible house and this gate wide open. We enter, they watch us on a camera and we're put down for the count at the bend in the road. I don't like it!"

Mie was drumming her fingers on her bag. To deny that Brady was right would have been a mistake. And now that she was at the gate, she also sensed a real danger.

Brady felt her hesitating. "Before charging in there, I think we should check out these pillars."

As always, he spoke and acted at the same time. He bent down and carefully examined the cement. His eyes wandered over them for a minute and then fixed on a thin plate of glass embedded 20 inches in the ground.

"Come and look at this, Mrs. Beffort."

He was whispering as he stepped slowly backwards. Mie took his place, saw the plate and noticed that it had a faint bluish glow.

"If we cross the ray," she said, "the alarm will sound in the house. Okay, we have to inform my husband!"

They went back to the car and Brady got rid of his machine gun as he slid behind the wheel. Mie sat next to him, feeling uneasy, sure that they were being watched. She rolled a cigarette with her trembling fingers, but forgot to light it.

"Gourmet to 6289," Brady called.

"I'm listening, Gourmet," Stutton answered immediately. "Where are you?"

"The property here is suspicious, Ralph," Brady instinctively lowered his voice.

"Belof still there?" Stutton shot out.

"Yes. At this juncture we've got to give him a long leash, right?"

"Exactly what the boss wants," Stutton confirmed. "You lay low, Ben, if Mrs. Beffort agrees, of course." Mie nodded. Brady answered that he would take care of Belof and signed out.

Mie asked, "What did you mean by a long leash, Ben?"

"That's when we let a guy do whatever he wants, even kill all the folks he visits. That way, Yuri Belof might just lead us straight to Madame Atomos."

Mie sat there pondering. She did not understand how the Russian could have accepted working for the sinister Japanese woman. She refused to believe that he did so of his own free will.

Ben Brady moved the car, parking it discreetly in the nearest driveway, facing the road. From here they could clearly see the gate as well as the stretch of driveway. 30 minutes went by in utter silence before Belof's station wagon reappeared. The Russian was still at the wheel and this time turned north.

"The car seems loaded down," Mie was very observant and attentive.

"That's true," Brady agreed. He suddenly wondered if it wasn't a big mistake, if Belof wasn't just a salesman making deliveries and, which could very well be the case, exchanges for unsatisfied customers. Brady thought he had seen the top of a television in the station wagon's window and he felt more and more perplexed as he started the car.

Mie called Stutton, told him about Belof's departure and that he was heading north toward Milfort. Stutton said that the Green Dragon Force would take over watching the property and asked her to check in as often as possible with their position.

Yuri Belof veered off toward the northeast and entered Columbus at 5 p.m. He stopped to get gas at the edge of town. Since the Gourmet's radio could not reach Cincinnati from this distance, nor receive calls, Brady took the opportunity to call 555-6289 by phone and got Beffort on the line.

"What are you doing, Ben?" the G-man exploded. "We haven't heard from you in 30 minutes!"

"We're in Columbus, boss. The station wagon's driven like hell since it left and if it didn't stop to get gas..."

"Got it," Smith cut him off. "In five minutes you'll be picked up by headquarters in Springfield. Does Belof seem like he's getting close to his destination?"

"No. We're on Highway 62."

"That doesn't mean anything."

"Okay, but why would he get gas if his trip's almost over? On 62 there's gas stations galore, right? I think Belof's still got 500 clicks before he's going to let up. Hey, he's leaving!"

"Don't lose him, Ben," Beffort concluded, "and be extremely careful. I'll talk to you again when I have the relay from Springfield."

Brady hung up and sprinted back to the car where Mie was fiddling impatiently as she watched the station wagon driving off. He jumped in, closed the door when the Mie peeled out, and said, "Mr. Beffort is at dispatch. In a few minutes we'll be picked up by headquarters in Springfield."

"If my husband went back to Cincinnati," Mie figured, "it's because Doug Egerton's hat didn't tell him anything. You know, Ben, I think we've got the only lead."

Ten minutes later, they got Stutton's call and they gave their position. Now they were between Johnstown and Utica, still on 62, and the clock on the dashboard read 5:40 p.m.

Meanwhile in San Francisco, Max Ritter continued his investigation after the death of Arthur Trigg. The way he had been killed was of no more interest to him than the name of the killer. That was police business. On the other hand, Ritter's job was to establish whether or not Trigg had any relations with the mysterious A.O.F.M.A.

He took a trip down to the Pacific National Bank of San Francisco with a team of experts and sifted through the Trigg accounts over the past two years. It was very easy to find the transaction for the purchase of the Garrani sawmill, but the trail went cold right afterward. However, in one week Trigg signed 300 checks! Nose to the grindstone!

"It's weird," one of the experts remarked, "Trigg readily signed a bunch of medium-sized checks to the same person rather than just one big check. Wow, this Mrs. Surrey got 10,000 dollars in seven days, all in 1,000-dollar checks with the ambiguous note *Various Supplies*."

"She's not the only one," his colleague added. "I've got 20 people here who Trigg paid off in the same way."

Ritter asked, "What would he get out of that?"

"Nothing financially. Maybe it's a way not to attract the attention of any would-be investigators into such and such operation."

"Fraud?"

"Not at all. I think Trigg wanted to hide the fact as long as possible that he was paying huge amounts of money to the same people. We just have to see who these people are and where the money came from that Trigg squandered so glibly. Since we're here already, let's start with the second question."

They got back to work. First of all, Trigg had a personal fortune to spend. Then came the income from the hotels. After that, and this was where things started getting interesting, the accounts showed that Trigg was regularly receiving very large sums from different parts of the United States. In all, the deposits balanced out the checks and it would appear that Trigg had very little in his pocket.

"That's some organization!" Ritter admired. "I'd love to get a gander at his books and unless I'm mistaken, we'll find out what's been going on."

Of course, the Trigg Company books had no trace of these curious transactions. One of the experts remarked, "Everything seems to indicate that Trigg was the middleman in a huge movement of funds outside of fiscal control and that he performed this strange trafficking without any personal gain. I wondered what that means?"

Ritter did not enlighten him. Now he was sure that Trigg had been the treasurer, or at least one of the treasurers, of the A.O.F.M.A.

Chapter X

At nightfall, the Oldsmobile Vista Cruiser driven by Yuri Belof entered Canton, still on Highway 62. It crossed the town and pulled up at a roadside diner that was big enough to hold 200 cars. At the moment, around 50 vehicles were parked between the concrete paths reserved for the waitresses. Girls in miniskirts and on roller skates were speeding around, doing their job in a fascinating ballet of long legs and fishnet stockings that was sure to leave no normal man unaffected.

When Belof got his plate, Mie slipped the Gourmet into a free space in the first row. A waitress raced over immediately so Ben Brady had to wait until Mie ordered before calling dispatch. He hid the mic behind his handkerchief and signed in. Beffort answered quickly, which proved how important this tail was. On the map of Ohio, Belof's route was marked with pushpins and it was heading straight for Chardon!

"We just got into Canton," Brady said, eyeing the waitress who was filling up two plates. "Belof's taking a snack break, which means he's still on the road for a while."

"What's he acting like?" Beffort asked.

"Like he hasn't got a care in the world. You see how long it took him to cover these 200 clicks? Just taking a stroll."

"No cars following him?"

"Nada. It's like Belof's…" Brady saw the waitress swivel on her skates and said, "Hold the line, boss. Be right back."

Beffort kept silent. Brady put down the mic and watched the waitress bolt over, balancing a plate in each hand. She stopped short next to the driver, hooked the first plate over the window and shot around the car to do the same for Brady. After that she sailed off, slapping a number on the windshield. Brady picked up the microphone again.

"An alarm?" Beffort sounded worried.

"No, just a cute waitress in a miniskirt. We're at a diner, 20 yards away from Belof who's eating like a tourist."

"Don't lose him," Beffort advised. "The guy we captured at the Garrani sawmill was staying in a hideout around Chardon..."

"Chardon?"

"A little town in northern Ohio that's only 60 miles away from you. According to our man Hank Seurer, the hideout is right around Chardon. So stay on your toes, Ben!"

"Okay. Do you want to talk to Mrs. Beffort?"

"There's no need to draw attention to yourselves from anyone around you by talking too long. I repeat that you must be careful. The danger gets graver the closer you get to the goal. Belof knows my wife. If he spots her, who knows what he'll do? Stay quiet and stay vigilant. And don't use the radio until you leave the diner. Bon appétit. Talk to you soon."

Brady hung up the mic, but left the radio on. Mie grabbed his arm. "Look, Ben! Yuri Belof's walking off."

The Russian took a few steps toward the road before walking back to the building while Brady got ready to follow him. When he entered the restroom, Brady relaxed. "It's nothing," he said. "He's been driving nonstop since Columbus. Nature calls..."

Two minutes went by. Mie and Brady ate as they watched the restroom door rather anxiously. Belof could have left the building through a hidden door and escaped in another car...

A waitress suddenly sprang out from the counter and rolled between the cars holding up a slate with an airhorn. She turned in front of the Gourmet and showed the slate on which was written, *Telephone for Mrs. Beffort. Urgent. Booth 9.*

"What's the meaning of this?" Brady barked.

Mie was already opening the door. She stopped the waitress to tell her that the message was for her. The girl smiled and took off.

"You're not going to answer that, Mrs. Beffort! No one knows you're here!"

"I think I know what it's about," she said calmly. "Stay here, Ben, this won't take long."

She got out of the car and hastened to the telephone booths before Brady could protest. When she entered booth 9, she saw the phone off the hook. She put it to her ear. "Mrs. Beffort here. Who is this?"

"Yuri Belof," the Russian whispered. "I'm in the restroom and this is the only way I figured out how to talk to you without putting you in danger. I don't think the Atomos gang is watching me, but I wouldn't swear to it..."

"I knew that you were the only one who could be asking for me," Mie declared. "Are you finally going to tell me what you're still doing in the United States? And also how..."

"I called you to tell you my story. When you approached me in Cincinnati, I couldn't talk because I was expected by Madame Atomos."

Mie controlled her alarm. "My God, she was in our hands and you..."

"Listen to me. And do me the favor of believing that I'm not a willing slave of this criminal. I thought I was free after the operation on my brain and for a while I really was. When my recovery was over, I went to my embassy to go back home. My driver didn't say a word, but he turned on a recording that said that my wife and children would be killed if I didn't obey Madame Atomos' instructions. I don't have time to tell you everything. But you can understand that I've been living in terror for the past three years and that I never dared to ask for your help out of fear of retaliation against my family."

"That's awful, Yuri," Mie was terrified. "But your family could be very well protected by the soviet police."

"Sure, you say that when it comes to someone else," the Russian said bitterly. "Do you think the murder of your son and Dr. Soblen gave me hope?"

"Since then Madame Atomos has lost her power."

"She's lost power, but not all her power! Even under the worst circumstances there are people ready to help her. Believe me, Mie Azusa, this woman is demoniacal and I would never have tried to disobey her if you hadn't recognized me in Cincinnati. Since the harm is done, since you seem determined to follow me in spite of the dangers you're facing, I have to take a stand! Even if it means sacrificing my wife and children..."

"Stop talking nonsense, Yuri Belof! I'm going to inform my husband and in less than an hour, your wife and children will be under the protection of the soviet police."

"That would be fabulous."

"You've underestimated us, Yuri," Mie's voice was full of regret. "With your help, we could have crushed

Madame Atomos a long time ago! And so, regarding this building in Cincinnati…"

"No," the Russian interjected. "She's no longer there. Besides, I'm not sure she ever was there."

"Didn't you have an appointment with her?"

Beffort snickered over the phone. "Have you ever seen Madame Atomos have a conversation other than through some machine? Of course she gave me instructions through a speaker, so I wasn't really with her. If you think about it, she could have been in the next room or a thousand miles away."

Mie did not deny the Russian's theory. If Madame Atomos was still alive, it was due to the fact that she always took extraordinary precautions.

"In the end," Belof continued, "even though I've accomplished several missions for her organization, I don't know any more about her than you or Mr. Beffort. However, I recently heard Scarlett talking about a freight train. Do you know who Scarlett is?"

"It's in our files, as well as Keating. But let's get back to this freight train."

"Scarlett said that it would be in Cincinnati soon and that they would remember him for it. That's all I know about it."

"When did you hear this, Yuri?"

"This morning in Tobasco when I went to load this weird machine that you certainly noticed in my station wagon."

"What's it for?" Mie asked, trying to understand a lot of things in a short time.

"I don't know," Belof regretted, "but they made me cross all of Ohio just to bring them this machine. At first sight, even with all its packaging, it looks like a television. Say, Mie, we've been talking a long time, haven't we?"

"That's true. Let's wrap it up," Mie decided after looking at her watch. "Where are you going?"

"Someone told me to go to Chardon. I have be there at 10 p.m. and then phone someone called John and he'll tell me where I have to take it."

Mie did not hesitate. "Will you do what I tell you, Yuri?"

"I trust you."

"Thanks. Here's what you're going to do: at Chardon, when this mysterious John character gives you the last leg of your trip, you'll call 555-6289 in Cincinnati immediately. Smith Beffort will be on the line. He'll take your information and also tell you what's been done for your family in Moscow. Then you'll abandon the station wagon and take a taxi to go to the FBI."

"If I'm being watched..."

"Don't worry about that," Mie interrupted. "We'll fix it so that it will look like you got back on the road after the first phone call. My husband will make the arrangements when he's got all the information. I'll just ask you to choose a telephone booth without glass and to park for ten minutes in front of it before entering."

"In short," the Russian asked, "I'm going to disappear?"

"Exactly. A G-man will already be in the booth when you enter. He'll look like you and be wearing the same clothes and he'll be the one leaving after you call John. He'll get in your station wagon and draw any would-be tails. Meanwhile, you'll talk with Smith Beffort... Is that okay, Yuri?"

"Okay."

"Remember, it's 555-6289 in Cincinnati and don't forget to choose a booth without windows."

"I understand everything. Don't worry. The G-man will have time to enter the booth before the people watching me know that I'm going to call."

"Good. Leave now," Mie said. Belof hung up and left the restroom.

Mie waited a few seconds, left in turn and went back to sit next to Brady. She explained the unexpected turn of events that had just taken place and then called Smith Beffort just when the Russian's station wagon got back on Highway 62.

Brady started the car. He was expecting to leave quickly, so the waitress had taken away their plates a while ago. While the Gourmet was following the station wagon at a respectable distance, Mie explained to Smith the plan that she had just set up with Yuri Belof. Smith let her talk without interrupting even once in order not to muddle the recording that was taping every word.

Finally he said, "It's all a little risky but doable. Let's hope that the gang isn't watching Belof."

"No one knows. Are you going to call Chardon, Smith?"

"Soon. First I'd like to know more about this freight train."

"Belof told me everything he knows. You'd have to capture Scarlett to get all the details."

"Right, but I just learned that the property in Tobasco is empty," Smith barked. "The gang members who were there must have skedaddled right after Belof left while the Green Dragon was still on the way. And of course they left nothing behind…"

"So our only hope lies in Yuri?"

"Unfortunately yes! Nobody here has received an invitation to death and it appears that Madame Atomos has decided to abandon her deadly project. But if she has, it's certainly because her plan was successful. I'm speaking about the lab…"

"Is it really set up in Chardon?"

"Apparently," Beffort mumbled. "She built it in three months with the help of foreign workers and Seurer painted the walls. Which means that the big work is finished. Now all they have to do is equip the laboratory itself."

"The machine that Belof is hauling would be part of the installation. We have to blow the whole thing up, Smith, or else she'll start all over again."

Beffort kept silent for a few seconds. He felt like the culmination of Operation Ohio was fast approaching and it was going to end in a terrible disaster if the Belof lead did not pan out.

"Everything's going to happen tonight, Mie. How far are you from Chardon?"

"Around 50 miles. Belof isn't driving very fast so that he doesn't arrive too early."

"I'm going to hop on a plane and be there for the switch in the telephone booth," Beffort decided on the spot.

"Yuri's going to panic if he can't talk to you when he calls dispatch."

"Silver will keep him calm. Expect to see the Yellow Mask when you get to Chardon."

"How are you going to transport the Malibu?" Mie was astonished.

Beffort laughed. "Don't you worry about that, Mie. Today a jet can carry a tank. We have a date in Chardon!"

Beffort signed out and turned to Akamatsu who was waiting with Bernitz and Silver. "Who wants to deal with the train?"

"I'll take it," Akamatsu said. Then he advised, "You should take our friend Owen to Chardon. He knows best how to back you up when it comes to working the Yellow Mask."

Beffort shook his head. "Owen will be more useful here. He can help you figure out this freight train puzzle. In my opinion, there's a serious danger looming over Cincinnati, Yosho. We have to find out about the train fast and see what's inside it. Silver, I'm counting on you to take care of Belof. Call Moscow, get his wife and kids protected and…"

"I heard your wife," Silver jumped in. "You have to go now. You don't have much time to get to Chardon before Belof."

Beffort nodded and as he opened the door he pointed to Ralph Stutton and said, "Remember that Ralph is coordinating all our actions. Every message, without exception, should go through him. Good luck!"

He left, climbed into the Malibu and headed for the Greater Cincinnati airport located on the other side of Ohio.

After Beffort left, Akamatsu and Owen went straight to the train station. The information they got was vague and they found nothing about the origin of the train. They did not even know if it was already in the Cincinnati station or if it was supposed to arrive soon.

"I'm racking my brain," Owen said, "but I can't see how a train can be dangerous."

"It all depends on the freight it's carrying," Akamatsu answered.

"Okay. Let's say that the cars are packed with dynamite and let's imagine they explode. That would make a lot of noise, but not too much damage to the city. You see how far the yard is from downtown!"

Akamatsu said nothing. He went to the office where they controlled all the train schedules. Having been forewarned by Silver, the network chief was ready and waiting for the two men. Akamatsu explained to him the purpose of their visit and the man dove into his books. He searched for a minute and then stood up straight.

"No weapons transport," he said.

"Even over the next few days."

"Nothing for a month."

Akamatsu was perplexed. Then he asked, "Chemical products?"

"Aha! That's different. We have the 402 coming in at midnight. A daily. 50 cars of chlorine, ten of propane and five of ammonia."

He spoke calmly. Akamatsu thought it best not to alarm him. If the train blew up and the wind blew right, all of Cincinnati could be intoxicated by the chlorine fumes.

Chapter XI

Without getting out of his Malibu, Smith Beffort traveled the 275 miles between Cincinnati and Chardon in the belly of a US Air Force transport plane. 30 minutes after he left, he was driving 125 miles an hour down a long, straight highway. At this breakneck speed he contacted the headquarters in Chardon and found out that everything was ready for Yuri Belof's disappearance. They also told him that the Gourmet was only ten minutes away from the city and that Moscow had responded very favorably to their request for the Belof family protection.

Reassured, Beffort skirted around Chardon, took Highway 62 for a short while and then parked the Yellow Mask on a little side road. He turned off his lights and tried to contact the Gourmet on the radio.

His first attempts got static before Mie's voice got the better of the interference and came over surprisingly clear. Their conversation was short. It was agreed that Mie and Ben Brady would join Smith in the Malibu after the Belof switch.

A moment passed and Beffort saw the Oldsmobile Vista Cruiser go by, driven by the Russian. 15 seconds later the Gourmet came rolling along. Beffort made sure that no one else was following and then fell in behind.

At 9:40 p.m. the station wagon entered Chardon. Belof had timed it perfectly, letting the federal agents position themselves and bring in his replacement. At 9:50, ten minutes before he was supposed to make his call, Belof stopped on Wilson Avenue, turned on his interior light and started looking at a road map. 100 yards away, Mie and Brady abandoned their Chevy and joined

Beffort. There was very little traffic and practically no pedestrians.

"Where's the phone booth?" Mie asked.

Beffort pointed to the other side of the street. "In that alcove. Belof followed your instructions to the letter, but I'm afraid his replacement can be spotted."

At that moment, a group of night owls showed up. There were both men and women, all a little tipsy. In spite of being so few, they made a lot of noise, whooping it up all over the sidewalk.

"Not bad," Beffort commented. "We can see them but can't count them."

The group passed by the telephone booth and continued down the sidewalk without stopping. There was one less. However, it was not noticeable because he had been carefully hidden by his colleagues. The group turned the corner and climbed into three cars that looked like they had been parked there for a long time. In truth, headquarters had just performed a marvelous improvisation, staging the whole thing against the city backdrop. Wilson Avenue was the stage and the streets the wings.

At 9:58, Yuri Belof got out of the station wagon, crossed the street and disappeared into the telephone booth whose door faced the building. The man inside the booth was squatting in the corner. He was holding the phone and obviously talking to a third party.

"John's number?" is all he said.

Belof looked at his notepad and answered, "555-0600."

The stranger repeated the number into the phone and Belof noticed that he was the same size as him and wearing the same clothes, the same hat... His face was different, but the darkness would easily hide it when he left the booth.

The G-man hung up. "You're up," he mumbled. "John will be quietly under wraps before dawn."

Belof said nothing before calling 555-0600. He was awfully nervous. Right now his freedom was at stake, as well as the life of his wife and children. If Madame Atomos spotted the fake, the worst was to be feared.

At the other end of the line, the phone rang only once. As he was told he said, "Doctor Spenk here."

"Good evening," the jolly voice answered. "Thanks for calling. The conference will start in one hour."

"Where?" Belof asked.

"It's hard to explain exactly because the place is very remote. Take Highway 6 to Andover and then turn right as if you were heading to Williamsfield. Someone will be waiting for you there in a green Plymouth."

"Okay. A green Plymouth. And then?"

"You'll follow the car that will lead you to the destination. Hey, is everything okay, doctor?" John was keeping updated, asking casually if Belof had been followed during his trip.

The Russian said that everything was fine.

John said, "I think you're at home there on Wilson Avenue?"

Belof and the G-man glanced at each other. Even though all appearances were to the contrary, the Atomos gang knew where Belof was calling from.

"That's right," the Russian's voice was choked.

"Great! You'll be there quickly. I'll tell your colleagues that you're coming. Have a good trip, Dr. Spenk."

"Thanks."

John hung up. Belof too. The G-man grabbed his arm and said, "I'm leaving. Wait a minute before calling

Cincinnati and stay here until my colleagues come to get you. The key is in the ignition?"

Belof was too emotional to talk; he nodded. The G-man winked at him and left the booth. He scurried across the street, climbed into the station wagon and left.

Smith Beffort gave him some distance. He was just about to pull out when he a saw a big Buick shoot out of a nearby side street and jump on the wagon's tail. At that very second headquarters came over the radio and asked how the scene played out.

"The substitution went off without a hitch, but there's a Buick following the station wagon now."

"You're on it, right?" the operator asked confidently.

"I'd feel better if I knew where this ride was ending," Beffort confessed as he let the Malibu take off. The car literally sprang onto the road and Beffort had to lighten his foot. He was still surprised by the power and bite of the engine.

The man at headquarters said, "We'll pick up Yuri Belof in a minute. He knows where the car's going. Right now he's telling your agent on Cincinnati."

"And what about John?"

"Stuck in a house in South Aguilla. We're about to arrest him right now."

"You're kidding! This guy has to be in touch with Madame Atomos. Leave him alone until we know where the laboratory is. And by the way, alert General Salem immediately. We're going to need his B-52s very soon."

"Got it, Yellow Mask. Location?"

"We're leaving the city on Highway 6," Beffort informed him. "The Buick is on the station wagon. Who's the guy doubling for Belof?"

"Harry Sherman. A vet in the service."

"He's in the worst spot. Too bad the station wagon doesn't have a radio."

The operator laughed but spoke in all seriousness, "Sherman's carrying a transmitter and we're following his route on a screen in Ashtabula. Moreover, James Edward Evans has given orders from Washington and ten heavily armed "birds" are ready to take off from Warren."

Beffort groaned. J.E.E. could not help sticking his nose in the affair. But he had to admit that it was a good move. Ten helicopters could do a lot of damage when it was time to attack.

"Instructions?" the operator asked politely.

"Nothing until further orders," Beffort said. "I'll give my position every five minutes. On your side, just watch over Belof and call me when Cincinnati has news about the train. Over and out."

In truth, and even though nobody was really paying attention, this new battle against Madame Atomos was unfolding on three fronts. While Beffort was nearing the laboratory and Akamatsu and Bernitz were waiting for the 402 freight train, Ritter was doing work just as important in San Francisco. On one side they were striking at Madame Atomos by destroying her troops and weapons. On the other, her economic power was under attack.

It was 10:30 p.m. when Ritter and five of his men showed up at 19 Lombard Street and rang the bell for Mrs. Surrey, who had recently received 10,000 dollars from Trigg.

Lombard Street is one of the busiest streets in San Francisco and Mrs. Surrey's building was still noisy in spite of the late hour. The bell rang and rang amidst the din, lost in the police sirens coming over the TV on every floor. Ritter waited for Eliot Ness to empty his gun and pressed again, longer.

Slippers scuffled over the parquet, the lock jiggled and an old woman appeared. She was dirty, toothless, and her hair looked like bundle of candles.

"Mrs. Surrey?" Ritter asked without believing it.

"No, she don't live here. Is that it?" She watched Ritter and his men in a daze, finding herself face to face with these modern *Untouchables*; she could not get over it.

"What's her new address?" Ritter asked.

The old lady shrugged. "Don't know, Mister. Well, not really..." Ritter stuck his hand in his pocket and brought out a five-dollar bill. He did not have to repeat the question. "She's in Cincinnati."

Ritter forced himself to stay calm, still holding the money. "What does Mrs. Surrey look like?"

"A woman looks like a woman, don't she?"

Without the promise of another bill, she would not say anything else. Ritter added another five dollars and held it out to the woman, who cracked a smile.

"Young?" Ritter offered.

"Uh, more yellow than young," she laughed, no doubt thinking that was funny and not awkward. "If she stayed any longer, I'd have left! Wasn't my place no more, you know! These Chinese think they can do anything."

Ritter's cool was starting to crumble. This woman was leading him to believe that Madame Atomos had been her roommate for a while. It was unbelievable!

"How did this Asian woman happen to be here?"

The old lady smiled and eyed his pockets.

"No," Ritter said. "I just lost my good mood. Answer!"

His voice was not the same, but the old lady was not versed in psychology. She barked, "I'm at home here! I'm watching TV! You come and get in my face... really, sometimes..."

Ritter raised a finger. Two G-men jumped on either side of the woman, lifted her up and carried her down the stairs. At headquarters, under the iodized lights she had no desire to talk nonsense. She talked a lot, said that Mrs. Surrey was introduced to her by someone named Linder, a waiter at the restaurant in the Trigg Palace Hotel in San Francisco. Mrs. Surrey was hiding from her husband, a violent brute who refused to divorce her. Brings tears to your eyes!

Ritter sent the old woman home, climbed into his car with his five bullies and went to knock on Linder's door. The guy had just fallen asleep and was having a hard time keeping his train of thought.

"Mrs. Surrey? I don't think..." With a good, strong slap Ritter shook his memory. "It's Mr. Trigg who asked me to help Mrs. Surrey hid herself."

His apartment was too ritzy. Ritter slapped him again and he stumbled into the arms of his men. Barefoot and in pajamas, Linder was easy prey. They stepped on his foot, jostled his ribs, and to top off his bad luck, the elastic on his pajamas snapped.

"What's going on, Bobby?" Another young man popped his head in through the door. Pink pajamas, fluffy slippers, ruby red lips. Nice couple!

"Go back to bed, Sonny!" Linder snarled. "I told you not to come in here!"

Ritter had enough and packed up the two of them. At headquarters Linder cracked, confessed that he collected the funds for the A.O.F.M.A. account, said that Arthur Trigg was one of the directors. He told them so much that Ritter was quickly aware that he was trying to cloud the issue.

"Let's get back to Mrs. Surrey. She was Japanese, wasn't she?"

"Yes," Linder whispered.

"She lives in Cincinnati?"

The little man started trembling. From head to toe, feebly. He was panicking.

"Madame Atomos, huh?" Ritter slipped in.

"No! You're crazy! I didn't..."

"Quiet!" Ritter shouted, seeing the beginning of a nervous breakdown.

His outburst frightened Linder. From one fear to another, he turned pale. It was the longest night of his life.

Ritter shouted again, "You're working for the A.O.F.M.A.! You hid Madame Atomos and you helped her run away to Ohio! It's the gas chamber for you, boy!"

Linder wept. One of the G-man, the one who had stuck him in the ribs, said, "Give him a chance, boss. If he talks, maybe you could talk about extenuating circumstances. After all he was only following his boss' orders. Isn't that right, Bobby? Mr. Trigg forced you to do it?"

He was over doing it, playing his bit part like a ham actor, but Linder fell for it with astounding ease.

"That's right," he sniffled. "Arthur was the boss and threatened to fire me if I refused to collaborate. What could I do?"

"I don't give a damn," Ritter spit out, still playing the bad cop. "I want to know where Madame Atomos is! And don't tell me you don't know the other bosses of the A.O.F.M.A.!"

"But I don't know. I don't know! I never even saw Madame Atomos myself. She used my name to get in with that old lady on Lombard Street, but Arthur took care of everything."

Ritter was expecting this. Madame Atomos would have been crazy to trust this pathetic boy. In hysterics, Linder continued to confess. "It's the same for the A.O.F.M.A. Arthur gave me a list of names and addresses. My mission was to make the collections twice a week..."

"You're going to give us this list!"

"It's at home, in the desk drawer. Take it, take whatever you want, but don't send me to prison, Sir! I'm begging you! Anything, but not prison! I'll die there!"

Ritter left him sobbing when he went back to the apartment with his men. Ten minutes later they discovered the list, two vials of LSD, a packet of pure cocaine and a roll of bills. Ritter counted them and whistled softly.

"60,000 dollars. Well, subtract that from Madame Atomos' account. I have the feeling that we're going to find a lot more money before the night's over." Then he pointed at the list and asked, "Any tips on these guys, Galloway?"

"At first sight, I only recognize two of them. Gloria Bailey runs a club in Chinatown. Strippers, escorts, porn films, etc. The other is Alec Maitland. He also runs a club. Very special kind: transvestites, marijuana, highly erotic shows in the private room on the second floor."

Ritter nodded. He was feeling dirty and wanted to get out of the apartment fast. A rich love nest for queers. Blue, lacey sheets, pink tile, curtains and drapes... everything soft to the touch.

"Come on, boys, I'm suffocating here. Madame Atomos is making the whole underworld march to her drum, using threats, drugs and money! Sickening!"

"Yeah," Galloway said. "But now we know where we have to look."

And that was the most important thing.

Chapter XII

In the train yard in East Cincinnati, Akamatsu and Bernitz were waiting for the freight train. The clock showed 11:05 p.m. Not much traffic. Sometimes a passenger train rumbled by, gloriously, on the central track, ignoring the ghostly cars behind it that switched all alone from one track to another.

Repair shops, loading docks, engine changes... a muffled but constant noise. Bernitz did not like it.

"Too much space to watch," he said grouchily. "With all this hubbub, how are we going to spot a sabotage?"

He and Akamatsu were in the shadows, far from the switch operators, but close to track 12 where the 402 would arrive before being uncoupled. At night the yard had a very special ambiance. Everything worked by signals and except for a team of men taking care of the uncoupling, the night shift worked at their posts with orders from the dispatch.

At the end of the line, an engine touched a car to push it to a new location. The car went through a series of switches and passed in front of the two men. It bore its destination marker: Tampa, Florida, arriving directly from Bismarck, North Dakota. When it reached its destination, it will have crossed practically the whole US from west to east. Musing on this, Akamatsu watched it roll, very quickly out of sight because of the darkness, but he heard it hitting the buffer of another car. In the night sky, lights went on and off. The switches creaked while new cars filed down the track, miraculously crossing each other without even a scrape. A pretty fascinating sight.

"There's someone," Owen whispered.

The man was a little ways off, high-stepping it over the rails, and a gust of wind blew the scent of coffee that he was carrying in a can. On track 2 another man was on the move, swinging a light and bending over the switches.

"If they all start strolling around," Bernitz complained, his bad mood getting worse, "we'll never get out of the woods."

He was right. The train yard was the ideal place for sabotage. To throw a bomb into a train was child's play. Akamatsu saw it as it was: an explosion, burning trains and the chlorine gas spreading out right away around the blaze. An accident of this kind happened on November 19, 1967 in Newton, Alabama[5]. The firemen could not do anything to contain the blaze because of the intense heat and they had to stop the traffic on the roads and rails and declare a state of emergency within a three-mile radius.

Akamatsu suddenly spoke up, "We're not doing any good here. We have to be on the 402 when it arrives on track 12. 50 cars of chlorine, 10 of propane, 5 of ammonia… In my opinion, they'll hit the propane, but not before the train has stopped."

Bernitz did not understand. "If nothing can happen before the 402 stops," he said logically, "we might as well stay here."

"A timer."

"Oh, I see," Bernitz said and then after thinking about it, he said, "I don't agree. The 402 is supposed to arrive here at midnight, but it's not a given fact. For one

---

[5] True. The 2,500 inhabitants of Newton were evacuated to Ozark and Dotham under the threat of the chlorine gas.

reason or another it could be late, stuck on a sidetrack for ten minutes or an hour. No way to control a timer under these conditions, right? Now, if it was me doing the job, I'd wait for the cars to stop moving and be left alone."

"Exactly," Akamatsu countered. "The network chief said the train would be uncoupled in 30 minutes after it's registered and the Atomos gang can't ignore that. Plus, we're waiting for the 402. If a saboteur wants to succeed, he has to act fast and watch out for us. By sitting here, we're making it harder for him. We have to make it easier for him in order to catch him. Because in the end, that's what counts. Come on, Owen, we're going to hop on the 402."

The two men went back to the station and up to the network chief. 20 minutes later, the engine carrying them stopped at mile 42, at the top of a long uphill grade that the 402 was slowly climbing.

"The ten propane cars are at the back of the train," the machinist reminded them. "Going back toward the engine, there's the 50 chlorine tanks, then the 5 ammonia cars. The propane's in cans on flat cars. Here we go, the 402!"

Knowing what was being planned, he was nervous and in a hurry to get back on his route to Chillicothe. Akamatsu and Bernitz climbed onto the ballast and let it roll on the slope that the 402 was struggling up, unbelievably slow. The two men hid while the engine and the first 55 cars filed past. Bernitz jumped onto the first propane car and Akamatsu on the second.

When it got back on the flat track, it picked up speed. It was on time when it entered the yard at midnight sharp and stopped on track 12. The engine rolled alone slowly toward the service hangar. Silence fell over the rest of the cars that were buried in the night.

Between the canisters, paralyzing pistol in hand, Akamatsu and Bernitz were all eyes and ears. They were guarding the propane, but what would happen if they decided to attack the chlorine directly?

A little while passed in complete silence before Yosho Akamatsu spotted two men hopping along next to a moving car and finally veering off toward the 402. A low whistle informed the Japanese that Bernitz had also seen them.

Akamatsu slid a few feet between the canisters, climbed down and under the car. The two men were coming in from the rear. Each was carrying a heavy postal bag and... wearing railroad uniforms. Yosho started having doubts, but stayed on his toes. The Atomos gang could look like anything; their members could dress up as nuns if need be.

Owen had sneaked around to back him up. In spite of his size (height and width) he prowled around the cars with amazing dexterity, reaching the next to last platform when the two fake employees started emptying their sacks. At first sight Akamatsu could see that they had enough explosives to blow up two trains like the 402.

Just then Owen joined him. "We knock 'em out?" he whispered.

Akamatsu waved affirmatively, stood up at the same time as Bernitz and said, "So, the little boys like to play with trains?"

The men jumped, dug their hands into the pockets, but it was too late. Akamatsu and Bernitz had pressed their triggers simultaneously...

Not long after that, in the station chief's office, the two gang members were identified. One was called Bauer and played only a minor role in the new organization. But the other was Keating. He was one of Madame Atomos' bodyguards and his presence in Cincinnati proved that the sinister Japanese woman was still in the city. It was rather by chance, but thousands of miles away from each other, the Akamatsu-Bernitz team on one side and Ritter on the other had just come to the same conclusion.

If Madame Atomos' hideout were not discovered before the next morning, it would be most surprising.

Meanwhile, Yuri Belof's station wagon (driven by the G-man Harry Sherman) had made good time and was well on the road from Andover to Williamsfield. The gang's Buick was sticking close behind it without worrying too much about being noticed. Farther back, but still in sight came Smith Beffort's Malibu, which was keeping in radio contact with headquarters in Chardon and so was informed about the exact situation on the other two fronts. He knew through Ritter via Stutton and Chardon how Madame Atomos was recruiting her new troops among the most corrupt people in San Francisco. Later, but just as clearly, he knew about the capture of Keating in the train yard.

"Down there," the Chardon operator announced, "they're absolutely sure that Madame Atomos is hiding in the city or its suburbs."

"Apparently," Beffort grumbled. "Except that whenever they start getting certain about something, it's already too late. The 402 train didn't blow and Keating and his accomplice have disappeared. Do you think that Madame Atomos is going to sit around waiting for us to arrest her? Not me!"

"Silver swears that Keating will talk."

"Yes, but not during the next hour before the effects of the paralyzing ray wear off. In the meantime, Madame Atomos will have changed her strategy. Tell Stutton to get the Green Dragon Force, the local police and all the G-man available to guard Ritter during his questionings and tell him to go hard. Among the directors of the A.O.F.M.A. someone must have been in touch with Madame Atomos since Trigg's death."

"Why 'must'?"

"The money!" Beffort exploded. "Do you think it's going to drop into Madame Atomos' hands through the force of the Holy Spirit? Ritter has to find an address, a bank account or post office box! Get on it, Chardon? Every minute is playing into our enemy's hands. Over and out!"

He slammed the mic down, but kept the radio on.

"Never seen such a scattering of our forces," he said bitterly. "If Belof didn't talk, we'd be crawling along gloriously! Where are we, Ben?"

Brady looked at the road map that he had unfolded on the back seat, made a quick check and answered, "Theoretically we're coming up on the point where the green Plymouth should take over the station wagon."

"What's the land like?"

"Hills, valleys and Lake Pymatuning about two miles due west."

Beffort and Mie exchanged glances. Madame Atomos was a maniac. She could never set up her refuges far from a lake, river or the sea. Until now it had worked; Madame Atomos had often saved herself by fleeing on board a submarine or speedboat.

"This time," Mie commented, "she's set up around Lake Pymatuning just a few miles from Lake Erie."

Beffort grinned. "She's not so sure of herself. She had to double her means of escape. Surprising that she let herself get trapped in Cincinnati."

Mie shot him a sideways glance. "Who'll swear to that, Smith? You're going to tell me that I'm relying on my sixth sense again, but I feel like every second rolling by is bringing us closer to Madame Atomos."

Beffort did not smile. He knew that Mie had her personal radar since the death of their son. Moreover, immediately after the tragedy in Williamsburg, Mie had found the trail of Madame Atomos when everyone else thought the sinister woman had been disintegrated on Atomos Island and she launched herself on an extraordinary hunt. Practically without any clues, without anything to guide her, Mie had literally tracked her mortal enemy all the way to Billings... It was miraculous.

"In Cincinnati," Mie continued, "I never felt her and I think that emptiness caused my apathy, that discouragement I couldn't fight."

Beffort kept silent and Ben Brady imitated him on instinct.

Mie went on, "Yuri Belof said himself that Madame Atomos had pre-recorded the instructions he got in Cincinnati. Now I'm sure she's controlling everything from a distance."

"But the telephone call to the Garrani sawmill?" Smith Beffort objected.

Mie shrugged. "Her way of talking to Yosho could lead one to believe that she was calling from nearby, but if Keating and Scarlett kept her informed, she could just as well have been calling from her laboratory. Along the same lines, she could have written all her 'invitations to death' beforehand to Tiger, Judge Stark and Max Powell... And using a powerful relay, she could even have followed the events by radio, got minute to minute up-dates and so given the impression that she was there."

Mie was back in the swing of things and her reason-ing was strong. Beffort thought she was close to the truth. Madame Atomos had done everything to make them believe she was in Cincinnati. Ritter's and Akamatsu's reports testified to it, but she would have been quite happy to leave the diversion work to her un-derlings so she could supervise the finishing touches to her laboratory.

"Slow down," Brady warned. "Looks like the Plymouth is showing up."

In front of them the Buick and the station wagon had just stopped behind another car. Beffort slowed down, let a truck pass and then parked on the shoulder, turning off his lights.

Until then tailing the cars had posed no serious dif-ficulties because it was in traffic. The Malibu had played hide and seek with the Buick in front of it and Beffort would have bet that the gang members had seen only his headlights. But from now on, it would get complicated if the trip took a less frequented route. In the end, it was the G-man Sherman who was taking the biggest risk. His life would not be worth a slug nickel if the gang identi-fied him.

"It's okay," Brady was relieved. "No one's getting out and the Plymouth is taking off. Sherman must be getting white hairs, eh?"

Beffort nodded, neglected to turn on his headlights and started after them. Less than a mile down the road the Plymouth turned left and entered some woods. The station wagon and the Buick followed. Beffort sped up and turned in the same place. It was a small, well main-tained forest road but narrow and winding.

"Mie," Beffort requested, "call headquarters in Chardon."

The young lady signed in and the operator's voice instantly sprang out of the speaker. "Chardon here. Where are you, Yellow Mask?"

Smith took the microphone. "We're getting there. Alert the base in Warren. The helicopters should zero in on my radio signal. We're off the 95, less than two miles from Lake Pymatuning. Got it?"

"Got it, Yellow Mask. The map shows a forest of fir trees, forestry area 30.15, ten hectares of pastureland, a hill 1,500 feet high. Farther east, on the 125 side, there's the valley of Lake Pymatuning... Whoa! Warren just sent his ten birds, Yellow Mask!"

"Arms?"

"Rockets and 12.5 mm machine guns. If that's not enough, I can send you a group of B-52s directed by General Salem. It'll only take them five minutes to take off from Franklin. In 30 seconds you'll be in direct contact with the Air Force through Ashtabula: code name Bluebird. Do I stay?"

"No. Sign out, Chardon. I'll take the line to Ashtabula. Over and out."

Chardon's cutoff shook the speakers. There was a little dead time and then a voice spoke curtly, "Warren here. Bluebird to Yellow Mask."

"Got you," Beffort said.

"I'm on Kinsman branch, seven minutes from 95. Need precise targets."

Tired and bored with the pidgin English, Beffort simply said, "I don't know, friend. I'll tell you when I'm sitting on it. If visibility is good up there, you'll see a farm on open land not far from a hill. Right now the farm and the hill will be your target. But don't do anything before I give the signal."

"A-OK! I'm standing by! Over and out."

As the radio went dead again, Beffort got closer to the Buick whose taillights were shining between the trees. In the station wagon, Sherman must have been on pins and needles. Without a radio, he obviously had no information and might be thinking his FBI colleagues had lost him.

Beffort let off the gas when he was 50 yards from the Buick and said, "Ben, get ready to open your door. Sherman isn't going to go quietly and will start shooting as soon as the Plymouth stops. That's when you have to hit them hard."

"The alarm will be given at the same time," Brady said.

"Possibly," Beffort said calmly, "but Sherman's life is our number one priority, Ben. When he sees you coming at him, he'll react defensively since he doesn't know us. You have to make him understand that we're on his side. My wife and I will be busy with the radio and the battle with the other cars. Get ready! I see the farm!"

They were out of the forest and entering a big spread of open space. The farm was pretty much in the middle, not far from the famous hill that was partly hidden in the night.

Beffort turned on the headlights, leaned on the horn and slammed on the accelerator.

Chapter XIII

Madame Atomos was in her future laboratory. She had arrived so discreetly that no one had detected her presence yet. Naturally, the room she occupied was underground. At the start of the work, three months earlier, in the snow and bitter cold, there was only a group of Italians working here. They had been hired by the A.O.F.M.A. on contracts that nobody could match, to dig out a hill and lay the foundations of a new NASA laboratory. The project chief, a member of the gang given precise instructions, had carefully avoided digging deeper than needed so that Madame Atomos' former refuge not suffer the slightest damage.

This refuge dated back to the great Atomos period when it still contained extraordinary machines that the Great Brain ran. Now none of this served any purpose, but Madame Atomos had not lost hope. One day, soon perhaps, she would get some of her power back. She and she alone possessed the formula for the terrifying disintegrator ray. And Madame Atomos was living through fascinating times because since her self-disintegration, amazing things had happened.

Disintegrated on Atomia Island, reconstructed in the antiques shop in Savannah, Madame Atomos had felt unusually tired. Already from her first disintegration in the police headquarters in Canby she had been stricken with weird problems: headaches, memory loss, lethargy, deep sleep...

When she got back to Atomia she had consulted Doctor Minao who prescribed complete rest. It was all due to menopause, had nothing to do with the two disintegrations. Of course, Madame Atomos figured that the doctor was lying to her in good faith and so her condition must have been serious, if not desperate.

Later, after the disappearance of Atomia, Madame Atomos felt better. In Billings she had totally recovered her health. Then she stopped thinking about her body, proof that everything was all right. Until the day she happened to look into a mirror.

It was something that did not happen often, but this time the terrible woman had experienced the biggest surprise of her life. *For, she was growing younger!*

The mutation was quick and undeniable. The woman in front of Madame Atomos looked ten years younger.

Fascinated, Madame Atomos watched her own transformation week after week. She saw her wrinkles fade, her skin tighten, her flesh firm up. On the inside it was even more miraculous, impossible to describe.

This unexpected rejuvenation was necessarily the result of the two disintegrations. It was like her human genetic code had gone through a remarkable purge during the teleportation! Regeneration of cells, purification of blood, softening of the arteries, cleansing of the heart, lungs, brain, etc.

Now, that is to say four months after the start of the process, Madame Atomos did not recognize herself. Her step was lively and her movements precise. She had found her former appetite, a certain joie de vivre, and other sexual needs that were disturbing her quite a bit. In short, Madame Atomos had got 20 years of life back and was feeling like she was 30 again!

An ordinary woman would have been thinking of her beauty. Madame Atomos was just thinking that she would live longer and this would give her the time to carry out her vengeance against the Befforts and the

United States. Because even though her body had changed, her state of mind and her experience had undergone no modifications. The monster was still there and with the change of appearance it was even more dangerous.

Who now would be able to identify Madame Atomos?

A criminal can hide, wear a disguise, change his voice, move out of the country, etc. But no one could imagine such a fantastic transformation. Only one fly in the ointment: without gloves Madame Atomos ran the risk of being suspected, if not recognized, because of the tip of her right index finger being cut off[6].

But all things being equal, it was a minor detail. A detail like fingerprints, for example. Or the tone of her voice, the color of her eyes, the shape of her ears, the size of her shoes or of her body…

Even in growing younger, Madame Atomos was still herself. Moreover, no one could know about it. That is why Scarlett and Keating had not seen their boss again after she had fled Billings. That is why Madame Atomos was watching over things from her secret room in the laboratory at the very moment that Beffort chose to attack with the Yellow Mask.

In the past, Madame Atomos would have been notified immediately. But cameras and microphones, radars and domesticated atoms were no longer part of her arsenal. Now she could count only on her men to ring a ridiculous alarm in case of emergency. Well, the Malibu charged so suddenly that everyone was caught off guard.

---

[6] See *The Sinister Madame Atomos* in *The Terror of Madame Atomos*.

Everyone except the G-man Sherman, that is, who realized that his colleagues had finally come to the rescue. He jumped out of the station wagon and ran for the Malibu. In the Plymouth and the Buick, the gang members balked. They still thought he was Yuri Belof.

"Over here!" Brady shouted, swinging open the rear door.

Sherman sprinted and literally dove into the car just when Scarlett pulled the trigger of his machine gun. The flashes lit up the night and the sound of gunfire echoed all the way down to Lake Pymatuning. Scarlett was shooting from the hayloft, giving the alarm signal at the same time and then devoted himself to putting the Malibu out of commission as it continued rolling merrily on its way toward the hill.

The problem in this affair was that the workers knew nothing about the situation. The A.O.F.M.A. had hired them because they were all basically hiding from the immigration services, which guaranteed a mute worker who would go to Canada once the work was finished. But in the dormitories, the Malibu's horn and Scarlett's gunfire threw them into a panic. The 40 men were thinking only of the police, of deportation and some of them of extradition. They ran to the ground floor and then to the garage where two trucks were parked.

Being outnumbered, Scarlett and his team ended up losing their head as well. Nothing is more contagious than panic. The Malibu was seen as the vanguard of greater forces. And to top things off, Madame Atomos had not shown up.

In 30 seconds, Scarlett and his killers were piled into two cars. They headed for the woods, abandoning men and materials. They had heard the sound of engines rumbling in the air…

On Beffort's orders, the ten helicopters answering to Warren's Bluebird code attacked the farm targeting the trucks that were stupidly driving with all their lights on. Machine guns and rockets! You imagine they would take potshots at the Atomos gang? They killed the poor guys whose only crime was being on the wrong road at the wrong time.

On the hillside, the Beffort group was making their way through the mounds of earth full of rubble and debris that the grass would soon grow over but for the moment led straight to the brown wall of the laboratory. A cement wall stuck to the hill, with no windows and no door to be seen. Apparently the side of a cube buried in the land, like a plug in a wall.

"Where's the entrance?" Beffort was on edge.

Mie found it 15 seconds later while the helicopters were sowing death. The group entered a door as thick as a dam. Cream-colored cement, ventilation pipes, but not a single piece of furniture.

Mie's nostrils flared. "The heat and electricity are working," she murmured. "Whose if for if not Madame Atomos?"

Her voice, though quiet, echoed loudly through the empty rooms. Beffort led the small crowd to the lowest floor, which could be considered the ground floor or the basement. They found the boiler room with its turbines, the ventilation system, the generator working at full power.

"All this is turned on for nothing," Sherman said, "because there's no one in the building."

Without a word, tight as a drum, Beffort started flipping switches by pure chance. One by one he turned off the heating, ventilation and electricity to no avail. In the darkness the silence was so thick you could almost touch it. A necropolis where the brain and eyes became empty.

Beffort leaned forward and asked, "Do you see something too?"

"A faint yellow glow," Mie responded. "It's a microscopic point, invisible in the light but sitting somewhere in the middle of the heating controls."

Mie stepped forward in the dark and put her finger on the light to be able to locate it afterward. Beffort switched on the current and the electric brightness flooded the basement.

Ben Brady raised his voice, "Look! Here! Now there's an opening!"

In the corner of the room, behind the motors, there were in fact six square feet of floor missing. By cutting off the faint ray of yellow light, Mie had probably activated a secret mechanism. Smith Beffort found the rungs that led to another basement and climbed straight down to another landing that opened onto the underground.

No cement, less light. The corridor was not industrial made; it was shored up only by planks and now and again some metal props. It gave the impression of being unfinished, unlike the perfect constructions of the ex-Atomos Organization.

"Weird," Beffort groaned, who was starting to have doubts. "Madame Atomos doesn't usually trust her life to such a precarious setups…"

Holding her pistol Mie was already striding down the corridor. They followed her until they reached a gap. The corridor continued east, but Mie stopped to open a metal door that she had just found and she went straight into a kind of cabin. A cot, a telephone, a two-way radio, some food and a dressing table full of bottles and creams. And in a recess in the wall was a folding closet containing an extraordinary wardrobe.

"Madame Atomos' lair?" Sherman asked.

Beffort and Mie examined the clothes. The young lady uncovered a peg holding a baby-blue outfit. She frowned and said in disbelief, "Madame Atomos never dressed like this. Smith, all these dresses are the latest fashion… I have the same ones!"

Confused, Beffort was mindlessly fingering a low-cut blouse. "At 50 years old Madame Atomos could not wear such a thing without looking ridiculous. So?"

Mie continued her search, opened a drawer, took out some silk stockings, sexy panties and then showed them a pair of stiletto-heeled pumps.

"Heck," Brady said, "I'd love to meet the pin-up who's wearing that!"

Beffort and Mie dropped it. They did not understand and even in their wildest thoughts they had no chance of coming close to the truth. Beffort turned on the radio, tuned to the Chardon channel and signed in.

"Chardon here," headquarters answered right away. "Where are you, Yellow Mask?"

"I'm in the lab," Beffort stated. "Actually right now I'm in a basement dug under the hill. There's a fully equipped refuge here. Madame Atomos must have used it recently because the heat, ventilation and generator were all on when we got here. Let the dogs loose, Chardon. Close off the area and put Owen Bernitz and his men on Lake Pymatuning. Immediate surveillance of all roads and waterways. All passenger and commercial flights cancelled in Northern Ohio and Pennsylvania. Do it! Over and out!"

It was abrupt, but Chardon asked for no extra information. Beffort turned around and said, "Ben, you go back and get the Malibu while we follow the underground passage. Try to get around the hill and wait for us in the valley."

"That valley's huge!" Brady objected.

"Sure, but I think we'll come out on the 125 side, between the hill and the lake. Madame Atomos always escapes toward water and she's too old to change her habits. Then get in touch with the helicopters. They'll be watching for our lights and you can give them our exact position. Go on, Ben, we're playing speed chess here!"

Brady bolted up the metal ladder.

Beffort, Mie and Sherman left the small room and continued down the underground passage. After around 400 yards the group arrived at a dead end where another ladder brought them to another landing 50 feet below. The corridor was like the other and led to a third landing where a series of giant steps, like dam locks, led up.

"Rather than dig out a sloping tunnel," Beffort explained, "the Atomos Organization preferred to level it out, to progress in steps... I wonder why?"

Farther along and for the first time they noticed that there was a cement block to hermetically seal one of the vertical junctions. Nearby there was also an intake valve for water. But the installation was not finished: there was no water and no mechanism to push the cement block into place. It was obviously a system meant to flood the corridors separately in case of an attack, but without inundating the entire setup.

"It's diabolical," Sherman observed. "If the contraption were working, we'd already be dead, wouldn't we?"

Beffort nodded. "You can be sure of that. Later, Madame Atomos would drain the corridors, pumping out the water, and we'd become new servants of the Organization. Fortunately that time has passed, but we have to make sure that a new laboratory isn't built. You can see that Madame Atomos isn't giving up. From what I know of her, she's capable of constructing several laboratories at the same time in different parts of the United States. What we've just discovered here will be taken down, but who knows if she isn't in the middle of another one already?"

Beffort could not be accused of pessimism. The terrible Japanese woman had sufficiently proven that she had the means at her disposal, even after the destruction of Atomia.

"I feel fresh air," Mie said.

She was not mistaken. Five minutes later the small group surfaced in the kitchen of a deserted house. Through the window Beffort could see the calm water of Lake Pymatuning twinkling. He spotted the dark ribbon of a narrow road stretching along the Ohio-Pennsylvania border.

The house was rundown. It was only one story, but it had a shed where a car could park. It was all typical Atomos. Beffort and Mie were almost expecting... Nevertheless, in a way, the situation had taken an unexpected turn.

"If she used a car," Beffort said, "it wasn't to go to the lake. She could have done that on foot. So she fled inland, deliberately avoiding Pennsylvania. That's strangely reckless of her."

A big car was cruising down the road, headlights beaming. Beffort recognized the Malibu and signaled to it with his pocket flashlight. The car stopped.

"I thought you got lost," Ben Brady. "I've been driving all over the 125 for the past 30 minutes and the helicopters had to give up because they were running out of fuel."

"What's the word from Chardon?" Beffort asked.

"The road blocks around the hot zone are in place, but they're still searching for this guy Scarlett. The farm burned down, but the Bluebird guys only nailed the workers while the killers went on the lam."

"And Cincinnati?"

"Keating told what he knew, but his confession could fit on a postage stamp. Since the affair in Billings he hasn't seen Madame Atomos again. He and Scarlett got their orders over the phone or radio, but of the two of them it was certainly Keating who was doing the grunt work. Akamatsu has the feeling that the real contacts are in San Francisco."

"And what's Ritter saying over there?"

"He's pursuing his investigations. His last report was less than 15 minutes ago. He says he's sure that Madame Atomos had been replaced by an Asian woman, approximately the same age, at the old lady's place on Lombard Street. In fact, nobody knows now who Mrs. Surrey is. In short, Ritter's investigation is going too slowly. By the time he's questioned all the people on the list, the big boys will have had plenty of time to get away."

It was not a pretty picture.

There was still the fresh trail of Madame Atomos. Beffort talked with Chardon again. A Japanese woman in a car—that could not be too hard to spot.

Chapter XIV

Madame Atomos drove flat out until Padanaram, a small town stuck on the west shore of Lake Pymatuning, and pulled her '65 Chevrolet into a legal parking space. The clock on the dashboard read 2 a.m. She turned on the interior light and looked in the visor mirror. When the alarm sounded she was in the process of making herself look older. Then she had to quickly change her plans, wipe off the makeup and keep her new face. She fled with only a small suitcase. The image of a seductive, young, dark woman stared back at her from the mirror; the eyes were barely slanted and the lips were full. Her gaze was a little hard, but when she smiled, the hardness faded.

To tell the truth, Madame Atomos was drowning in narcissism and she was craving to test out her charm. 20 years ago, when she looked like this, she was preoccupied with creating the means to get her revenge. Now, and totally by chance, she realized that she had wasted her youth.

If youth had known, if old age were able...

So, destiny was giving Madame Atomos both knowledge and ability. No one before her had made this fantastic experiment. No one had been able to start their life over again. It was exhilarating and Madame Atomos was feeling a storm of desires, which she forced herself to resist, but which were rapidly becoming uncontrollable.

Madame Atomos took a deep breath, turned off the car light, grabbed her suitcase and got out of the Chevrolet. The car belonged to Miss Icho Fuji, a journalist presently assigned to the Tourist Information Center, Kyoto branch, in the Kyoto Tower Building, Higashi-Shiokojicho, Shimogyo-ku in Kyoto, Japan. Of course, Miss Icho Fuji had her papers and press pass with the photograph and fingerprints of Madame Atomos. New face, new identity. A practicably full-proof cover if the FBI requested information about Miss Icho Fuji, one of the employees of the Tourist Information Center would vouch for the young lady.

Madame Atomos, aka Icho Fuji, crossed the street and entered the lobby of the Triadelphia Hotel, second class, bar, restaurant, air conditioning, bathroom, telephone. The front desk clerk looked up and saw a ravishing creature walking towards him. Automatically, he straightened up. Madame Atomos read the admiration in the young man's eyes. This one was a shocker. She had to get used to seeing men undress her with their eyes.

Right now she was a little embarrassed by her provocative breasts, her short dress and the sensuality that her body exuded. She went up to him and said, "I'd like a quiet, comfortable room."

The clerk told her that he had exactly what she wanted and he gave her a form, standing up as he did so to get a better view of her cleavage while she filled in the registration form. Madame Atomos almost blushed when she caught him, but she kept on signing in with her new name, forcing herself to ignore the eyes that were burning her skin.

Then the clerk gave her a key with the number 9 on it and said that the room was on the third floor, with a view of the lake. He led her to the elevator and held the door open for her. Madame Atomos said good night to the young man, trying to soften her husky voice, and pressed the button.

When she got to her room, she locked the door, put her suitcase on the bed and rushed to the window. She was disturbed by these new sensations, but she had not forgotten that Smith Beffort, the FBI and the Green Dragon Force were after her. A moment passed, and then a few police cars drove slowly by. Patrols...

Lost in thought, Madame Atomos unpacked her suitcase, putting her clothes away after drawing the curtains and then standing naked in front of the mirror for a long time. Her perfect body could become an effective weapon if she used it right. In the meantime, she had to act normally in order not to make anyone suspicious.

She slipped on a see-through nightgown, went to bed and turned off the lights.

At that very hour, four G-men were arresting the mysterious John whom Yuri Belof had called and taking him from South Aguila to the FBI headquarters in Chardon.

The man did not open his mouth, so they left him alone. They were counting on a call from Washington and the presence of Yosho Akamatsu to loosen his tongue. Washington came over the radio around 3 a.m. John was really Douglas Hopper, escaped from Bellaire, sentenced to life for armed robbery and other similar little indiscretions.

Yosho Akamatsu arrived at that moment. He had come directly from Cincinnati with Owen Bernitz and most of the Green Dragon Force, stopping in Chardon with the sole purpose of making John confess.

At headquarters, Akamatsu ran through Douglas Hopper's file and scanned the messages out of Ashtabula. They had not yet found Scarlett and his team of killers and Madame Atomos' trail ended at Lake Pymatuning. On the wall map a thick line stretched from

Cleveland to Warren, passed into Pennsylvania to Greenville and went up to Lake City before dropping along the shore of Lake Erie to rejoin Cleveland. This line represented thousands of men on the land. It was an impassable wall that was closing in by the hour while the police cars patrolled inside the barrier. It might take a day or two, but this time it was eight to ten that Madame Atomos would not escape.

Akamatsu brought in Douglas Hopper without much hope of learning anything new. After interrogating Keating, he understood that Madame Atomos trusted no one, especially the gang members with an FBI file.

Hopper had the walk and talk of a preacher and was smart enough to know on what side his bread was buttered on. He talked when he found out they knew who he really was.

"After Belof's telephone call," he said, "I called Scarlett to confirm that everything was all right. My role stopped there for the night. However, and this is where you're going to regret arresting me, I was supposed to stay by the phone in case Madame Atomos needed me."

Akamatsu shook under the blow. He suddenly understood what the house in South Aguila was being used for and he wondered what obscure reason had made Beffort order Hopper to be arrested. When asked about it, the bureau chief in Chardon said that he was only following orders and he showed a message from HQ in Ashtabula ordering all the forces to immediately neutralize anyone attached to the Atomos gang. Smith Beffort had written it and everything seemed in order. Still, Akamatsu wanted to clear his conscience. He went to the radio room, called the Yellow Mask, was put directly through to Beffort and told him the news.

"What!" Smith exploded. "I never mentioned John in the message! All I said was to leave him alone! Give me the operator, Yosho!"

The operator turned a little red when he took the microphone. "Sorry, Mr. Beffort," he started in, "but you were specific that they should leave John alone as long as the lab wasn't found..."

"I didn't say that!" Beffort contested.

Without a word the operator turned back the recording and replayed the tape. Beffort's voice could be heard very clearly: "And what about John?" Then the operator answered, "Stuck in a house in South Aguila. We about to arrest him right now." And Beffort's recommendation, "You're kidding! This guy has to be in touch with Madame Atomos. Leave him alone until we know where the laboratory is..."

After that was a little silence. Finally Beffort said, "Okay, Chardon, I made a mistake."

"No big deal for the moment, Mr. Beffort," the operator assured him. "The G-man watching South Aguila hasn't received any telephone calls. If we took Hopper back there..."

"QED, my boy! If I collaborate, of course."

"That's all he needs," Akamatsu interjected. "Say, Smith, I'd love to get back in the hunt when Hopper's at his post again. Where are you?"

Beffort was in a kind of slump. He had lost all trace of Madame Atomos and given confusing instructions about John. He felt the need to get back on top of things and do something truly effective.

He said, "It's agreed, Yosho. You're going to take care of the Ashtabula sector. I'll take Trumbull and Owen Bernitz and his men can have Lake and Geauga Counties. Naturally you'll have carte blanche over

Ashtabula. Go on and we'll keep in touch through headquarters in Chardon."

It was undoubtedly by chance, pure coincidence, but Yosho Akamatsu was inheriting the very sector that contained the small town of Padanaram and the Triadelphia Hotel where a certain Miss Icho Fuji was staying.

In their Plymouth and Buick Scarlett and his killers were having a hard time. When they first hit the road they got unusually lucky and were now 125 miles to the west, not far from Painesville. Close by to the north was Lake Erie; to the south, Chardon; farther west was Cleveland. A mortal triangle now swarming with police, occupied by the army, flown over by observation planes, blocked off like a war zone...

In case of danger Scarlett had received orders to go to Fairport Harbor, get on a yacht called the *Washtucana* and hide out until things calmed down. Later Madame Atomos would call on the radio to tell them what to do next. It was clean and simple, but Scarlett had the feeling that he would never make it to the *Washtucana*. Between him and the yacht there were already too many obstacles.

While he was watching the road from some woods, one of his men complained, "Well, Scarlett, have you made up your mind?"

The six others were becoming just as nervous. If caught, they would go back to prison and probably see their sentences increased. On the other hand, Madame Atomos had not shown herself for a long time and rumors were starting to run wild... The ex-Atomos Organization had been made up of robots. The current Atomos gang was thinking, criticizing, working only because of money and terror. Scarlett knew that the whole gang could fall apart at the smallest bump.

His answer was late in coming. "Okay. I've made up my mind. We're going to leave the cars and split up. In teams of two we'll have a better chance. Robson, you come with me. You others try to get to the shore."

He had not divulged the final destination of their trip so none of them knew about the *Washtucana*.

"What part of the shore?" one of the killers asked.

Scarlett had a crooked smile. It was every man for himself now. "Willowick," he said, "at the station's cafeteria. Sit at different tables. The first to arrive should wait for the others." He unfolded a road map and pointed to Willowick. "Only 17 miles and we'll be scot free. Everything's ready for us there. Don't forget, meet at the station's cafeteria!"

Scarlett knew that he was sacrificing them. However, he could not logically do otherwise, especially not tell them about Fairport Harbor and the yacht. One or more of them might be arrested. Being interrogated, with nothing left to lose or hope for except maybe a dose of leniency for cooperating, any one of them would play ball.

"It's five in the morning," Scarlett said, looking at his watch. "In a few minutes, it'll be daytime and we'll really be in trouble. Let's split up now. Robson and I will take the road to Painesville. The rest of you choose your routes."

He had purposefully given the impression of choosing the worst direction by turning through Painesville. In reality, since his final goal was Fairport Harbor, this was the shortest way to get to the *Washtucana* yacht.

The six others had a short pow-wow to divide into pairs and then finally headed back into the woods. They were going straight to Willowick. Scarlett watched them vanish in the darkness, turned around and said, "Let's

147

go, Robson. Each of us on different sides of the road. If a car comes, dive into the ditch."

Robson crossed the road that was bathed in the hazy light of the nascent dawn and the two men started walking. At 5:30, without knowing about the red alert, they entered Painesville. The town was occupied by the army and police, but a good number of people were going to work as usual, which created some hustle and bustle that the two killers could use to their advantage. When they got downtown, they stopped in a crowded diner where they learned that the police were checking identities in the north of Painesville and the road heading to Lake Erie was being closely watched.

"Lucky that we're going west," Robson whispered.

"No," Scarlett said coldly. "We're going to Fairport Harbor."

Robson stared hard at him, eyes half-closed. "The others?"

"We'd be nabbed if there were eight of us."

Robson understood quickly and he was not particularly sentimental. He did not ask questions, just drummed lightly on the butt of his pistol. Scarlett shook his head. "No trouble, Rob, or else we're done for. The police are going to find the cars any minute now that there's daylight. I hope they'll follow the fresh trail that our 'friends' have left on the ground in the woods. We're going to play our last hand in peace and quiet, no guns, but with a snack and dressed up as workers."

"Easier said than done!"

"Just listen to what they're saying around here," Scarlett advised. "We're at a bus station and all these guys are waiting to go to the Headlands factory. They leave in ten minutes. So, we have time to knock out a couple of guys, grab their passes and switch clothes. In the bathroom it should be relatively easy. Come on."

Robson followed him through the crowd. At 6 a.m. the ten buses for the Headlands factory stopped in front of the cafeteria and loaded the 450 workers who were waiting there. Unarmed and disguised in overalls, Scarlett and Robson joined the last group in the tenth bus after showing their passes. They were not as calm as they looked, knowing that their escape was hanging by a thread. In the first place it was clear that they would soon discover their victims locked in one of the stalls in the bathroom. Then there was that damned identity check to get out of Painesville...

"Where's this factory with respect to Fairport Harbor?" Robson asked softly.

"I have no idea," Scarlett answered. "Let's hope that the name of the factory has something to do with Headlands Beach. If so, we'll only be a mile away from Fairport Harbor."

Robson smirked and crossed his fingers to ward off bad luck. Five minutes later the convoy stopped to go through the police barrier. Faced with 450 men, it would not be a simple formality. They ended up just asking the driver if their passengers had all presented their passes and then they let the buses go.

Another 20 minutes of crawling through the winding county roads and the convoy entered the factory property. As the buses rolled out of the parking lot, the workers spread out. Scarlett and Robson walked through the workshops and had no problem reaching the northernmost shop in the factory. They simply walked out, jumped in a truck and headed for the wharf.

At 7 a.m. the two men climbed on board the *Washtucana*, which was being guarded by a very small crew, and stretched out on the cots in the starboard cabin. Madame Atomos had not sent them a message and the yacht was sitting at the pier until orders arrived. Scarlett fell asleep instantly. Now he had no more worries because the *Washtucana* was obviously the last refuge for Madame Atomos and was perfectly in order, so the boat could not be suspected by the police.

Chapter XV

At 8 a.m. Smith Beffort received a message from
Ashtabula informing him that six men from the Atomos
gang had just been killed in a fierce fight. It happened
one hour ago in the Willowick station cafeteria. The G-
men had arrived in Willowick after finding the Buick
and Plymouth abandoned in some woods outside of
Painesville.

The message added that Scarlett was not among the
victims, but that a new trail was coming out of a cafeteria in Painesville. Anyway, the bureau in charge of the
Lake sector was sure that no one had breached the forbidden zone, except made to go deeper inside and therefore Scarlett and his partner would fall into their hands
sooner or later. This was not an empty promise because
the Washtucana was, in fact, moored inside the famous
forbidden zone, far from the limits of American territori-
al waters, but the authorities were obviously unaware of
this detail.

As for Madame Atomos herself, there was absolutely no information. The terrible woman seemed to have
vanished into thin air. And in a region that was very difficult to go unnoticed. They had blocked the roads,
stopped the trains, cancelled flights and searched all
abandoned vehicles in vain. Now they were going
through a systematic inspection of hotel registers, boarding houses, anywhere an Asian woman might have taken
a room for the night.

In the course of this tedious operation, Yosho
Akamatsu and a bunch of policemen were going over
Lake Pymatuning with a fine-toothed comb. Through the
newspapers and radio the HG in Ashtabula had informed

the population that Madame Atomos might be traveling or hiding in their town and that they should contact the nearest police station immediately if a woman answering to her description (even slightly) was seen anywhere. According to Madame Atomos' "identity card," of course. Under the heading of individual marks they specified that the sinister Japanese woman had the tip of her right index finger cut off. On the front page of all the dailies appeared the fingerprints and photograph of Kanoto Yoshimuta, aka Madame Atomos, which Akamatsu had long ago obtained in Japan. This made a strong impression on the Americans, but Akamatsu, Beffort and Mie knew that no one could swear that these fingerprints actually belonged to Madame Atomos.

In fact, a few months before, in the Canby police station, they had photographed Madame Atomos before her self-disintegration, but they did not have time to take her fingerprints. And to be straight, Beffort and Akamatsu had to admit that they were never absolutely sure that Madame Atomos was really Kanoto Yoshimuta. Indeed, only the photograph and the right index finger were in the archives. The rest was only guesswork, unsubstantiated evidence.

At 9 a.m. Akamatsu arrived in Padanaram to question a Japanese woman who was staying at the Triadelphia Hotel. She was a young Japanese journalist named Icho Fuji, working for the Tourist Information Center in Kyoto. Akamatsu was not very enthusiastic when he entered the hotel. He only came to put his mind at rest, already certain that this woman could not be Madame Atomos. Plus, Akamatsu was tired. He had been on his feet for 24 hours and would have loved to rent a room and take a rest if the situation allowed.

At the front desk he learned that Miss Icho Fuji had not yet come down, but that was no surprise because she had gone to bed at 2:30 in the morning. Akamatsu was startled. The arrival of the journalist coincided with the disappearance of Madame Atomos to the second.

"What's she like, this Icho Fuji?" he asked.

The clerk's hands drew suggestive curves in the air. "Like this!"

Akamatsu cracked a smile as he glanced at the picture of Madame Atomos in the newspaper lying on the counter.

The clerk shrugged his shoulders. "Not a chance," he said.

"Let me see her registration." He saw that Miss Icho Fuji was 30 years old and had not been long in the United States, her permanent residence being in Kyoto. As the clerk rightly said, this young lady could not be Madame Atomos, but Akamatsu still had to question her. An immutable law decreed by Smith Beffort and J.E.E. in the hope of thwarting their enemy's diabolical tricks.

"Ring her room," he said, "and tell her that an FBI agent would like to speak with her."

The young man rang the room, waited, and rang again. There was a click and Akamatsu heard a nasally voice. The clerk said, "Sorry to wake you, Miss, but there's a G-man here who wants to talk to you... Okay, I'll tell him." He hung up, turned to Akamatsu and said, "You can go up. Room 9 on the third floor."

He clearly thought the G-man was damn lucky and his voice unconsciously expressed his envy, with a hint of jealously. Akamatsu was starting to be intrigued. To affect the clerk like this, Miss Icho Fuji must really be something special.

The elevator brought him to the third floor and was immediately taken by a guy who looked like a wrestler. His ears stuck out, his eyes were small and round and he had a flattop haircut over his narrow forehead. As he stepped aside Akamatsu had the feeling that he had seen the man before and he racked his brains trying to remember where, but to no avail. He gave up before he reached room 9.

The bell echoed in the strange silence of the Triadelphia before a melodious voice invited him in. Akamatsu turned the knob, walked through the door and closed it behind him. He was standing in a small entranceway and could see the foot of the bed through the door that was left ajar.

"Come in, please."

Akamatsu pushed the door open and was suddenly alone with Miss Icho Fuji. She was still in bed, had not even taken the trouble to open the curtains. The room was still dark and steeped in the young lady's perfume. On the chair lay a dress, women's underwear and a typical Japanese kimono.

Miss Icho Fuji reached out and a veiled light lit the room with its frosty glow. "Excuse me for seeing you like this, but you would have waited too long if I had to get up…"

She was exactly the kind of beauty that hooks men and she knew how to play with her provocative modesty to a tee. Then Miss Icho Fuji propped herself up on an elbow, forgetting to pull up the sheet as it slipped off her shoulder, and exclaimed, "But you're Japanese!" She said this in Japanese and the sheet slipped even more to reveal her generous breasts barely hidden by the see-through nightgown.

Akamatsu felt a gust of heat rise into his head as he introduced himself with unnecessary stiffness. "Yosho Akamatsu, special agent of the *Tokkoka*[7], representing Japan in the fight against Madame Atomos and currently working with the FBI."

It was pompous. Miss Icho Fuji pulled up the sheet and laughed a little teasingly. "Mr. Akamatsu in the flesh and blood! I never thought I'd have the honor of seeing such a celebrity in my bedroom when I woke up! Do you know that you're the talk of the town in Kyoto? Don't you want to sit down? Here on the side of the bed."

Akamatsu sat. He was both charmed and confounded.

Miss Icho Fuji snatched up a pack of Lucky Strike and a box of matches with a Chinzan-So ad in red letters. "Do you smoke?"

Akamatsu accepted, striking a match and lighting the cigarette that the young lady was holding between her lips. The dancing flame briefly lit up her oval face and black eyes, revealing at the same time that the right hand of Miss Icho Fuji was missing the tip of the index finger.

Madame Atomos saw Akamatsu flinch. She was leaving herself open in the first round, but not without taking precautions. One of her gorillas (the man Akamatsu had passed) was listening at the door. And under the sheets her left hand was gripping a heavy automatic pistol. Since she could not hold the weapon, cigarette and sheet with one hand, the latter slipped again off her stunning chest. Akamatsu's eye wandered off the

---

[7] Japan's special police.

finger and down into her cleavage just when the match went out.

Miss Icho Fuji whispered melodramatically, "Search no further, inspector, I am Madame Atomos."

Akamatsu smiled. "Your finger?"

"A car accident when I was a child. Except for that, do you think I look like her?"

"Maybe in her younger days," Akamatsu recognized. "Why are you in the USA?"

Madame Atomos heard the elevator door close and knew that her gorilla could see that she was in no danger. She buried the automatic between the mattress and box spring and leaned back into the pillow, pulling up the sheet but not up her neck. "A report on Madame Atomos," she said softly.

Akamatsu raised an eyebrow. "For the Tourist Information Center?"

"No, I'm also working for three magazines…"

She was almost whispering, puckering her lips to blow smoke to the ceiling and sinking deeper into her pillow. The ambiance was becoming really very intimate. Akamatsu was talking in his native language to a pretty girl who was also concerned with Madame Atomos and he was slowly forgetting why he had come to Padanaram. Besides, there were thousands of men looking for Madame Atomos. His temporary absence would not change a thing…

"I was in New York when the radio announced that you were looking for Madame Atomos in Ohio. I drove almost all night to get here… Sincerely, I didn't think I'd be able to get past the roadblocks, but they let me through with no trouble. Say, have you eaten?"

"No, I was driving all night too."

Icho Fuji's gentle hand touched his. "Would you call down for a couple of breakfasts? I've been feeling a little lonely since I came to the United States."

An offer was being made that Akamatsu had not seen in years. He was thinking of the clerk's face when he picked up the phone and then, kind of absent-mindedly, of Smith Beffort when he would tell him...

"Front desk," a voice said.

"Could you send up two breakfasts to Miss Fuji," Akamatsu asked in a very dignified voice.

A heavy silence followed before the stunned voice of the young clerk asked, "Coffee or tea?"

"Tea," Akamatsu stated after a sign from Icho Fuji.

Then he hung up and went back to sit on the bed, just a little closer to her this time, and picked up where they had left off.

"Are you staying in Padanaram for a few days?"

"That depends."

"On Madame Atomos?"

Miss Icho Fuji could not hold back a little smile. It was an incredible situation for her. One of her grand enemies was flirting with her and even though she hated him she found it quite nice. In fact, she hoped with all her being that they could continue. To become the mistress of Yosho Akamatsu might just be her greatest victory: introduce her into the Beffort clan and at the same time fulfill the purely sensual pleasures that her rejuvenated body was so needy for. Why not unite the practical and the enjoyable?

Provided that Akamatsu was falling in love with her!

Madame Atomos shivered in thinking of the fantastic vistas that this last supposition opened up. Akamatsu was single, free as a bird...

"That depends on Madame Atomos?" Yosho repeated.

"Partly..." She sat up and her breasts stretched the light fabric. She turned on her charm, offered her lips, eyes half-closed. Akamatsu put his arms around her, leaned forward and... a discreet knock at the door.

"Breakfast," Miss Fuji whispered in a quavering voice.

Akamatsu got up to open the door, took the heavy tray and locked the door again. After that he put the tray on the folding table, took off his coat and went back to the bed where Madame Atomos was waiting for him.

At four in the afternoon that same day, the HQ in Ashtabula, following the orders of Smith Beffort, sent out a series of radio messages to the heads of the police, army and air force to return to their respective bases or stations. An entire region could not be blocked off any longer. Washington was already ranting and the President had received an incredible number of delegations in protest. The blockade was bad for both business and tourism.

J.E.E. had pressured Beffort who was forced to give in, sick at heart.

"You understand, Smith," J.E.E. had said, "Madame Atomos isn't a serious threat to the country anymore. It's not possible to paralyze Ohio and Pennsylvania for a simple criminal!"

The reaction was human.

The army and air force evacuated the area, but the FBI and the Green Dragon Force remained. Of course the police, although limited in its actions, were collaborating in the hunt and all together they were still a substantial force.

At 7 p.m. no one had found any trace of Madame Atomos or of Scarlett. In San Francisco Ritter was trudging along, still unaware of who was using the contributions and how it was getting to its user. In truth, he had hit a wall of silence or ignorance and saw that the A.O.F.M.A. was superbly organized, modeled on a spy network with its completely independent compartments. Arthur Trigg had been the head of one of these compartments, but his death had taken away all possibility for Ritter to climb the ladder because he had dealt only with underlings. It would take weeks or more to get any results!

In Chardon Smith Beffort and his wife were pacing around the radio room in FBI headquarters where the hustle and bustle had been replaced with calm and quiet. Sitting by a window, J.E.E. was chewing on a cigar stub. He had landed in Chardon that afternoon. Official business: to guarantee that the White House orders were carried out to the letter. Unofficially J.E.E. had come to be present at the capture of Madame Atomos.

Beffort said to him, "It won't be this time, Evans. Over the course of the night our men have visited all the hotels, boarding houses, anywhere Madame Atomos might be hiding out. Plus, she hasn't called the house in South Aguila that we were thinking was her home base. I'm waiting for news from Bernitz and Akamatsu, but I'm not getting my hopes up."

"The laboratory?"

"Destroyed," Beffort said wearily.

"And the machine in the station wagon?"

"The specialists are studying it, but none of them know what it's used for yet."

30 minutes later Owen Bernitz informed them that the trail of Scarlett and his partner went cold at the

159

Headlands factory. The Green Dragon Force had been scouring the Lake in vain since morning...

At 8 p.m. Yosho Akamatsu called from Padanaram. He was at the police station and was holding the negative search results from the Ashtabula sector.

Beffort groaned and said, "We're beaten, Yosho. Madame Atomos has slipped between our fingers again. You can come back."

"Do you need me?"

"Not at the moment," Beffort admitted.

"Well, I'm going to take a few days vacation." It was so unexpected that Beffort was speechless. Somewhat embarrassed, Akamatsu added, "Just between you and me, Smith, I've met a Japanese girl."

"Oh, I see!" Beffort was astonished.

"You're going to tell me that this isn't the time, but..."

"Do what you want, my friend. Take all the time you need. Is it serious?"

"Uh... See you later, Smith."

Beffort heard a click and slowly hung up the phone. For the first time, Akamatsu had stunned him.

At Padanaram the Japanese special agent left the police station right away and climbed into his car. He went back to the hotel where Miss Icho Fuji was waiting for him. Before Beffort had mentioned it, he had not considered the possibility, but now he truly believed that things might just get serious.

In the Triadelphia Hotel Madame Atomos was gloating. If Akamatsu could hear her giggling, it would have given him goose bumps.

André Caroff

Mme ATOMOS FAIT DU CHARME

ANGOISSE

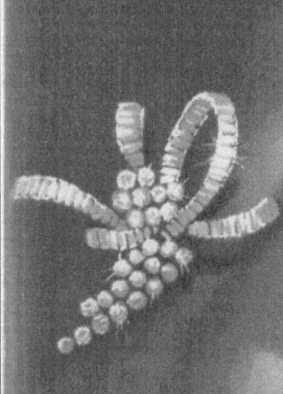

FLEUVE NOIR

THE SEDUCTION OF MADAME ATOMOS

Chapter I

One month had passed since the disappearance of Madame Atomos and no one could understand how the sinister woman had managed to escape the steel trap set up in northern Ohio[8]. As always in such a case the search lost steam as time went on and by the end of June only the Green Dragon Force backed up by a few local FBI agents remained in place.

However, Smith Beffort also stayed in the area when he should have gone back to Washington D.C. and this was very intriguing to James Edward Evans who called him almost every day.

"You say you've got no lead, Smith, but you're standing guard in Chardon like you were waiting for something to happen. Madame Atomos is long gone by now!"

"Could be, Evans, could be."

"Don't get all secretive with me, okay?"

"I give you my word that I've got no secrets. Given the circumstances, I just figure that I might as well wait here as in my office."

"Wait for what?"

---

[8] See *The Resurrection of Madame Atomos.*

"For Madame Atomos to reappear. What do you think? Mie and I aren't on vacation!"

"There are a few little things that don't fly, Smith. After every Atomos attack, you hurry back to Washington to use our information network. This time you're sitting there in Chardon like a lump on a log and your Green Dragon Force is standing around arms at the ready. Tell me the truth!"

Smith Beffort looked at his wife. She was listening to J.E.E. through the speakerphone, but did not seem very interested. In fact, Mie was somewhere else. She was like a clairvoyant in a divinatory trance and this state had lasted exactly four weeks.

"Listen, Evans," Beffort decided on the spot, "I'm not moving from Chardon because Mie feels that Madame Atomos is close by. Does that satisfy you?"

J.E.E. cleared his throat. He thought it a hard pill to swallow. He said, "Mie feels Madame Atomos, that's what you mean to tell me?"

"Yeah. She literally feels her, like a hound sniffing out game."

"Marvelous!" J.E.E. laughed.

"I know you don't understand," Beffort spoke softly, "but it just so happens that Mie has never been wrong since the death our son. Moreover, if you take the trouble to think about it, you'll clearly see that Madame Atomos had no way of leaving Ohio. So, she's still here. That goes without saying, doesn't it?"

Evans did not argue. Since the death of Bob and Dr. Soblen, the Befforts had behaved strangely, preferring psychic information to good old-fashioned investigation. But when it came to Madame Atomos, who could say what the best method of fighting her was? The terrible woman herself used extraordinary methods, scientific of course, but sometimes parapsychological, too, so that no one so far had been able to match her.

"Okay, Smith. I hope that Mie is right and that Madame Atomos is still in Ohio... By the way, what's become of our friend Yosho Akamatsu?" Evans wanted to change the subject. He knew perfectly well that Akamatsu was on vacation and that a ravishing Japanese woman was helping him pass the time.

Smith Beffort laughed and said ironically, "He's making the perfect couple with a journalist from Kyoto. I think he's completely forgotten about Madame Atomos. He's lucky!"

"Where is he?" J.E.E. asked.

"In Padanaram at the Triadelphia Hotel, room 9, and the girl's name is Icho Fuji. Any other questions, Evans?"

"No, thanks," Evans refused politely. He could hear that Beffort was extremely nervous and he did not want to be his punching bag. Beffort wanted to believe that Madame Atomos was living in Ohio and that she would end up coming out of hiding, but the inaction must have been eating him up. Evans easily imagined him pacing around Chardon, waiting for reports from Owen Bernitz or farther away from Ritter who was tirelessly (and unsuccessfully) investigating the A.O.F.M.A. in San Francisco. Yes, Beffort must have been growing white hairs.

Evans said, "How long will you be staying there, Smith?"

"I don't know," Beffort grumbled. "But to prove to you that in spite of everything I'm still working on concrete issues, I can tell you that the Green Dragon is sniffing out the trail of Scarlett and his partner. They, too, have to stay in Ohio."

Evans sighed. "Madame Atomos vanished around Lake Pymatuning. Scarlett led his hunters to the shores of Lake Erie, more precisely to Fairport Harbor. In both cases, there was probably a boat or..."

"No!" Beffort cut him off. "Forget about that! For the past month no boat has lifted anchor without being inspected from mast to keel."

"I know, I know," Evans muttered. "Don't get all worked up... I still think you're wasting your time in Chardon. Our bureau in Sterling, Colorado informed me about some cases of poisoning."

"Poisoning?"

"Children," Evans said reluctantly, "only children. Weird, isn't it?"

"Poisoned by what?"

"The bureau is investigating. Which of course means that no one knows what's happening. It seems that a dozen kids have died. Anyway, it's got nothing to do with you, right?"

Beffort did not answer.

Hypocritically, Evans added, "Who would want to see children die? They were all between six and ten years old. Really harmless, don't you think, Smith?"

"When did this happen?"

"This morning. Coming out of school," Evans spoke more seriously. "The bureau says that every kid was at a different school. What do you think?"

"Nothing," Beffort forced himself to say. "It's a matter for the Sterling police. I know that you're trying to get me to believe that Madame Atomos is responsible, but..."

"Oh sorry," Evans interrupted, "I completely forgot to tell you that witnesses had seen a Japanese woman prowling around the schools in the morning. She was an older woman who…"

"Hogwash!" Beffort barked. "Don't tell me that Madame Atomos has been reduced to that! And certainly don't try to make me believe that she would do it herself!"

Evans laughed politely. "I said nothing of the kind, Smith. I'm just giving you the facts. Moreover, they have no idea what kind of poison it was. Now you know everything."

"If they can't find traces of poison in the kids' stomachs," Beffort objected, "how do they know they were poisoned?"

"Convulsions, drooling, horrible pain," Evans enumerated briefly. "Plus, these kids were in good health and the exams showed that they didn't die of anything else. So that's what I have to tell you today. Would you talk to Mie about it and see if she'll change her mind about where Madame Atomos is right now? Goodbye, Smith, 'til tomorrow."

He hung up and Smith did the same. "Did you hear that, Mie?"

The young lady nodded. She was clearly troubled by J.E.E.'s news and obviously starting to wonder if her intuition might be mistaken.

Since she remained silent, Smith said, "It's undeniable that these ten simultaneous poisonings can only be the work of a lunatic or Madame Atomos. Personally I'm leaning toward the second hypothesis because of the publicity that the press will soon be giving this affair. Sterling is located in Colorado, but on the border of Nebraska. Now, we've both seen how attracted Madame Atomos is by borders since she lost her formidable power. In case of danger, it makes it easier for her to escape

167

and harder for us to chase her. There's always been a lack of coordination between the state police, so like gangsters in the 30s Madame Atomos uses every weakness to get away from us."

Smith was pacing rapidly up and down. He stopped, turned to his wife and said, "J.E.E. is right, Mie! We're wasting our time gathering dust here."

The young lady looked gloomily at her husband. "Just now you were saying that it was unlikely that Madame Atomos would do it herself. Can you see her strolling around in front of the schools in Sterling while every policeman in the US has her face stamped on his memory? That would be suicidal!"

"Kids died and witnesses saw a Japanese woman prowling around the area..."

"It's a trap, Smith. It's been months since Madame Atomos has shown her face and Keating, her number one lieutenant we arrested, said that he hadn't seen her since the affair in Billings[9]. After taking so many precautions, why would she change her MO all of a sudden?"

Beffort shrugged. "It's hard enough for me to anticipate her actions let alone worrying about the deep, dark reasons behind them. If Madame Atomos is seen in New York, I'm going to New York. Today they're talking about her in Sterling and so I'm going to Sterling. Pack your bags, Mie, I'll tell Owen Bernitz and Akamatsu. We can leave in 30 minutes."

Mie stood up. "For Colorado?"

---

[9] See *The Evil of Madame Atomos* in *The Revenge of Madame Atomos*.

Beffort nodded and left without a word. Mie opened the suitcases and started filling them up. She was used to it.

At the Triadelphia Hotel, room 9 on the third floor, overlooking Lake Pymatuning, very comfortable, peaceful and quiet...

Yosho Akamatsu was on the fourth week of his honeymoon with the splendid Icho Fuji and still had not the slightest suspicion about her. But how could he? Who could have imagined that Madame Atomos had grown 20 years younger and that she had become Miss Fuji, a journalist from Kyoto working for the Tourist Information Center and a few magazines that have her writing—what a coincidence!—a report on Madame Atomos?

Yes, who could have imagined this? Even at the time of the conquest of the moon, it was so unthinkable, so improbable that Madame Atomos was the first to be surprised at seeing herself grow younger day after day. Now she was used to it, even felt good being in the arms of Akamatsu, although in the beginning the sinister woman had felt uncomfortable in her new skin. It was like a dress that was too tight, too low-cut and too short. The wrinkles, the fat and cellulite had disappeared. Her legs were hard and shapely, her waist thin and supple, her chest firm and provocative.

In a word, Madame Atomos did not go unnoticed as Miss Icho Fuji. She turned the heads of men and sometimes women because she was really a gorgeous creature. With Akamatsu's caresses added to the mix these details had made Madame Atomos lose her head a little. Over the course of four weeks she had not really thought about her vengeance against the Befforts and the United States.

Hiroshima and Nagasaki were far away. Japan was on the other side of the world and Madame Atomos no longer existed.

But, since all good things must come to an end, the sinister woman had to come back to down to reality someday. She had ordered the ten poisonings in Sterling by telephone and it was also on her orders that a Japanese woman from the A.O.F.M.A. was seen by witnesses there. Thus, no one would ever suspect the truth. From time to time someone would see a woman who looked like the old Madame Atomos, preferably somewhere far away from Miss Icho Fuji so that no one would suspect who she really was. It was devious, but Madame Atomos was devious.

Around 4 p.m. the telephone rang. Akamatsu and his adorable mistress were just coming back from a long walk along the lake. The weather was nice, almost hot, and Akamatsu was savoring the rest and relaxation without thinking too much about what the future held.

He casually answered the phone and stiffened up on hearing Smith Beffort's voice. "Sorry to disturb you, Yosho, but J.E.E. just told me that Madame Atomos is in Sterling, Colorado."

Akamatsu crashed. He felt like he had suddenly woken up from a deep sleep. "No way," he said flatly.

"Ten kids were poisoned this morning," Beffort snapped back, "and you know that anything's possible when they examine the bodies in the Sterling morgue. Are you up to going over there with me?"

"Right now?"

Beffort laughed dryly and said, "Madame Atomos won't wait, you know. I understand your surprise, but Evans called me less than an hour ago. I don't want to meddle in other people's business, but can I suggest that you authorize your young compatriot to follow the investigation? After all, that's why she's in the USA, isn't it?"

Akamatsu relaxed. "Thanks, Smith. I wanted to ask. Where are we going to meet?"

"You can meet us at the FBI headquarters in Sterling, if you want," Beffort proposed, "but I was hoping we could travel together."

"You caught me a little off guard," Akamatsu glanced toward the bathroom where Icho Fuji was taking a shower.

"There's no doubt about it, Yosho," Beffort's voice was a little sharp, "you've changed in the last four weeks. Not so long ago you would have been the first to jump on a plane for Colorado! Would it be improper for me to ask if it's serious between you two?"

Because of the noise from the shower Akamatsu was sure that Icho Fuji was not listening. He said, "She's charming, but I don't think our little adventure will last long. She's pretty secretive and there are parts of her that are completely foreign to me. Truthfully, Smith, she seems to have lived a lot and she knows a bunch of things that she shouldn't. You know what I mean?"

"No, but it doesn't matter, my friend. I gave up trying to understand women a long time ago, especially my wife! Still, I'm happy to see that you haven't lost your mind. So, rendezvous at Sterling headquarters tonight?"

"Okay. What hotel will you be at?"

"Certainly the Statler. The food's good and the single rooms are only 11 dollars. But are you going to take an 11 dollar room?"

"Um..."

"In that case, the rooms for two people are 20 dollars," Beffort said kindly. "Maybe your young lady and my wife will become friends?"

"Maybe," Akamatsu said evasively.

His tone surprised Beffort who said, "Are you acting strangely because you're in love or because she's weird?"

"It's a ready-made solution, eh?" Akamatsu complained, his voice still drowned by the shower. "Really, Smith, I feel like I've got myself in a fix that I'm not ready to get out of. Icho Fuji..."

"No forced confessions, okay? I'm not asking you anything."

"Don't worry, I'll feel better. This woman is like a maze. Sometimes she's sweet and charming, absolutely adorable, but other times she's mysterious, authoritative and almost hideous..."

Beffort laughed aloud. "You sound like a kid, Yosho! And I was thinking Japanese women were submissive! Another illusion shot to hell! I'm curious to meet this girl who you're so wrapped up in. See you tonight in Sterling?"

"Okay, Smith. We'll hop on the first plane."

Beffort hung up and hurried back to his bedroom where Mie was closing the suitcases. He said, "Owen Bernitz and his team are heading for Sterling right away. Akamatsu will join us a little later with his sweetheart."

Mie's eyes went wide. "Is he going to get married?"

Beffort shrugged his shoulders. "I don't know, but she's already putting him through the wringer. In his place I'd give her up. He doesn't know how lucky he is to be single."

Mie smiled. When Smith teased her, it meant he was in a good mood.

Chapter II

Smith Beffort and Mie got off the plane at the Crosson Field Airport in Sterling, walked five minutes and happily found their formidable Chevrolet Chevelle Malibu, a gift from the members of the Green Dragon Force and almost hand-made. The car was armored, soundproof, air-conditioned to be able to sit for two hours in the middle of a cloud of mustard gas or any other toxic fumes; puncture-proof tires, bulletproof glass; radio, telephone (code name "Yellow Mask"), four perfectly camouflaged machine guns and a swiveling paralyzing cannon mounted under the chassis. The bumpers were strong enough to pulverize a 15-inch cement wall. The all-wheel drive could keep rolling sideways at 40 miles an hour. Besides all this, the Malibu cruised at 150, weighed more than two tons and its shiny hood hid 400 hp and three Holley double pumper carbs and a special camshaft.

As big Owen Bernitz had rightly said, "This bucket is no bicycle!" And Smith had had the opportunity to test it during a terrifying battle against some bulldozers and cars driven by members of the Atomos gang.

Smith put the suitcases in the spacious trunk, sat behind the wheel and straightaway got on the radio. "Yellow Mask calling 555-6289."

There was cracking and sizzling and the very distinct voice of Ralph Stutton shook the speaker, "6289 here, boss!"

"Everything okay, Ralph?"

"It's okay, boss! We've been here since 7 o'clock. The dispatch is set up at 500 North Division Avenue. Bernitz rented a house there. It has a yard big enough to stick a base of Saturn rockets and a second exit onto Washington Street."

"The men?"

"Twenty or so here with their radio-equipped cars. The rest are scattered around the city and in the closest suburbs, Padroni and Atwood."

Beffort nodded mentally. It was not easy to hide the arrival of 300 men and almost as many radio cars from the inhabitants of a small city, but Owen Bernitz had become a master at it.

"Did you reserve my room?" he asked.

"With a bathroom and sitting room at the Statler Hotel," Ralph Stutton confirmed. "You're on the fourth floor, number 46. I think Bernitz is already waiting for you there."

"Thanks, Ralph. Out." Beffort hung up the mic, but keep the radio on. The men of the Green Dragon Force must have been working since the minute they arrived. They were looking for Madame Atomos all over town so an urgent message might come to Beffort at any moment.

In ten minutes the Malibu covered the distance between the airport and the Statler Hotel. Beffort and Mie left the car in the parking lot and went immediately up to the fourth floor. When they pushed open the door of room 46, Owen Bernitz clambered out of the armchair where he had been sitting comfortably. He took the eternally unlit cigar stub out of his mouth and said, "Glad to see you."

His greeting was short and sweet, but his smile showed the real joy he felt at seeing Smith and Mie again.

"How's it going, Owen?" Smith asked, shaking his hand.

174

"Slowly, boss. Ohio was starting to bore us, so this move was a windfall. Well, Mama What's-Her-Face is on the warpath again, is she?"

Owen had his way of talking and did not mince words. Beffort and Mie were used to it.

Beffort nodded. "Evans called me this afternoon to give me the information from the Sterling FBI. Ten kids were poisoned and they saw a Japanese woman strolling around in the area. You know that already, but I'm repeating it so you can tell me what you think."

"And that's exactly what I'm going to do," Owen said frankly. "I don't think Madame Atomos is crazy enough to show up out in the open right now. If there weren't these ten kids, it would look like a jumbo prank."

Mie looked up. "See, Smith, just like I think."

Bernitz stared at Beffort. "Look, boss, don't tell me you're buying it. It's obvious that Madame Atomos is doing her Cincinnati all over again. While we're floundering around here, she's building a laboratory somewhere else and if we keep on, we'll go down in flames pretty soon."

Beffort lit a cigarette. "I know all that, Owen, but there's no other way to act effectively. In every investigation you have to start from the beginning of the trail. In a month, in spite of all our efforts, we've been reduced to utter inactivity. Today Madame Atomos is holding out a carrot, like she did in Cincinnati, but she's running a risk in this one. And lastly, during the last adventure, Madame Atomos didn't come out unscathed: the destruction of a refuge and a laboratory that was almost finished, the arrest of Keating and his accomplice at the train yard in Cincinnati, the elimination of six men in Willowick, the death of Trigg, etc. And to top it all off, do I have to remind you that Madame Atomos was almost caught?"

Mie stopped unpacking the bags, turned to him, narrowed her eyes and said pensively, "By the way, Smith, remember the yellow dresses and sexy underwear we found in the underground refuge?"

"Of course. All of that belonged to a younger woman and we discussed it."

"Let's discuss it again, okay?" Mie asked with abrupt authority. "I've thought a lot about it over the past month and I've come to the conclusion that the woman we were chasing was not Madame Atomos."

Beffort and Owen stared at her in amazement.

Mie continued, "You agree with me that no one's seen Madame Atomos for a very long time and that's not normal. She doesn't show up on the scene anymore but lets the members of her organization act instead and that's not her way. In Ohio a woman hides out in the underground refuge. She runs away when we get close, but can only do it at the last minute. Madame Atomos is 50 years old. Do you think she can run that fast for over a mile? Do you think she's spry enough to shimmy up iron ladders, and lift a heavy trap door before speeding away in a fast car?"

"Why not?" Beffort said. "She had quite a head start on us. We had to look for a long time before finding the entrance to the underground."

"No more than five minutes," Mie said precisely. "Then we lost five minutes in the refuge. Still, when we came back out in the open air, Ben Brady told us that no car had passed by on the road for 20 minutes. In my opinion, it was physically impossible for Madame Atomos to move at such blistering speed!"

Beffort let out a weary sigh. "Okay, Mie, okay. Conclusion?"

"I'm sure," Mie pronounced slowly, "that Madame Atomos had temporarily given all her power to a younger woman. A second Miss Atomos![10] Is that so hard to believe?"

Beffort sat down and puffed on his cigarette. It was hard for him to believe. However, putting aside his own opinions, he had to admit that his wife's hypothesis was not so far-fetched.

Mie sat across from him. "Look, Smith, let's be logical. All of northern Ohio was gone over with a fine-toothed comb. Every house, every field, every nook and cranny of ground was inspected meticulously. The people helped and the police and army were everywhere. The roads, waterways, train and bus stations, the airports were all being watched and no vehicle could move without special authorization. In spite of all this Madame Atomos managed to hide and then disappear. Me, I'm think that's impossible. A young woman fled from the refuge and got away because we weren't searching for her! It's that simple!"

Smith and Owen glanced at each other.

"Mrs. Beffort," Owen grumbled, "I hope you're wrong because if you're right, we're not out of the woods yet. We don't have Mama Atomos cornered like we thought. Well, just think of the racket if we have to fight a Miss Atomos we've never seen! Yellow dresses and sexy underwear… any girl could be wearing that!"

The telephone interrupted Bernitz' outburst. Beffort picked up. It was Akamatsu.

"Good evening, Smith, we're in Sterling."

---

[10] See *Miss Atomos*.

"Great, Yosho. Where are you exactly?"

"Maybe 50 feet away from you in room 12. Can I pay you a visit?"

"Of course! What's got into you? You're being so formal! Do you plan to introduce us to the charming Icho Fuji?"

"No! At least not right now. She's already in town trying to get information about Madame Atomos. By the way, Smith, don't you find this whole thing a little astonishing?"

"Yes," Smith responded. "Everyone finds it astonishing and I'm no different. As if Madame Atomos has only done normal things. People have forgotten that she flew around in flying saucers like we take taxis, that she disintegrated steel plates with her ray guns and that she lived in an unimaginable city. Well, now they're surprised that she's taking the risk of showing her face after poisoning a bunch of children."

"It's okay, don't get upset. I'm coming over."

Beffort hung up, stubbed out his cigarette and asked Bernitz, "What are your men doing, Owen?"

"The usual rounds," the big man answered cynically. "Visiting the hotels, the boarding houses, basically anyplace Madame Atomos can scurry into. We gotta wait a while before we get any results... Any special instructions?"

"No, it's too early to make any decisions."

"In that case, I'll go back to dispatch. Good night." He left and closed the door gently.

Mie murmured, "You're going to think I'm crazy, Smith, but I have the feeling that Madame Atomos is very close to us. A lot closer than she was in Ohio."

Beffort looked at her gravely. He was convinced that Mie had a gift, a special internal radar capable of

178

detecting Madame Atomos when she entered her zone of influence. Maybe that was due to the fact that she was living only to revenge her son. Still, in both Billings and Cincinnati she really had felt the presence of her enemy before anyone else.

"She must be thinking of me as much as I am of her," Mie resumed, "and our hatred is facing off by telepathy. When she's far away from me, my senses are weaker and I feel calm and relaxed. Right now I have the feeling that if just close my eyes I'll see her."

Beffort was careful to show no reaction. He stayed perfectly still, hoping that she would continue on her own.

Mie lowered her eyes, stayed silent for a minute, then furrowed her brow and said, "There's something different about her. Before she gave off only hatred and all the waves that she emitted were bad. Now she's lighter, sparkling with some kind of joy. I don't know what's happened, Smith, but Madame Atomos isn't the bitter woman we used to know. However, her animosity is still there... I don't understand!"

The doorbell made her jump. Smith got up and went to let Akamatsu in. When he waved to Mie, she instantly noticed his utter weariness and said, "The air in Ohio isn't doing you well, Yosho. You've lost weight and..."

"Come on," Beffort cut in cheerfully, "let's not forget that our friend is almost a newlywed. At a time like this, no one ever gets fat! A little Cutty Sark, Yosho?"

Akamatsu accepted and flopped into the armchair. "That'll pick me up," he remarked, "because Mie is right. I'm going through a bad spell."

Beffort poured the whiskey and with feigned indifference asked, "The start of a flu?"

"No, it's more like general fatigue. I feel sluggish, no energy and no will. And I have lost weight."

"That's just a feeling," Beffort said, holding out the glass. "It happens to me sometimes. There are days when I feel old and ugly and I hurt everywhere. When you feel like that, you cut yourself shaving and bump into every piece of furniture... It'll pass."

"I've lost six or seven pounds," Akamatsu said, "and I always want to sleep."

His voice was so mournful that Smith broke out laughing. "Your sickness is called Miss Icho Fuji, my friend! Come on, drink up and stop complaining."

Mie intervened, smiling. "Don't be mean, Smith. It's true that our friend is going through a hard period. Yosho, you should see a doctor. It often takes nothing at all to get back on your feet."

"Okay," Akamatsu said, "I'll see someone tomorrow. Now can we talk about something else, Smith? Madame Atomos for example?"

Smith wet his whistle with the amber liquid. "We can talk about it if you want to, but as things stand now our conversation will revolve only around the past, specifically the ten poisonings in Sterling. But even about this I don't have all the information yet. A few dead children. We still don't know what they ingested or how they got it or how they all took it at the same time in ten different places. In and of itself that's a mystery... The director of the Sterling FBI is Danvers. It's not too late to go see him. You want to go, Mie?"

"I'm ready." The young lady grabbed her handbag.

Beffort picked up his hat, searched his pockets and asked, "Do you have any money on you, Mie? I've got to go to the bank."

Mie opened her bag and pulled out a handful of bills. Then her eyes bugged out. "What's this?" Between her fingers she was holding a magnificent brooch. It was a beautiful piece of jewelry and obviously very expensive.

Beffort examined it and whistled softly. "Hey, this thing is worth a small fortune. You didn't tell me you bought it?"

Mie looked extremely surprised. "But I didn't buy it, Smith. This is the first time I've seen it. Anyway, it wasn't in my bag when we left Chardon." She narrowed her eyes and stared at her husband. "Funny way of giving me a present, don't you think?"

"Don't look at me," he defended himself. "I'm really sorry but something like this never enters my mind except at our anniversary."

Yosho Akamatsu took his turn to examine the brooch. "Very beautiful piece," he assessed. "Where was your bag during the trip?"

"In the overhead."

"Well," the Japanese suggested, "probably another passenger made a mistake. Maybe mistook your bag for one just like it?"

"That's the only logical explanation," Beffort admitted. "We can pass by the airport and tell them what you found, Mie."

The young lady pinned the brooch on her blouse and looked at it in the mirror. The jewelry sparkled so brilliantly that Beffort declared, "It must be glass. They make wonderful imitations nowadays."

"Even if it is a fake," Mie murmured, "I think it's extraordinary. Notice how it looks like it's made for me?"

Beffort and Akamatsu winked at each other.

Mie asked, "While we're waiting for someone to claim it, can I wear it, Smith?"

"As long as you don't lose it, I don't see why not. It really does look great on you, but don't get too attached to it because you're certainly going to be returning it to its rightful owner." He looked at his watch. "Now let's hurry up and go see Danvers before he leaves his office."

He opened the door and as Mie stepped through the doorway, she said, "I hope nobody claims the brooch."

Akamatsu smiled and Beffort whispered to him, "You don't understand Icho Fuji, do you? Me, I don't understand how a G-man's wife wants to keep something that doesn't belong to her. When I told you that we would never understand anything about women, I wasn't joking…"

In the Chevy Malibu, Mie fingered the brooch tenderly.

Chapter III

Danvers was scrawny and skeletal. His bare skull was like an oiled billiard ball and his strangely smooth face would have looked like custard if it did not have that thick moustache slashing across it. When he talked, his Adam's apple bobbed up and down his skinny neck like a restless elevator; and his round eyes bounced like Mexican jumping beans.

Danvers was pleasant, but his nervousness was contagious. Just watching him Beffort, in spite of himself, compared him to an erupting volcano and wanted to beg the man to sit down and stay calm.

"And finally," Danvers was reeling off like a sportscaster, "the coroner reports told us that the children all bore traces of a small prick on their faces. Since no one approached them when they left school or their house, we figured that some kind of projectile had been shot at them with an air gun. This projectile might be a tiny poisoned dart that..."

"Why might be?" Beffort interrupted.

"Because the coroners didn't find anything!" Danvers said, continuing to pace around the office. "Therefore, I think that these darts must dissolve with body heat. Since the specialists haven't been able to determine the nature of the poison, we have no clues to pursue the investigation. They say this Japanese woman might be Madame Atomos. I certainly hope so, but how can we be sure? There are a lot of Asians in Sterling and this woman spotted in the vicinity before, during and after the schools got out might not be the same person."

"I thought the witnesses corroborated on her description?"

Danvers lifted his arms to the sky. "The witnesses! Let's talk about them! They saw an older woman, an Asian, but she's not the same height or weight and they all say she was wearing something different! Besides, it's all the result of collective psychosis. If they weren't talking so much about Madame Atomos, I'd bet my bottom dollar that nobody would have noticed this Japanese woman!"

All of a sudden he stopped talking and walking. He sat down and gave each of his three visitors a hard, insistent, awkward stare. Danvers was a weird guy, unstable, and Beffort wondered how he could have risen to the position he occupied.

Distant and uncomfortable, Akamatsu said, "No one can kill ten children so quickly and cruelly unless they're crazy or named Madame Atomos. Personally I think the latter is the author of the massacre and that this is only the beginning."

"I won't argue with that!" Danvers barked. "I'm just saying that I have no proof. You came to me to get information and I can't give you any. Someone killed children. Who is it? That's the question. The rest is just guesswork. There you go."

Beffort changed his opinion about Danvers. The man was a ball of nerves, but his apparent tendency to fantasy and disorder was just a front. He must, in reality, have been terribly effective because he relied only on the facts and his offhand manner was his way of refusing to be smug or melodramatic. In front of Beffort, the Washington representative and supreme chief of the Anti-Atomos Army, Danvers could have tried to toot his own horn by saying that his investigation was moving full steam ahead. But he admitted his inability to shed any light on the affair. It was a sign of courage.

Beffort said, "I understand how things look, Danvers, but in every criminal matter there's a potential perpetrator. In the present, Madame Atomos is at the top of the list. You're aware that she's trying to construct a laboratory to make one or more of the dreadful weapons she used to have before the destruction of Atomia Island. Knowing that we're on her trail, she'll do anything she can to throw us off track. We know it and on this premise it is very possible that this Japanese woman is not Madame Atomos. But supposing that the witnesses believed they saw the same woman everywhere, even if they were different women, doesn't change our investigation in any way. The first thing we have to do is catch a member of the gang and trace back to Madame Atomos."

"I fully understand," Danvers assured. "Give me the order to arrest all the Japanese in Sterling. You have the power for that, not me. Except before getting any results, you understand that we'll have to line up hundreds of women before the witnesses?"

Beffort smiled coldly. "Arrest whoever you want and bring them before the witnesses in the community center. Maybe nothing will come of it, but our minds will be at rest. In the meantime tell your men to watch the elementary and high schools, etc. In the next few days the mortality rate in Sterling is going to skyrocket!"

Danvers nodded and picked up the phone. On the desk Beffort put a card with his telephone number at the Statler as well his radio contact for the Yellow Mask.

"You can reach me day or night at one or the other."

"Got it," Danvers said. Then he looked at Mie and said, "You have the same brooch as my wife, Mrs. Beffort..." Mie smiled politely. Danvers added, "Except my wife found it this morning in the gutter. Pretty lucky, don't you think? Especially since no one's claimed it. Hello? Danvers here at headquarters..."

He winked at Beffort to excuse himself for cutting off their conversation so abruptly. Beffort waved him off and then waved goodbye, dragging Mie and Akamatsu in his wake.

Once in the Malibu Mie said, "Strange coincidence, isn't it?"

"Indeed," Beffort responded as he started the car. "You found a brooch in your handbag and Mrs. Danvers found the same kind in the gutter... it's like some mistimed publicity stunt. Hey, here's a jewelry store. Let's clear this up."

He pulled the Malibu up to the curb and got out while Mie and Akamatsu preferred to wait in the car. After he entered the store the jeweler glanced at the brooch and said, "Worthless. It's glass, but I must say that this piece is very original. Where'd you buy it?"

"Family heirloom," Beffort lied. "Thanks."

Now the matter was closed for him. In fact, the whole thing seemed so unimportant to him, not knowing that the expert Atomos hand was behind it all.

Mie did not raise her hackles or arch her back because she was not a cat, but she did get goose bumps when Akamatsu introduced her to Miss Icho Fuji in the restaurant of the Statler Hotel. When the two couples sat in a booth Akamatsu turned very formal.

"Mrs. Mie Beffort, this is Miss Icho Fuji. Mr. Beffort..."

"Glad to meet you," Smith said.

"Me, too," Mie said.

"I'm thrilled!" Icho Fuji responded. "I even heard about you in Japan! You're exactly like I imagined." Then with a dazzling smile she added, "In my country we admire you a great deal. Without you Madame Atomos would certainly have destroyed the United States, right?"

Akamatsu intervened, "Don't put their modesty to the test, Icho."

"I'm sorry," Miss Fuji apologized, bowing slightly.

She was charming, exquisitely friendly, and Mie wondered why she was so ruffled. She fought against the feeling, started a conversation with her in Japanese, but could not manage to chase away the utter dislike the woman inspired in her.

"So, Miss Fuji," Beffort asked, "how's your report on Madame Atomos coming along?"

The young lady frowned. "Rather badly. I was counting on getting some new information about her, but I see that my American colleagues have already said everything. If you don't give me some tips, my employers will be very disappointed."

Beffort looked down at his steak and tried to dodge the remark, "Yosho knows as much as I do."

He did not particularly want to confide in her. Akamatsu's girlfriend made him feel strangely uncomfortable. Beneath her friendly façade he detected extraordinary cunning. By what fantastic set of circumstances had Akamatsu the Wise got himself hooked by a tigress like this?

"Me," Yosho spoke softly, "I don't know anything. We're no better off than you are, Icho. For a good article you'll have to wait for something new, just like your colleagues, and that all depends on Madame Atomos."

Mie tilted her head, watching the young Japanese girl like a pigeon inspecting a grain of rice. She spoke very sweetly, "You must be passionate about your job, Miss Fuji. Excuse my ignorance, but I imagine you must be a famous journalist if Japan sent you to the USA?"

"Not Japan, Mrs. Beffort," the so-called Icho Fuji corrected, "just two magazines in Kyoto. But I'm afraid I was chosen only because I'm fluent in English."

"It's true that you speak with almost no accent," Mie complimented. "Have you been in the United States before?"

"No, but there are a lot of Americans in our country and talking to them helped me a lot." Madame Atomos was enjoying herself immensely. She had never thought she would be able to talk in peace with her most relentless enemies.

While Mie continued to chat with her in Japanese, Akamatsu leaned over to Beffort and whispered, "What do you think of her, Smith?"

"Charming, pal, really charming."

Akamatsu relaxed in his chair.

"Aren't you eating?" Beffort asked him.

"I'm not hungry. But I could do with a nap right now. I'm beat."

He did not need to say it; anybody could see it. Beffort made no comment, just watched him out of the corner of his eye. Akamatsu's eyelids were heavy and he was obviously forcing himself to stay awake. From time to time he unconsciously rubbed his wrist where Beffort could see that he was wearing a new square watch that showed the day and date on a luminous face. It must have been too tight because all around it his skin was blotched.

As the conversation started lagging after they had finished eating, Smith said, "I think it's high time we got to bed. We have a lot on our plate for tomorrow. Good night, Yosho. Good night, Miss Fuji."

Icho Fuji held Mie's hand. "I'm so happy to have had the chance to talk with you. I hope we can become friends."

Mie said that they already were and then she took Smith's arm. They flew up to the fourth floor in the elevator and went to their room. Mie collapsed on the bed right away. "That girl gets on my nerves, Smith," she said under her breath.

Beffort took off his jacket and emptied his pockets. "What?" he was surprised. "But she's nice and pretty to boot. You aren't jealous, are you, Mie?"

"Don't be stupid!" the young lady protested. She got up, put the brooch on the table and took off her blouse and skirt before going into the bathroom. As the water started running, Smith untied his shoes and could hear, "That Icho Fuji is more devious than she lets on."

Beffort saw that his wife had the same opinion about Miss Fuji, but he said nothing.

"Akamatsu met her in Padanaram, right?"

"Yes."

There was a long silence. Mie had just made a suggestion that Beffort would not accept and neither of them wanted to delve deeper into the matter for the moment. Both of them were clearly thinking about the yellow dresses and sexy underwear found in Madame Atomos' refuge. Miss Icho Fuji was dressed like that, but as Owen Bernitz had said, so were all the young ladies.

The Mie's thoughts drifted. In the mirror she had just noticed a red spot on her chest. Right between her breasts at the point where her blouse closed.

Madame Atomos did not sleep much. She woke up at two in the morning, listened to the slow, regular breathing of Akamatsu, who was sleeping next to her, and slowly parted her sensual lips. At the rate things were going he would not be living much longer—maybe 30 or 40 days.

Madame Atomos got quietly out of bed and carried the telephone into the bathroom. The wire, however, kept the door from closing, but she knew that Akamatsu would not wake up for hours. She picked up the receiver and tapped to get the front desk to request a number in Sterling. She heard the dial turning and the phone ringing five times before a female voice answered and was connected directly to room 82. Madame Atomos waited until she was sure no one was listening and then said, "Mrs. Yshinari?"

"Yes, who's this?"

Madame Atomos spoke in her normal voice, "It's me. You know who I am. No names!"

"I know who you are," Mrs. Yshinari said respectfully.

"Good. I want to congratulate you for your work on the students. Where are you with the brooches?"

"A hundred have already gone out," Mrs. Yshinari informed her in a nasally voice, "and I think I can get another hundred out tomorrow. You said it's not dangerous, right?" She was worried.

Madame Atomos smiled in the dark. "That's right."

"But I have them all with me and I have to fiddle with so many."

"There's no danger if you follow the safety instructions to the letter," Madame Atomos said flatly. "Besides, you're fully aware that the brooches only work when they're very close up. Use tweezers and keep them eight inches from your body."

"Okay, I'll be careful."

"You'll also have to speed things up so that they can all work at the same time. Use taxis, grocery stores, the movies... Women always keep what they find in those places. And get the A.O.F.M.A. team under Scarlett to help you. You know how to contact them?"

"Yes. He called me the day before yesterday to tell me he'd arrived in Sterling. He wanted me to tell you that he needs money. And he's starting to worry about not hearing from you."

Madame Atomos bit her lip. By necessity she had neglected the members of her gang for the past month and the new organization was obviously starting to unravel a little.

"Tell Scarlett that you spoke to me and that he has to get the A.O.F.M.A. to give him money. Also tell him that everything is fine and the construction of the laboratory is almost finished. If he happens to be in your room tomorrow night, I'll call back then."

"He'll be here, Madame."

Madame Atomos opened the bathroom door a little more. Akamatsu was still sleeping like a log. She said, "What have you heard about the police?"

"They're very busy," Mrs. Yshinari said, "and I think that all the Asian women are going to be arrested very soon. The local FBI director is going to line them up before the witnesses."

"What's his name?"

"Danvers."

"He has to disappear," Madame Atomos said softly. "Use the same method as you did with the students. It's quick and leaves no trace."

"You said that I wouldn't have to…"

"Danvers will be the last one to die like that," Madame Atomos cut her short. "It's an emergency. I don't want to create a stir, but this is unavoidable. We can't let the witnesses recognize you. If need be, we'll eliminate them, too. Find out about them. Get their names and addresses. I'll call you tomorrow night."

She hung up just like that and went back into the bedroom. She put the telephone back in place after carefully rolling the wire up at the foot of the nightstand. Then she went back to bed and tried unsuccessfully to fall to sleep. She was thinking too much about the laboratory that would give her back her infernal power.

Chapter IV

Danvers got out of his car, closed the door and crossed the street. The parking lot was across from the FBI headquarters and the director did not have far to walk to get to his office. He hated this because he wanted exercise. Even if he was not being squeezed by fat, his arteries were still clogging up like a neglected drainpipe and his heart raced every time he made a physical effort.

On the sidewalk Danvers felt something sting his left cheek. He automatically raised his hand to chase away a mosquito as he entered the federal building and then waved to the guard. He reached his office at 9 a.m. on the dot, started working and died at 9:22. It was a flawless execution.

Madame Atomos' killer was Kazuo Meguro. He belonged to the A.O.F.M.A. strike force and was one of those who had murdered the ten school children. A passionate follower of Madame Atomos, he was sorry not to know her, but nevertheless served her cause with exemplary devotion. Being a naturalized American citizen for a long time, Kazuo Meguro was a prime candidate because he was practicably beyond suspicion.

He lived and worked in Sterling, had a wife and two kids, and his life could not be more banal. In terms of espionage, he was the quintessential sleeping cell. With respect to the police and in case he happened to be listed as a possible suspect, Kazuo Meguro had the best chance of exonerating himself because he would be assumed not to know his victims and thus have no interest in seeing them disappear.

Therefore, after shooting the tiny poisoned dart at Danvers—from

ten yards away, sitting in his old Ford—Kazuo Meguro, in all likelihood, should have left the scene without a problem. Except that 300 men of the Green Dragon Force had been watching the city for a day. One of them, Ben Brady, was stopped on Poplar Street when the old Ford passed by him at 8:30 a.m. For Ben Brady, any yellow face was synonymous with the Atomos gang. Moreover, he was in the city trying to find an older Japanese woman, but barring that he would make do with a Japanese man.

He saw the Ford park not far from the FBI headquarters, so he turned around, parked his own car and waited.

At 8:50 he noticed that the Ford's driver was fidgeting around behind the wheel. Five minutes later Brady saw the thin bald man arrive. The man crossed the street, stepped onto the sidewalk and headed for the door of the federal building. At that moment the Ford's occupant hunched over in his seat. He leaned out the window, tilted his head and froze. Brady saw nothing else, but it really looked to him like the Japanese had just taken a shooting position. And yet, nothing happened. The bald man disappeared inside the building and the Japanese sat back in a normal position. Then he started his car and drove off.

Brady hesitated, but finally decided to follow the car for only one reason: the Japanese man had come there directly and parked for 15 minutes before leaving again without, apparently, doing anything. It was bizarre.

Brady tailed the Ford all the way to 330 Pioneer Road where he saw the Japanese enter a restaurant using a key. He deduced that he was the manager or owner of the place. Brady jotted down the Ford's license plate in his notebook along with the name and address of the restaurant, then he headed back to Poplar Street. He had done his job, that was all, and was not really expecting to get anything out of it.

At 9:30 he spotted a Japanese woman in a taxi. She was rather young, but Brady followed her all the same. Even though Madame Atomos was 50 years old, she did not look her age and he could not overlook anything. The taxi cruised to the corner of Broadway and the woman got out, paid the fare and hurried into a store.

A little later Brady saw her through the window dressed as a sales clerk. He used his notebook again, restarted the car and drove slowly down the street hugging the curb.

At 10 a.m. Ralph Stutton's voice exploded over the radio speaker. Brady turned the volume down and listened to the dispatch launch a general alert:

"The FBI director of Sterling has just been murdered in his office at headquarters. Someone stuck a poisoned dart in his left cheek. Smith Beffort wants you to be extra careful when watching the schools. Over and out."

It took a few seconds for the news to sink in. Brady got on the radio. "Car 63 here. At 9 a.m. I was in front of the FBI headquarters. Is the director skinny and bald?"

"That's right, Brady. You have something?"

"I'd say! I think I just watched the murder without even knowing it." He described the scene he had witnessed and gave the information about the restaurant on Pioneer Road. All of a sudden dispatch put him in direct contact with Yellow Mask.

"Where are you, Brady?" Beffort asked from his Malibu.

"Somewhere around Broadway."

"Turn around. I'll meet you in ten minutes at the corner of Pioneer and Sidney. You'll recognize the man, I suppose?"

"And how! It's like I photographed him."

At the meeting point, Ben Brady acted out the scene for Beffort, Mie and Owen Bernitz.

"Danvers was there. The Ford here. Danvers was walking in that direction, so his left side was to the Japanese. In my opinion there's no doubt about it. Good God, if I'd known!"

Beffort waved that off. "One miracle at a time, Ben. Because it's already one that you were there. Is that the restaurant?"

"No, it's farther down at number 330. Look, you can see the Ford from here. The Japanese went in through the front door. It looked like he owned the place and I wouldn't be surprised if he's living on the second floor."

Beffort had a detailed map of the neighborhood. He made sure that the building did not have another exit that the Japanese might use to escape and then gave the green light. At this point in the investigation Beffort had a choice between two solutions: the first was to put the suspect under surveillance and follow him for a few days to see where we went; the second was more direct—arrest him immediately, take him by surprise and make him admit, in any way possible, his connection to the Atomos gang.

Beffort had decided on the latter because he knew that time was on Madame Atomos' side. Somewhere in the shadows the terrible woman must have been putting the finishing touches on her laboratory. If she succeeded in realizing her plans, a dreadful menace would loom over the United States once again. The disintegrator ray, electromagnetic shield, paralyzing ray, motor brains, etc. It gave Beffort the shivers!

When they got close to the restaurant Beffort stopped and said, "Mie, you go and ring the bell. It's too early for them to open up without a reason and he'll figure that something's not right if he sees us all in front of the window. Speak to him in Japanese. Tell him that you have an urgent message for him. Act all mysterious... Don't let him think. The guy is certainly a fanatic. If he thinks the FBI is after him, he might kill himself. So go easy."

Mie nodded. "You can count on me, Smith."

She glided down the sidewalk and stopped in front of the door, putting her finger on the ringer. She did not hear the bell, but a shadow shifted inside the restaurant. She rang again. This time the shadow darkened the window and a hand moved the curtain decorated with silver lotus flowers. Under the glowering scrutiny of the Japanese, Mie felt less bold. The man was suspicious and would probably not fall for the urgent message trap.

She smiled and said loudly, "I'd like to reserve a table if it's possible?" That was much more reasonable.

The man opened right away and then faded away. Mie entered, but stayed in front of the open door so that the man could not close it at the last minute. Then she said in Japanese, "It would be for tomorrow night. There are four of us. Hold on, here are my friends."

Beffort, Owen and Brady came through the door. Beffort pulled out his weapon and ordered, "Don't move!"

Kazuo Meguro turned pale. "Who are you?"

"FBI. I'm arresting you for the murder of William Danvers. Get your coat and don't try anything. Is that him, Ben?"

"In the flesh," Brady testified.

Owen Bernitz slipped behind Meguro, who was petrified, put him in an arm lock and searched him with an expert hand. "No gun on him. Gotta look somewhere else."

Just then a small, round woman came out of the office. She, too, was Japanese and had heard the doorbell. Because of the bad lighting she could not see very well what was happening in the front of the room. She came forward, squinting, and babbled, "What's going on, Kazuo?"

The man spoke firmly. "It's the police. They say I killed someone."

The small, round woman said nothing. She simply leaned on a table and waited, fatalist, almost apathetic.

Owen," Beffort said, "watch this guy. Ben and I are going to try to find the murder weapon. Blowpipe or air gun, Meguro?" He had seen his name at the top of a menu.

The Japanese was startled, but shrugged his shoulders with contempt. "I don't know what you're talking about. You must have the wrong address and the wrong person. I'm not the only Meguro in the neighborhood."

Beffort ignored him and started an orderly search with Ben Brady. On the first floor they found nothing, so they went with Mrs. Meguro, still impassive, up to the second floor. Three rooms, a kitchen and bathroom. They found an address book, which Beffort snatched up, a list of telephone numbers, which he also pocketed, but no object even resembling an air gun or blowpipe.

Beffort let Brady finish the search and went up to the small fat woman. "Your husband left this morning, didn't he, Mrs. Meguro?"

"He leaves every morning. He takes the car and goes shopping for the restaurant. Before we had a car he used to take a taxi. He goes to bed late and wakes up early. He's a good husband. He helps the children with their homework…"

She was just talking and Beffort knew that in spite of her cold exterior she must have been terrified. She obviously did not know about all her husband's activities and if that were true the shock would be terrible.

"This morning," Beffort pressed, "he wasn't here at 9 a.m."

The woman shook her head and said, "He came back later. He was at his cousin's who has a restaurant on Front Street."

Brady reappeared with empty hands. Beffort turned his back on the confused woman and went back down to the first floor. Kazuo Meguro had put on his coat and was standing stiff and motionless under the watchful eye of Owen Bernitz.

"Let's go," Beffort ordered. He took the Japanese by the arm and led him out to the sidewalk asking, "Where's your car?"

The man pointed to a Buick that was parked across the street. Beffort smiled and said, "You wife says you own a Ford."

Meguro lowered his head. He had tried to keep the danger at bay, but had failed. Beffort pointed to the Ford and told Brady, "Look in the glove compartment and under the seats, Ben. I'm sure the weapon's in the car."

Brady opened the door and searched for five minutes before pulling out a big air gun and a case con-

199

taining 50 tiny, hollow darts. Beffort did not know what they were made of, but it looked like wax. He let go of the Japanese to examine them more closely and Kazuo took advantage of the diversion to run down the sidewalk. He reacted with extraordinary speed, but could not run faster than the paralyzing ray that struck him. He rolled on the sidewalk before coming to a stop in the middle of a group of bystanders.

Smith put away the weapon and said, "That's too bad. Now he won't wake up for an hour. Come on, we have to get him out of here."

Kazuo Meguro had been sleeping on a bench at headquarters for 30 minutes when Akamatsu and Miss Icho Fuji joined Beffort's group.

"Sorry for being late," Akamatsu apologized, "but I couldn't wake up this morning."

"No problem," Smith responded. "How did you find out?"

"Stutton alerted me. It looks like you made a good catch."

"Absolutely, Yosho. We've got the murderer of poor Danvers."

Icho Fuji turned slightly pale, but no one noticed.

"Except," Beffort continued, "he tried to escape and I had to paralyze him. In 30 minutes I think he'll be able to give us quite a bit of information. You see, Miss Fuji, you've got your scoop! There's no other journalist in the building."

The young lady smiled and took a notepad and pen out of her bag. Icho Fuji was playing her role as journalist, but Madame Atomos was boiling inside. She said, "Could you give me some information about this man?"

"Talk to Ben Brady," Beffort said.

The so-called journalist turned to Brady and fired off questions. Smith Beffort, Mie, Akamatsu and Bernitz stood back from them. They were all in Danvers' office and Kazuo Meguro was in a room next door being guarded by two G-men.

Smith showed the address book and telephone numbers to Akamatsu. In this mess," he said, "I'll be damned if we don't find the names and addresses of the Atomos gang in Sterling. Yosho, you just woke up and your mind is clear. So, tell me why the Atomos gang killed Danvers?"

"Gosh, Smith, I have no idea. At first sight it looks like an act of gratuitous terrorism."

Beffort stared at him. "You're tired, pal. According to our evidence they killed Danvers because he was about to give the order to arrest all the Japanese women in town. The decision was made last night, but Danvers didn't have time to get the word out."

"Ridiculous!" Akamatsu said. "The order will be given this morning and the Atomos gang will still be faced with the problem."

"Of course," Beffort objected, "but it's gained some time! It's almost noon and the order was supposed to be sent out at 9 a.m. Why did the Atomos gang need three hours?"

Akamatsu did not answer. In a sudden rush of excitement Mie said, "The best thing to do apart from stopping all the Japanese from being arrested is to kill the witnesses who can identify the suspects in the line-up! Smith, we have to find a list of the witnesses right now!"

Beffort tossed his cigarette stub onto the floor and rushed to the operations center. Mie and Akamatsu were hot on his heels when he disappeared down the corridor.

"Are they coming back?" Miss Fuji asked.

"For sure," Brady assured her, "but not right away."

The Japanese girl smiled. "In that case, I'm going to take the time to cable my information to Kyoto. Can you tell Mr. Akamatsu that I went back to the hotel? Thank you and goodbye."

She headed for the exit and sped up when she was out of sight. Madame Atomos was off to warn Mrs. Yshinari.

Chapter V

There were 16 witnesses. Smith Beffort found their addresses very quickly through Seater, Danvers' assistant, who was trying the best he could to hold the reins while waiting for Washington to send a new director to Sterling. It was not easy. Danvers had been a hard worker and all the affairs, important or not, passed through his office before being handed out to the different federal services.

"No one's irreplaceable," Seater said, "but you have to admit that Danvers left a big hole in the organization. Whoever takes his place is going to have his hands full."

He was visibly shaken. Beffort gave him the list of witnesses and said, "So start filling up your hands right now. James Edward Evans will send someone later unless you prove that you can do the job, in which case I'll tell Evans to make you the director of this bureau. Get these 16 people under protection and send out the orders that Danvers didn't have time to. By this time tomorrow all the Japanese women in Sterling should be in a lineup. Get cracking, Seater, and fast!"

Leaving the assistant dumbstruck he went away and took Mie and Akamatsu to the room where they were keeping Kazuo Meguro. It was almost 12:30 and the man was starting to show signs of life.

Beffort asked Mie to sit down and said, "Yosho, you want to get the addresses and telephone numbers in the next room?"

Akamatsu went into Danvers' office where he was handed the two objects by Owen Bernitz. "Miss Fuji?" Akamatsu asked.

"She took off to cable the news to her rag," Bernitz told him. "She said she'll see you back at the hotel."

Akamatsu looked at the telephone. "She could have cabled from here, right?"

"Maybe she wasn't comfortable doing that?"

Akamatsu nodded and returned to Beffort. Meguro had just come around. He woke up almost immediately but even though lucid he had a hard time making the connection between the street where he had been put to sleep and this room where he was now.

"We're in FBI headquarters," Beffort told him, "and I can tell you that you're nowhere near leaving here, Kazuo. One of our men was present when you shot Danvers and his eyewitness report is your irrefutable condemnation. But you can still escape the death sentence if you collaborate with us. You might as well play ball because if you refuse we'll just give you a drug that will make you sing like a magpie. Are you ready to answer my questions?"

Kazuo Meguro nodded. He was smart enough to admit his defeat. Beffort turned to one of the G-men who was sitting behind a typewriter and made sure he was ready to take the Japanese man's deposition.

"Meguro," Beffort began, "who gave you the order to murder Danvers?"

"Mrs. Yshinari."

"Address?"

"555 Hamilton Street."

Akamatsu left the room. He was going to give the information immediately to Owen Bernitz, who would unleash the Green Dragon Force against Mrs. Yshinari.

"Could this woman be Madame Atomos?" Beffort continued interrogating.

"No," Kazuo said. "That's impossible! She's lived in Sterling for a long time and never leaves the city."

"If she's not Madame Atomos," Beffort concluded, "then she must be in touch with her. We'll soon find out. Except for her, who do you know?"

Kazuo loosened up. In a few words he had said practically everything he knew about the Atomos gang. "Nobody. Mrs. Yshinari hired me on behalf of the A.O.F.M.A., but I never had contact with any of its members. To tell you the truth they'd never used me before…"

He stopped and looked down. Beffort pushed him back up. "In your position, you don't have much to hide, Kazuo. If you killed Danvers, it's obvious that you could have killed one of the poor kids lying in the morgue."

"That's not true!"

"You're going to have a hard time convincing the judges of that," Beffort maintained. "The fact that you yourself have two children will surely play in your favor, but your cold-blooded murder of Danvers could prove that it wasn't your first time. Besides, there are three darts missing from the case that is supposed to hold 50… Do you admit that you murdered Danvers?"

Kazuo nodded affirmatively. From this moment on he was in the hands of justice and his case no longer interested Beffort. He left him to the G-men.

At 555 Hamilton Street, Bernitz' men had drawn a blank. Mrs. Yshinari had flown the coop a little while ago and in a great hurry. A thousand details proved it.

"It's weird," Beffort grumbled. "How did this woman learn that we were going to arrest her?"

"Meguro's wife?" Akamatsu suggested.

Beffort bit his lip. He did not like the explanation. Mrs. Meguro was not aware of her husband's secret activities; he was sure of that.

Mie said, "Maybe a member of the gang was there when we arrested him?"

"Possible but not probable," Smith stated. "Meguro was supposed to come through without a scratch and no one could have foreseen that Ben Brady would be present at the scene of the crime. On the other hand, I think that Kazuo telephoned Mrs. Yshinari to tell her that everything went fine... What are these cartons?"

There was a pile of them in the corner of the living room. They were empty and Beffort would not have paid any attention to them if it were not for the thin lead sheets inside.

"I don't know," Owen said, "but the delivery slip says that they contained samples. Sent out by train from Oakland, California and delivered only three days ago."

Beffort's ears tingled. "California again! Owen, take these crates to the FBI laboratory and tell the chief that I expect a report this evening. Yosho, call San Francisco and ask our friend Ritter to look into the sender. What's the receipt say about that?"

"It's a Weyerhauser," Owen read, "got a pad in Oakland, 408 Oak Street."

Akamatsu took the receipt and went to the phone. Bernitz and his men grabbed the cartons and disappeared. Mie, who had been searching the desk, triumphantly held up a photograph for her husband.

"In her hurry Mrs. Yshinari forgot this, Smith. This photo shows her on the sofa. Look, on the back, there's her name and the guy sitting next to her: D. Yshinari and J. Mimiko, on 5/5/1968."

"Damn, that's not long ago."

"Last month. Who's this Mimiko?"

"We'll know when we've got Mrs. Yshinari under lock and key," Beffort said. "We'll get this photograph out through the press. Yosho?"

Akamatsu finished his conversation with Ritter and rejoined his friends. He said that Ritter was going to get on the mysterious Weyerhauser right away. Beffort showed him the photo, but Akamatsu did not recognize Mrs. Yshinari or Mimiko.

"And yet," he hesitated, "his face looks kind of familiar."

Beffort and Mie almost dropped dead. Before meeting Icho Fuji Akamatsu had an extraordinary memory of names and faces. They were expecting a miracle, but nothing of the sort happened. The special agent of the *Tokkoka* looked like he was in a fog.

"No, I don' see…"

"You should see a doctor," Smith Beffort advised, deciding on the spot not to coddle him. "Since the day we meet, I've never seen you so tired. Between us, Yosho, as a friend, I think you're overdoing it with Miss Fuji."

Akamatsu grinned. "I wish it were so, Smith, believe me. I don't know how it happened, but I have to admit that I'm good for nothing on that score. I fall asleep as soon as my head hits the pillow and I wake up very late, against my will!"

"Before," Mie said, "the slightest noise used to wake you up."

Akamatsu spread his hands in bewilderment. "I've changed, that's all…"

Smith offered him a cigarette and said softly, "I may be completely off the mark, but it's obvious that all your troubles started in Padanaram, right?"

He was looking off to the side and Akamatsu could not catch his eyes or Mie's. "What exactly are you insinuating, Smith?"

This time Beffort stared him straight in the eyes. "I'm not insinuating anything, Yosho. I'm simply trying to figure out what's wearing you down."

"Don't exaggerate!" the Japanese retorted.

Beffort grabbed his arm and dragged him in front of the mirror. "Look at yourself, for God's sake! You look like a walking corpse!"

He shook him and Akamatsu almost fell over. Beffort shouted, "And you can barely stand up straight!"

"Smith!" Mie begged, "Leave him alone."

"That's it," Beffort barked, "I'll just close my eyes and leave him to his fate. Yosho, you're coming with me, like it or not."

Akamatsu smiled sadly. "I'll go, Smith. But where to?"

"To the nearest hospital, my friend. And I'm not leaving your side until a doctor examines you from head to toe."

"In the meantime, Mrs. Yshinari is getting away."

"Green Dragon will take care of her. Don't try to wriggle out of it. Come on, we're off!"

Smith and Mie waited for nearly an hour before an assistant came to tell them that the exams would take longer than they thought. Akamatsu would probably not leave the hospital before 6 p.m. And he was asking his friends to call Miss Fuji so that she would not worry that he was missing.

The Befforts went back to the Malibu after trying in vain to reach Miss Fuji at the Statler. Smith sounded concerned when he said, "If the doctors are keeping Akamatsu, it's because his condition is serious. We'll come back at six to pick him up. Right now we have time to pass by the lab."

They returned to headquarters, saw Seater and were struck by his paleness. Smith took him aside and asked, "What's going on, Seater?"

"A series of disasters, Mr. Beffort. Like we'd agreed, I sent men out to the witnesses' houses to protect them, but it turned out to be useless because they've all disappeared!"

"Goddamn!" Smith swore. "Are you sure?"

"Unfortunately yes. None of them came home but those who were eating in a cafeteria got phone calls telling them to return home urgently. Unless it was a coincidence…"

"With Madame Atomos," Beffort cut in, "there's no such thing as coincidence. If the 16 witnesses can't be found, it's because they've been kidnapped. First Mrs. Yshinari escapes and now again we're caught lagging. I can't believe it! It's like someone knows every decision we make right when we make it."

Seater was distraught. "Without any witnesses, arresting the Japanese women in Sterling would do us no good. I gave orders that they can't leave the city, but…"

"Okay," Beffort cut him off. "That's the right thing to do. Take this photo. It's of Mrs. Yshinari and some guy named Mimiko. Get copies of it and give them to all your men and the newspapers." He slapped him on the back amicably. "Don't panic, Seater, you're not responsible for any of this. Danvers couldn't have done any better. Do your job and everything will be fine. If you need me I'll be in the lab."

He left him there and took his wife to the elevator. Ten minutes later they were face to face with Mather, the head of the laboratory, who told them as soon as they

209

had entered, "We're ahead of schedule. I have the results of the analyses."

"Bravo! You work fast."

"Don't thank me," Mather smiled, "our Geiger counters were about to explode when we stuck them near the cartons. What was in them? Pocket-sized atomic bombs?"

Beffort grinded his teeth. "Radiation?"

"And how!" Mather exclaimed. "I haven't seen anything like it since Bikini! These cartons are literally impregnated with Strontium 90 in spite of the lead lining. And they're emitting more than 20 roentgens!"

Beffort took a deep breath. Mather was exaggerating. He said, "You're scaring me."

Mather did not smile. "20 roentgens is very serious. It only takes 1.5 roentgens to alter certain bacteria. Man can't put up with more than 5 roentgens of radiation a week. Personally I judged the cartons dangerous enough to lock them all up in our lead chamber. Come and see for yourself."

Smith and Mie followed the director down an endless corridor and into a white room with a very low ceiling where two specialists were working. There were complicated devices everywhere. Mather grabbed a Geiger counter and said to them, "Follow me, please."

He started walking again, pushed a button on his machine, and jumped on hearing the crackle. He put the counter on a table and stared at the screen.

"20 roentgens!" he was stunned.

Beffort and Mie approached and the amplifier instantly fired a series of discharges between the anode and cathode. Mather looked up at the couple and said, "Can you step back?"

Mie and Smith backed off and the counter quieted down as the needle dropped to zero. Mather asked again, "Come closer, Mr. Beffort."

Smith stepped forward, but the counter remained quiet.

"Your turn, Mrs. Beffort."

Mie approached. The counter started crackling and the needle in the screen slowly rose until it hovered around the number 20 when Mie was only a few inches away.

Beffort turned pale. "Is my wife emitting that, Mather?"

Mather lifted the counter and got a very strong amplification at Mie's chest. "It's not your wife, but surely that brooch. Take it off right away!"

Mie literally ripped the jewelry off her blouse and threw it on the table. Mather turned off the counter and wiped off the beads of sweat that were forming on his forehead, asking, "How long have you been wearing that damn thing, Mrs. Beffort?"

Mie could not answer. Her teeth were chattering and no sound could breach her lips. She was thinking of the little red spot between her breasts.

"Less 24 hours," Beffort answered.

"In that case," Mather sighed with relief, "there's no harm, but the radiation from the brooch is enough to cause leukemia in two to four months depending on the health of the subject. Mrs. Beffort, whoever offered you that jewelry wanted you dead."

Mie nodded and sat down on the table. Her legs were wobbly and the little red spot suddenly itched like mad. Mather saw her put her hand to her chest, saw the spot and said, "Don't worry about that. It'll go away in a few hours, but you can see that the epidermis is already infected."

"My wife found the brooch in her handbag," Beffort reeled off pensively, "and Danvers said that his wife had also found a brooch like it in a gutter. I wonder if the cartons didn't contain a whole stock of atomized brooches?"

Mather jumped. "Good God! I didn't think of that! That would bring it all back to Madame Atomos!"

Smith Beffort did not respond because he was already running toward the telephone.

Chapter VI

At 5 p.m. on that same day the pictures of Mrs. Yshinari and Mr. Mimiko were spread by the newspapers and broadcast on television along with a photograph and description of the radioactive brooch. On the purely informational level, it was a success concerning the jewelry. Almost 200 samples were returned and immediately isolated, but no news came in about Mrs. Yshinari and her friend.

Sterling was in a state of siege since the afternoon, but Mrs. Yshinari had certainly left the city in the morning. Moreover, federal agents could not find the slightest trace of the 16 witnesses who were all adults with families and seemed to have literally vanished into thin air between 11:30 a.m. and 1 p.m.

After the death of the ten school children as well as of Danvers, the matter of the brooches did nothing to calm the population. They knew that Madame Atomos was in the neighborhood. They were saying that she had recovered all her powers and they could now, definitely, expect the worst.

At 6 p.m. Mie and Smith Beffort went to the hospital where Akamatsu had been waiting a little while for them to come back. Smith asked, "Well, Yosho, what do the doctors have to say?"

The Japanese smiled derisively. "It seems I'm anemic. My white blood cells are eating up the red and I need to rest. Here's my prescription. When I've swallowed all these pills and got all these shots..."

"Don't start complaining," Beffort interrupted. "But tell me about the rash you have on your wrist."

"Oh, just some irritation."

"Caused by your watch?"

"That's right. Say, are you a doctor now, Smith?"

Beffort showed him the headlines and pointed to the photograph of the brooch.

Akamatsu was astonished. "But that's Mie's brooch!" Then he read the article and his expression changed.

Beffort said, "Mie wore that brooch for 24 hours. That's not long, but the irradiation had already started eating away at her skin. How long have you been wearing your watch, Yosho?"

The question was blunt and following the last statement, left no doubt about Beffort's thoughts. Akamatsu shrugged his shoulders. "Stop the melodrama, Smith, please. I've had this watch since the beginning of my stay in Padanaram."

"Did you buy it?"

"No, it was a gift from Icho Fuji. You see how ridiculous your innuendos are."

Beffort was perplexed, but decided to go all the way with his questioning. He said, "You didn't read the whole article, Yosho, otherwise you'd know that we wouldn't have known Mie's brooch was radioactive if a Geiger counter didn't pick it up by chance. Mather, the director of the FBI laboratories, stated that Mie could have died in three or four months if she kept wearing the brooch. Leukemia was the eventual result. Now, you've had this watch for a month and you're anemic."

Akamatsu's hackles were up again. "Are you insinuating that Icho…"

"No!" Beffort jumped back in. "It has nothing to do with Miss Fuji, who was certainly acting in good faith when she gave you the present. But I think that someone could have taken advantage of her... She was your friend—that was known—and they took the opportunity to attack you through her."

Akamatsu showed him the watch. "It's really quite beautiful, Smith, and who says it's radioactive?"

"Exactly," Smith replied. "We have to go to the laboratory and find out. Come on, the Malibu's engine is still running."

Miss Icho Fuji—Madame Atomos—was returning to the Statler when a newsboy attracted her attention. He was holding up a special edition, shouting that atomized brooches were menacing Sterling. Madame Atomos bought a paper and learned instantly that the situation was rapidly deteriorating for her. In fact, it was impossible that Mie and Smith Beffort had not made the connection between the brooches and Yosho Akamatsu's watch. The special agent's state of health only aggravated matters. No, Smith Beffort could not have ignored it.

At the Statler Icho Fuji knew that her fears were well founded when she saw the message Smith Beffort had left: *Yosho at the hospital for medical exams. He'll be back around 7 p.m.*

Madame Atomos clearly saw how things would develop when they found out that Akamatsu had been bombarded with radioactivity for a month through his watch, which was received as a gift in Padanaram. She would have difficulty defending herself, be unable to say where she had got the deadly watch and end up collapsing under Beffort's interrogation since she knew how dogged and skillful he was...

Of course the G-man could never prove that she was Madame Atomos, but a simple accusation of complicity would be enough to send her before a judge. So, for the security of Madame Atomos Icho Fuji had to escape all suspicion. Otherwise what good was her extraordinary mutation?

Madame Atomos needed to think, to put together a plan that would give her a belated alibi for the purchase of the watch. So, she needed some time. She asked for paper at the front desk, sat in plain sight at a table in the lobby and wrote:

Dear Yosho, I'm sorry I couldn't wait for you here, but after seeing the picture of Mrs. Yshinari in the paper, I got terribly worked up because I think I know where this woman is hiding. I can't tell you more at the moment. I'll call you when I'm sure.

She signed the message, slipped it into an envelope, which she sealed feverishly and she went to put it in the box of room 12. She was sorry that the front desk clerk did not pay attention to her drama, but she left anyway and hailed a taxi. If necessary she would sacrifice Mrs. Yshinari by giving her up to the police. But before that she had to find a plausible explanation for the atomized watch.

In the laboratory the counter's needle hit 20 roentgens when Mather put it next to the watch. The demonstration was so clear, so unquestionable that Akamatsu was floored.

"You were wearing your death on you," Mather said bluntly, "and it was just a matter of time! Get some rest and follow the doctor's orders to the letter. Even though it's not serious, your case is serious enough to warrant daily care for several weeks. To begin with you're going back to the hospital to tell the doctors your story."

"They already examined me!" Akamatsu protested.

"Yes, but they couldn't guess that you had suffered atomic radiation. You know, they still don't know where leukemia comes from. They might very well decide to keep you in the hospital now that we've found the source of your illness."

Akamatsu was pale, but Mie and Smith knew that it was not just his health that was bothering him. He was obviously thinking of Icho Fuji and the questions he was going to ask were no bed of roses.

"We should go," Beffort decided.

"Okay, but before going to the hospital, I have to stop by the Statler. I can be hospitalized for as long as is necessary if my mind is at rest. Do you understand?"

Mie and Beffort understood.

They left the laboratory, got back in the Malibu and pulled up in front of the Statler a little after 7 p.m. There were a lot of people in the lobby leaving the hotel with no vacancies. Most of these new guests were journalists. They came from all over the United States, hoarded the telephones and made a huge racket—a phenomenon that Madame Atomos always causes when she makes an appearance.

The Befforts and Akamatsu made their way through the crowd to the front desk. As Smith took the key to room 46 he saw Yosho opening a letter. Without worrying about his privacy, he approached. "You've got mail, Yosho?"

Akamatsu looked grimly at him and held out the message. Smith read the few lines and his face froze.

"Astonishing, isn't it?" Akamatsu murmured.

"More than you can imagine," Beffort responded. "I'd swear that this writing was the same as..."

He looked around and saw the journalists keeping an eye on him. He said, "Let's go up. We'll be more comfortable discussing this matter in our room."

They took the elevator up to the fourth floor and locked themselves in room 46, far from prying eyes and ears. Without a word Beffort searched through the briefcase that he never left behind and pulled out a photocopy. "Compare this, Yosho."

"It's the same writing," Akamatsu sighed.

"Yes, they're perfectly identical!"

"I don't understand," Akamatsu admitted. "Icho couldn't have written this photocopy you have."

Beffort sneered. "Icho Fuji apparently hasn't written anything, pal. All of this is by the hand of Madame Atomos."

Akamatsu flopped into an armchair, licking his lips. He was extremely tired and every question that came to mind demanded an immense effort by his brain.

"Don't wear yourself out," Beffort said. "The explanation is simple. Your little friend has been kidnapped by Madame Atomos or her gang members. They left this message so as not to alarm you, but when they call, it'll be to lure you into a trap."

Akamatsu nodded. He was devastated because he felt useless and in spite of his will, he could not fight against his numb and weary mind.

Mie caught his eye and said, "Do you have another explanation, Yosho?"

"No, Mie, none. Except that I find it surprising that Icho was kidnapped exactly when we were about to ask her where the watch came from."

Beffort coughed. Akamatsu was not as weak, mentally speaking, as he appeared. Without even trying, he had just highlighted the strange string of events that had saved Icho Fuji from an interrogation.

Mie said, "We'll have to ask the front desk who left the letter in Yosho's box."

"And if Icho calls in the meantime?" Akamatsu asked.

"Don't make a fuss, Yosho," Beffort implored. "You have to go to the hospital anyway. If your friend telephones, someone will take the call, don't worry."

He opened the door and Akamatsu followed Mie to the elevator. Downstairs it took Beffort some time to get alone with the clerk who thought long and hard before admitting that he knew nothing. Nevertheless, he remembered that Miss Fuji had asked him for some paper and an envelope, but his memory stopped there because right after that he was swamped with reservations.

Beffort called Ralph Stutton and asked him to send Art Baxter to the Statler. Baxter would take any call or message coming in for Akamatsu. After that, Mie and Smith drove Akamatsu to the hospital and accompanied him to the exam room where Beffort told them the story of the watch and the radiation. Akamatsu was wrapped up. "Stay calm," Beffort told him as the doctor dragged him away. "We'll bring you your things when we get a chance."

Akamatsu smirked and disappeared down the corridor. For an indeterminate length of time he was on the sidelines.

The problem with Madame Atomos' new situation was that she could not show herself to any member of the gang as Madame Atomos. She could continue to give orders over the phone and send any amount of money to fixed addresses, but she could not appear in the flesh and blood because no one would recognize her.

On the other hand, she could not betray her new personality by pretending to be Madame Atomos' delegate. At least as long as Beffort, Mie and Akamatsu were alive... afterward, it would not matter so much because she knew that she would never face such staunch enemies again.

For the moment, however, the problem was serious and Icho Fuji was more hesitant and worried than Madame Atomos had ever been. Should she continue to play the role of journalist or toss away the mask? It was a delicate question. Sterling is nothing like San Francisco so hiding here would be difficult. In Billings Madame Atomos had almost got caught precisely because it was a small town. Sterling presented the same problem and it is crawling with police and the Green Dragon Force.

At the intersection of Broadway and Sidney Avenue, two cops had stopped the taxi and Madame Atomos had to show them her Icho Fuji ID. Everything went smoothly, but would it be so easy at the next checkpoint?

Madame Atomos got out in front of the Burlington warehouse and took another cab to continue her wandering. For the first time she did not know what to do, but did not dare return to the Statler Hotel because she still had not come up with a logical explanation for the watch.

Around 8 p.m., riding in her eighth taxi, the driver turned on the radio to listen to the news. The newscaster instantly described the discovery of the brooches, spoke about Yosho Akamatsu's atomized watch and then was interrupted for a breaking bulletin. There was silence for a moment before the announcement:

"The FBI bureau in Sterling is telling us that Miss Icho Fuji, the fiancée of Mr. Akamatsu was kidnapped this afternoon by Madame Atomos around the Statler Hotel. For more information we'll go to Roy Adams who is at FBI headquarters right now. Roy?"

Madame Atomos could not move; she was petrified. There was more dead air before Roy's voice, more quietly, started in:

"As our friend Bob just said, I'm in the federal building right now and it's bustling with activity. The G-men are still looking for the 16 witnesses, without success it seems, and to complicate matters the news of Miss Icho Fuji's kidnapping has just been announced. They're saying that Smith Beffort found out about it first. Madame Atomos left a letter signed by Miss Fuji to make them believe that the young Japanese journalist was on the trail of Mrs. Yshinari, but our national hero recognized his sworn enemy's writing at first glance. The investigation..."

The driver turned down the volume, put on the brakes and turned around in his seat. "We're here. That's 10 dollars."

Madame Atomos gave him 12 dollars and got out. The taxi took off, leaving the terrible woman standing on the edge of the sidewalk. What was happening was beyond her wildest thoughts: she had kidnapped herself!

Then she realized that she had made a monumental mistake in writing that letter. She had acted too hastily in the fear of seeing the Befforts and Akamatsu stride into the Statler and her natural prudence had been tripped up. Now there was no turning back. If she showed up in front of Beffort, he would catch her just by making her write something down.

And then she realized how awful her situation was. Being a supposed victim, they were going to comb the city looking for her and right now she was a sitting duck on the sidewalk, in plain sight.

She backed away from the curb and entered a crowded drugstore. Hurriedly she found a telephone booth, dialed a number, let it ring twice and hung up. She gathered her coins and called again. This time she heard the voice of Mrs. Yshinari.

"It's me," Madame Atomos said.

"I thought so," Mrs. Yshinari said. "I..."

"Listen to me!" Madame Atomos cut her off. "I'm going to send you a young lady who's been working for me for a long time. You will hide her for as along as she needs and you will obey her as if she were me. Her name is Icho Fuji. If you were listening to the radio, you should know what it's about."

"I've heard, but I believed..."

"Believe only what I tell you! I have to disappear for a while and Icho Fuji is replacing me. Is that clear?"

"Loud and clear, Madame."

"Get ready for her. She'll be there in 30 minutes and will ring the bell six times. Goodbye, Mrs. Yshinari."

Madame Atomos hung up the phone, left the drugstore and hailed a cab. The dice were cast. She had to resume her life of adventure without a moment to spare. But as the taxi was carrying her away, a faint smile crossed her lips. Wasn't youth on her side?

Chapter VII

The taxi crossed Sterling from north to south, turned onto Main Street and headed for the airport. The traffic was pretty heavy so police checkpoints around the perimeter of the city were impossible. A roadblock would have created a monstrous traffic jam on Highway 6 and the bottlenecks were not making the verifications easier at the city limits.

Madame Atomos opened her bag, lit a cigarette and held out the open case to the cab driver. "If you smoke, help yourself."

"Thanks," the man said.

He used the lighter on the dashboard, took a long drag and said, "I've been watching you for a while in the rear view mirror."

"Is that right?" Madame Atomos said teasingly.

"Yes and I was telling myself that you very well could be Miss Fuji, if the Atomos gang hadn't kidnapped her. You look exactly like the description they gave over the radio. What a coincidence."

Laughter rippled out of Madame Atomos. "Don't worry, I'm a stewardess and I'm on my way to work. Drop me at 20 Hayes Street. Before going to the airport, I have to see my sister and put on my uniform."

She said this to avoid any immediate problems. If the driver became suspicious, he might, for example, stop at a police station and ask them to check his customer. By pretending to be a stewardess, she was putting him at ease and she could forget about the driver after that.

The cab turned onto Hayes Street and stopped in front of number 20. Madame Atomos paid the fare, got out and waited for the taxi to leave before ringing the bell of the bungalow.

Mrs. Yshinari answered right away. "Come in," she said in a frightened voice. "Why did you bring the taxi to my front door? That's pretty foolish!"

Madame Atomos entered and looked her hostess up and down. "I don't do anything foolish, Mrs. Yshinari," she snapped back. "The taxi driver will be dead in 15 minutes."

Mrs. Yshinari closed the door, locked it, and stared at Miss Icho Fuji with curiosity. "How do you know that he's going to die?"

"Right now he's smoking a cigarette laced with cyanide. When he drops dead, he'll be far away from here... Why are you looking at me like that?"

"You're very pretty, Miss Fuji. They were talking about you on the radio, but their description doesn't do you justice. Madame Atomos told me to be blindly obedient. What do you want?"

Miss Fuji smiled. "I don't want anything, Mrs. Yshinari. I'm only here to transmit the orders of our boss. Is Mr. Mimiko here?"

"He's in the basement with Scarlett. They had to dig for a long time before the ditch was big enough. Now they're pouring in the cement."

Madame Atomos really wanted to believe that it took a lot of work to bury 16 corpses and hundreds of radioactive brooches. She smiled with satisfaction and said, "Take me to a telephone. I have to tell Madame Atomos that I got here." She was beginning her disinformation campaign. For everyone, Madame Atomos would now be just a symbol, a distant voice that Icho Fuji alone had the ability to hear.

Seater wiped his forehead and stated, "No trace of the 16 witnesses or Mrs. Yshinari or Mr. Mimiko. On the other hand, everyone saw Miss Icho Fuji between 5 and 8 p.m. Eight taxi drivers said they took her to different places in Sterling and if we trace the itinerary that she supposedly followed, it makes no sense. She went from one end of the city to another eight different times without stopping for a single second, taking one taxi after another, without rhyme or reason, like a maniac."

Beffort grinned. "It looks unlikely, Seater. Miss Fuji was kidnapped in the middle of the afternoon."

"Unlikely perhaps," Seater admitted, "but all the cabbies described Miss Fuji just like you described her to me."

Mie crossed her legs, pulled down her skirt and said, "If eight people swore they drove Icho Fuji, that means Madame Atomos didn't kidnap her. We're missing something in this affair, Smith, and we'll never get it unless we admit that Miss Fuji is working for Madame Atomos."

Seater had a little jolt, but Smith Beffort did not flinch. He was on the same wavelength as Mie. "Come on, come on," Seater mumbled, "you're not serious, Mrs. Beffort?"

Mie smiled graciously. "I have never been more serious, Mr. Seater. My husband and I searched Miss Fuji's bags in the hotel room that she shared with Akamatsu and we discovered that the charming young lady had bought all her clothes in Cincinnati."

"What's the harm in that?" Seater asked.

"Nothing, but Miss Fuji told Akamatsu that she had come directly from New York. She herself said it was the first time she'd been in Ohio. But Cincinnati is in Ohio."

"Moreover," Smith continued, "it's in Cincinnati that Madame Atomos made her last show of force."

"And then," Mie added, "Miss Fuji arrived in Padanaram when the roadblocks were already up around the state borders. We didn't look into it, but it's about time to see whether Miss Fuji is registered on the checkpoint list between Ohio and Pennsylvania. While we're at it, you can get some information from Kyoto. Who is Miss Fuji writing for, Smith?"

Beffort consulted his notebook. "She's here on behalf of the Tourist Information Center but she gave no indication of the name of the magazines who sent her to the USA. Verification should be relatively easy. Seater, can you send a cable to the *Tokkoka* from Yosho Akamatsu? Ask for confirmation of the existence of Miss Icho Fuji and see whether she really works for the Tourist Information Center of Kyoto. Also try to get a set of fingerprints and a recent photograph of the young lady. I need all of it before midnight."

Seater called an assistant, gave him a paper he had just filled out, and ordered, "Number one priority. Answers in an hour."

The assistant nodded and dashed down the corridor. He had hardly disappeared when the telephone rang. Seater picked it up, waited a second and then turned on the speakerphone for the Befforts. Mie and Smith listened.

"The guy's name is George Harris. He's been dead for barely an hour and the coroner's initial examination shows that he was probably poisoned by a cyanide-laced cigarette. His taxi was parked on Main Street, ten minutes from the airport. That's all."

"Thanks," Seater hung up.

"A cyanide cigarette, huh?" Beffort mused. "You don't buy that in the drugstore... Call him back, Seater, and ask where the cabbie's body is."

Seater got the information instantly. Beffort jotted down the address and left headquarters with Mie.

In the Malibu the young lady asked, "What are you planning to do, Smith?"

"I want to know why they killed a taxi driver in that way. I want to know if they robbed him. I want to know the identity of the last guy or gal who rode in his cab."

Mie shot him a sideways glance. "Miss Fuji?"

"Oh, we can't say that yet, but we have to admit that there are a lot of taxis involved in this performance of little Icho Fuji. Eight cabbies drive her and recognized her. Maybe the ninth is the dead man?"

The corpse of poor George Harris had been brought directly to the morgue, right after the preliminary inquest and the photographs. The coroner welcomed the couple and offered, "Harris is in the fridge. Do you want me to take him out?"

"No, thanks," Smith declined. "But I would like to talk to the detective who called Seater."

"Come into my office. He's finishing his report."

The detective's name was Mannering. Beffort introduced himself and asked, "What is the apparent motive for the crime?"

"None," Mannering answered without hesitating. "Harris still had all his money on him and what's really weird is that his cab was empty when died. His 'light' showed that he was free and his flag was still up."

"How can you be so sure? His customer could have set that all up on leaving the taxi."

Mannering shook his head and explained, "Harris had a company cab with a new type of meter that records the hired miles and empty miles in order. On examining it, it only took me a few seconds to see that Harris had driven for a little over half a mile without a fare. Personally I think he was going home for dinner and given his position he was probably coming back from the airport. And there's this cyanide-laced cigarette. He had smoked almost all of it. A cigarette lasts around 15 minutes. The time corresponds with his mileage at reasonable speed."

"Therefore," Beffort concluded, "Harris smoked this cigarette in 15 minutes and around half a mile from where it was given to him. Apparently they poisoned him for no reason. Would it be crazy to imagine that they killed him so that he wouldn't tell where his last ride went?"

Mannering opened his eyes wide, totally in the dark. Beffort said, "You think Harris was going to dinner. Why?"

"Well, because it was time for dinner."

"Is it normal for a cabbie to come back empty from the airport where he has the best chance to pick up a customer?"

Mannering stumbled. He had obviously not examined the matter from this angle. Beffort looked at the map of Sterling and said, "Between the airport and this part of Main Street where you found him, is there a checkpoint?"

"No, but there's one on 4th Street at the end of Main. In fact, it's one of the patrols from this checkpoint that found Harris slumped over the wheel. Oh! I see! You think Harris was going to the checkpoint?"

"Exactly," Beffort confirmed. "Listen, Mannering, I believe that Harris had Miss Icho Fuji in his cab right before he died."

"What? You're talking about the young Japanese journalist who Madame Atomos kidnapped?"

"We were certain that Madame Atomos had kidnapped her," Beffort said softly, "except now we have eight taxi drivers who hauled Miss Fuji all over Sterling. I would appreciate it if you could lift some fingerprints from the taxi. We'll compare them with those of Icho Fuji."

Mannering took a long breath and said, "Okay, we'll get all the fingerprints you want, but I don't understand. If Madame Atomos didn't kidnap Icho Fuji, then she's free. And if she's free, there's no reason to go looking for her. So?"

"The fingerprints," Smith snapped. "That's all I'm asking of you. Leave the rest to me and don't worry about it. I don't know much more than you do at the moment."

He took Mie's arm and left. In the Malibu the radio was crackling non-stop. "6289 calling Yellow Mask!"

Beffort picked up. "Okay, Ralph, go ahead."

"Seater wants you back at headquarters on the double. Things are moving fast. He has the information from Japan."

"Okay. Tell him I'm on the way. Any news about the sender of the cartons?"

"No. Ritter only let us know that he's on it…"

At that very second, Ritter and his G-men showed up at Weyerhauser's, 408 Oak Street, Oakland, not far from the station. It was a huge building and Ritter winced when he saw the big sign over the gate: J. Weyerhauser and Co., Transportation, Transits, Storage.

When the bell rang, a dog barked like mad on the other side of the gate. Someone yelled at it to quiet down and then there was silence again. Ritter rang a second time.

"Okay, okay, I'm coming," a voice said.

Heavy shoes scraped over the ground and a man's face appeared in the little door. On seeing the group he stepped back. Ritter stuck his foot in the door and showed his identification, saying, "FBI. Are you Mr. Weyerhauser?"

"No, I'm just the watchman. If you want to see the boss, you gotta make an appointment, G-man."

Ritter always fooled people. He had a chubby baby-face and his voice was as soft as a harp. He smiled and asked, "What's Mr. Weyerhauser's home address, my friend?"

The watchman pointed to a house across the street. "He lives there on the second floor. You want to call him?"

Ritter waved him off, turned around and crossed Oak Street. The watchman wanted to close the gate door, but a G-man held him firmly by the sleeve. "Don't move, buddy."

"But on TV…"

"Tsk, tsk, you're staying right here, okay?" He had changed his tone of voice and the other G-man stepped up. The watchman leaned back against the wall, a little pale, a little anxious, not at all comfortable, and watched Ritter ring the bell across the street. After a short wait, the door opened onto a young woman standing in the doorway.

Ritter showed his identification and smiled. "Mr. Weyerhauser, please."

The young woman raised an eyebrow. She was dressed to go out and was carrying a small suitcase. She said, "If you want to ring at his door, he'll answer. I'm just passing through. Excuse me!"

She tried to slip around Ritter, but he did not budge. She stepped back and said, "This is ridiculous! I only know this Weyerhauser guy by sight!"

"Stay calm," Ritter advised as he opened the door wide. "You'll leave when Weyerhauser answers his door. What's in your suitcase?"

The young woman turned red but sounded miffed "Personal effects."

"You want to open it? Harker, check it. Don't worry, Miss, Harker is married and has two daughters about your age. He knows what women's lingerie looks like."

He rang again, but the interphone marked Weyerhauser stayed quiet.

"I'm in a big hurry," the young woman protested.

"Come on," Harker said, "this'll only take two minutes. If you'd opened the suitcase right away, we'd already be finished."

Her bad attitude started to intrigue him, as well as Ritter and the other men present. "Open your suitcase," Ritter repeated.

In a huff the young woman unlocked the suitcase and opened it, sticking it in Harker's face. "Well," he said, "get a load of this!" She was nude in all the photos. Harker closed the suitcase and looked at her in amazement.

She shrugged. "To prove you're a G-man, you have a badge. To prove I'm a stripper, I have these pictures. Got a problem with that?"

Harker shook his head. Ritter said, "You can go now, Miss."

She locked her suitcase and stomped toward her car. Harker said, "I would have bet that she was hiding something weird in that suitcase. Live and learn, right?"

Just then a big Ford stopped in front of the group and a thin, older man got out. At first hesitating, he stepped forward and asked, "What's going on here?"

"Nothing," Ritter said. "I'm just looking for Mr. Weyerhauser."

"That's me. What do you want?"

Chapter VIII

Ritter was surprised. He had already figured that Weyerhauser had run away after being warned by Madame Atomos or the A.O.F.M.A., but there he was standing calmly in front of him, probably coming back from having a few drinks with friends. As Harker had said: Live and Learn!

"I'm a federal agent," Ritter said, pulling out his identification again, "and I need to talk to you about a delivery that…"

"Please," Weyerhauser interrupted, "let's not talk on the sidewalk. Follow me."

He was very friendly, giving no sign of being worried or upset. Ritter accepted his offer and climbed up to the second floor. Harker followed them by habit.

Weyerhauser brought them into his apartment and then into his den. He invited them to sit down and asked, "So, what's this all about?"

Ritter and Harker both turned their eyes to the framed picture on his desk. They immediately recognized the girl with the suitcase and wondered what kind of link there was between the two of them.

Ritter said, "It's about a package addressed to a Mrs. Yshinari in Sterling, Colorado."

Weyerhauser nodded, grabbed a file and scanned down a long column of numbers before saying, "Mrs. Yshinari, Sterling, Colorado. I did, in fact, forward 25 cartons of samples, each weighing 11.5 pounds, marked fragile and urgent. Are we talking about the same thing?"

"That's the one," Ritter confirmed, "but you said 'forward'."

"Yes. The cartons were coming from... hold on a minute... there it is. They came from Tucson, Arizona!"

Ritter let out a sigh. "Who was the sender?"

"I don't know. I only know that they were sent from the Tucson station."

Ritter was expecting a snag like this. "Is it normal for you to forward packages like this? Wouldn't it be faster to send the packages directly to Sterling. Going through Oakland is a long detour and a big waste of time. Especially if it was supposed to be urgent."

Weyerhauser smiled. "You know, I stopped asking questions like that a long time ago. In my business I've seen enough not to be surprised at anything. Just like I store furniture for ten years without the owners coming to get it. As long as they pay the bill, I don't care."

"Who paid for the cartons?"

"Mrs. Yshinari," Weyerhauser said after consulting the file. "You want the number and amount of the check?"

"Thanks but there's no need," Ritter declined. "In your opinion, how should I go about finding out who sent the packages?"

He knew perfectly well how, but he wanted to see if Weyerhauser was on the up and up. Weyerhauser answered, "I think they should be able to tell you in Tucson if the person in question filled out the sender's receipt, which isn't mandatory."

Ritter got up. "That's what I was thinking." Then he pointed to the picture and asked, "Your daughter?"

"Dani, my only daughter. She's not yet 20 years old."

Ritter said that she looked older, that she must have been a little wild, and then, "I think I've seen her before. How about you, Harker?"

"Yeah," the G-man played along. "She left the building while we were waiting for Mr. Weyerhauser."

Weyerhauser shrugged wearily. "Night class," he said a little annoyed. "Kids work too hard nowadays. Dani never comes back before midnight. Even if she is studying medicine..."

Ritter and Harker nodded. A classic story: the mother had died, the father devoted himself to business and the daughter was given free range.

"Let's get back to this forwarding business," Ritter suggested. "Can you tell if these cartons stayed in your warehouse for a long time?"

"No more than two or three hours. We registered them, weighed them, and then got them on their way. Hey, can I ask you what..."

"No," Ritter said sharply. "Good night." And he dragged Harker behind him as he left.

They found Dani Weyerhauser in a club in San Francisco. Her picture was in the window, blending in with all the other strippers, but they could easily recognize the girl. Ritter and Harker entered the club and sat at a table in the dark. The show was a rather exclusive show, longer than in the "dives" in Oakland, and the clientele looked upscale.

Dani danced twice, as a bride and as a shepherdess. She was perfect, wonderful to watch for her youth, but also for the erotic intensity she exuded.

"She's studying medicine," Harker grumbled unapprovingly.

Ritter finished his five-dollar beer and said, "I wonder how this girl ended up here."

"Cash?" Harker suggested.

Ritter frowned. "Daddy Weyerhauser must give her enough allowance. I think maybe she's just in a tight spot. She's not an adult. This club doesn't have the right to hire her without parental consent. Now, we know that daddy doesn't know… Did you notice how bitter and aggressive Dani was? She didn't want to show us the photos and she blushed when we saw them, right?"

"She's a little vixen," Harker snapped. "This job is a goldmine and there's all kinds of men at her feet. It's a lot easier to take off your clothes than to study medicine."

Ritter grinned. "Try to forget about your daughters, Harker," he advised, "and look at it with an open mind. Mrs. Yshinari received radioactive brooches coming from Tucson, but the cartons were waylaid for two or three hours with Weyerhauser. Who knows if the brooches were even in the packages when it left Tucson?"

Harker looked askance at him. "Dani?"

"Why not? If she is being forced to strip, they could just as easily make her open some cartons and change the contents."

"Good God, can you imagine? A girl not even 20 years old!"

Ritter decided not to discuss it. Harker was starting to go nuts about his daughters and would end up not seeing the truth. Moreover, federal agents have to deal a lot with top-level crooks who are with young girls barely out of high school.

Ritter looked at his watch and said, "Let's get out of here. She should be ready now." It was 11:15 p.m.

Dani showed up at half past, without her suitcase, looking sad, and met a man who was waiting for her down the street. She passively let him kiss her. The man grabbed her arm and pushed her forward, into a nearby hotel. Harker groaned, but Ritter was a statue. He was starting to glimpse the truth.

At 12:10 Dani reappeared, alone and sadder than ever. She got into her car, started the engine and then jumped when she saw the two men sitting in the backseat.

"Don't be afraid, Miss Weyerhauser," Ritter said softly. "We're here to help you."

It had all started in high school, stupidly, with a few sticks of marijuana, and then there were the parties, the man in the Cadillac and the compromising photos that they threatened to send to daddy… After that was all downhill, then the big fall: stripping, drugs, prostitution…

"And the brooches?" Ritter asked.

"A stupid thing. Where I am, I don't care. Open some boxes to switch the contents. Say, you didn't say anything to my father, did you?"

"Who gave you the brooches?" Ritter evaded her question.

"Pat Ebbing. If you've been here for a while, then you saw him. We went to the hotel together."

Ritter slapped her hard. "Don't play the tough girl," he spoke softly, "or else I'll drag you in and you'll get 20 years. The brooches you were playing with were radioactive and were meant to kill hundreds of innocent people. Who's this Pat Ebbing?"

Now Dani was scared. "The club owner. Say, what's all this about the brooches?"

"You were working for Madame Atomos. You know what that means? You being a drug addict and a whore doesn't matter to her. That's what she wants!"

She broke down in tears. It had been building up for a long time and suddenly she cracked, turned back into the little girl that she had never stopped being. Harker was embarrassed and started fiddling with his tie. He was on the verge of comforting her.

Ritter smiled, a snide little smile, and Harker wondered how it was all going to end up. Ritter let Dani weep her eyes out and then said, "You're going to go home and go to bed as if nothing happened. Tomorrow you'll go back to the university with a briefcase or schoolbag, but not a little suitcase! I'm going to put you under surveillance. If you make the slightest move to get away, it's prison for you. Got it?"

She said yes. Ritter asked Harker to get out of the car. "Thanks," Dani said.

"Get out of here!" Ritter barked at her as she drove off.

Ritter raised an arm and several federal agents came out of the shadows. Ritter gave orders: "Ronson, you go and watch that girl. Get the police to help you. I want her protected 24/7. The A.O.F.M.A. or the Atomos gang will probably try to get rid of her after what she's told us. Shawn, take two of your colleagues and arrest this Pat Ebbing in the hotel he's still sitting in. You others, come with me."

"And me?" Harker asked.

"Call Sterling. Tell Beffort that we're onto something good here. If we're lucky, it might very well be that we discover where those brooches were made and irradiated. Get going! In Sterling they must be on red alert!"

In Sterling they really were on red alert, but calm and methodical. Beffort had just learned that Icho Fuji was a real person, but that her fingerprints and photograph bore no resemblance to the Icho Fuji he knew.

Moreover, the Tourist Information Center and the Japanese magazines denied sending anyone to the United States. They had local informants and the press agencies are completely worthless.

Then Mannering brought Beffort a wonderful set of fingerprints taken from the taxi and they were absolutely sure that they the so-called Icho Fuji was on the run and had certainly killed the poor taxi driver.

"Mie," Beffort congratulated sportingly, "you were right all along. She was the one we were chasing in the refuge at Lake Pymatuning."

Mie did not share his joy. "How could a woman like Madame Atomos give up all her power? That's what I don't understand, Smith."

"You're talking about a new Miss Atomos, right?"

"Yes, but the situation is different. I was Miss Atomos without knowing it, against my will. I had a motor-brain in my head and I unconsciously obeyed the orders of the Great Brain on Atomia Island. As things stand now, it's surprising that a young woman would accept running all the risks that Madame Atomos refuses. Because in the end Icho Fuji..."

"Who is not Icho Fuji," Smith noted.

"Let's keep calling her that since we don't know her true identity," Mie remarked. "So, Icho Fuji is literally risking her life in this adventure. I will never believe that she's acting solely out of self-interest."

Beffort threw away his cigarette butt, somewhat annoyed, and said, "The psychological aspect doesn't matter much. I know that Miss Fuji tried to kill us along with Yosho, that she got those radioactive brooches spread around the city, and that she's being accused of murdering the taxi driver."

Mie shot him a reproachful glance. "You surprise me, Smith. If you thought like that when I was Miss Atomos, I'd be dead now."

Beffort scratched his head. "Listen, Mie, let's agree on something. You were just saying that the situation is different. Are you suggesting now that Icho Fuji is acting against her will?"

"I'll wonder about it as long as I haven't found a viable reason to become the right hand of Madame Atomos," she said firmly. "Plus, we're not totally sure whether or not Madame Atomos has rebuilt her terrifying arsenal. How do you think she got those brooches irradiated?"

Beffort shook his head silently. He had asked himself the same question a hundred times, but could not come up with a satisfying answer.

"Let's admit," the young lady continued, "that Madame Atomos had got a new laboratory and that she is collaborating with surgeons capable of the same exploits as their predecessors. Let's admit that a team of surgeons..."

"Okay!" Smith intervened. "We can admit any absurdity. You're trying to prove to me that Icho Fuji could be remote-controlled and that she's the first model of a new line of servants. Hell, do you realize how much Madame Atomos must have accomplished for this? And where would she recruit all the surgeons and electronic specialists?"

It was Mie's turn to remain silent.

The case of Miss Icho Fuji clearly had an explanation, but the Befforts could not find it and both of them were trying to figure out what kind of energy was making the pseudo-journalist move.

Right then the telephone rang. When Smith picked it up, Seater spoke to him, "Mannering just made a quick investigation among the taxi drivers. He found a guy from the same company as Harris who was coming back from the airport. He claims to have seen Harris turning onto Hayes Street with a customer in the back. Maybe he's wrong, but the woman the driver described could very well be Icho Fuji."

"Damn!" Smith exclaimed. "Incredible! Now tell me that Hayes Street is about half a mile from where Harris died."

"That's right," Seater said coldly as he was starting to get comfortable being an FBI director. "Mannering checked it before alerting me. It's exactly 0.6 miles between the two points. Great, isn't it?"

Beffort forced himself to stay calm. If he could arrest Icho Fuji, he figured that Madame Atomos would have one foot in the grave. "Great," he admitted with sincerity. "What measures have you taken?"

"Nothing dramatic. The neighborhood is being blocked off by the police and the army..."

"Not dramatic?" Beffort groaned.

"No," Seater assured him, "because no one can see it until they cross the police barrier. Plus, the central switchboard is being operated by the feds who are listening to all conversations. I think it'd be hard to do any better."

Beffort took a deep breath. Seater was fishing for the director's job and could easily act with too much enthusiasm.

"Right now," Seater went on, "I'm waiting for your decision. If you give the word, the men are ready to enter the houses and apartments around Hayes Street."

"No! That would be the last thing to do! I'm sure that we can quickly select certain people to look at. Anybody's who been there more than 48 hours doesn't interest us first of all. It's likely that Icho Fuji and Mrs. Yshinari are in the same place. Wait for me. I'll be there in a jiffy."

He slammed the phone down and said, "Get up, Mie, I think we've got Icho Fuji trapped!"

"Unless she took another taxi after getting out of Harris'." Mie retorted in the same tone.

Beffort gritted his teeth and hurried out. Mie was becoming a pessimist, but she could still be right.

Chapter IX

The Malibu arrived in record time thanks to its powerful engine, but also because the streets of Sterling were as empty as a circus ring after closing day. Sterling was scared. Madame Atomos was within its walls with her criminal organization, her destructive machines, her domesticated atoms... None of this was true but like always people exaggerated. Contradictions spread from mouth to mouth. They said that eight cabbies had been murdered, that other things besides brooches are probably radioactive, etc.

On Main Street Beffort spotted several trucks parked along the curb and then he was stopped at the corner of Main and Hayes without really seeing the barrier before he was on top of it. He opened his door and was immediately staring into the eyes of Seater, accompanied by Detective Mannering.

"Bravo!" Beffort said. "That's good work. Where are your men?"

Seater made a sweeping gesture. "A little bit everywhere, but I feel like we're gathering an army to catch a fly."

"Don't fool yourself, pal. This Icho Fuji is without a doubt more clever than her boss. When she finds out her freedom is threatened, her reaction will be extremely violent and then maybe you won't have enough men. Have you started sorting out the people in the neighborhood?"

Mannering stepped forward and showed him a sheet crammed with small writing. "I followed your advice, but I went about it backwards. That is, I first got all the apartments and houses that were rented recently."

"Not bad," Beffort approved. "What's the result?"

"Nada," Mannering said. "Nothing was vacant in the area and the last rental, I mean the most recent, dates back to a year ago. In the meantime no one has moved. But..."

"No suspense, please," Beffort requested. "If you know something, tell me without wasting time. Every second counts."

Mannering hesitated. "I'm not sure about anything, but the Dewey Agency has a Japanese renter."

"Name?"

"Takijiro Inoguchi, single, painter, naturalized American for seven years," Mannering read. "He lives at 20 Hayes Street. A seven-room house with a garage and a yard. Seven rooms for a single man I figure is a little too much."

"His workshop might take up two or three rooms," Seater said, "but that still leaves four. And then he's Japanese."

Beffort nodded and asked, "Where's the house?"

Mannering turned around to face Hayes Street and said, "On the right about 100 yards down. It's right on the sidewalk with the yard in the back. We haven't had time to check it out, but we think the yard runs up against a four-story building behind which is Applewood Circle, which curves around to run back into Hayes Street. Therefore, it seems impossible to get away by this dead end. Now we just have to see if Takijiro Inoguchi is home at the moment."

Beffort's face was wrinkled in concentration. This Japanese man might be hiding Icho Fuji and Mrs. Yshinari. To go up and knock on the front door might be a mistake. And then there was the yard.

"Right now," Seater said, "it's not very easy to get people up and ask for information. Even if he is home, Inoguchi might not answer. Legally we have no right to break down his door before morning."

Beffort said, "It's his yard that bothers me, Seater. The airport is close by, right?"

"On the other side of Pioneer Park, just behind Applewood Circle," Mannering informed him. "But it's easy to surround the whole neighborhood?" He changed his proposition into a question through diplomacy toward Seater and Beffort.

Beffort murmured, "I won't hide the fact that I would far prefer to surround the house and yard of this Inoguchi. Between Hayes and Applewood and the four-story building, there's too many other houses and yards and hedges. If the painter is in on this, you can be sure that everything's been taken care of for escape if there's a snag. For example, why live so close to the airport? An artist needs calm to work, doesn't he?"

As if to prove his point, an airplane took off at that very second with a hell of a noise. The roar of its jets drowned out the entire neighborhood before the plane headed north and silence fell slowly over Hayes Street again.

"During the night there's not so much traffic," Smith added, "but during the day it must be unbearable. Inoguchi probably makes wave paintings... Mie, can you come over here?" The young lady stepped out of the Malibu. "You're going to cal Takijiro Inoguchi."

"And say what?"

"Say that you're the wife of Kazuo Meguro and that your husband left an envelope at home on which is written: *Important and Strictly Confidential* with Inoguchi's name. If he asks you why you didn't call earlier, tell him that it took you a long time to find his telephone number and address in the phone book. There's a booth on the corner..."

He paused and listened carefully. Through the open window of the Malibu he heard the calls from 6289.

"One minute," Beffort said. "Is it possible that Ralph Stutton has news..."

He got back in the car and picked up the radio. Stutton said, "I've just received a call from San Francisco. Ritter has arrested a Pat Ebbing who is responsible for sending the brooches. Ritter said he hopes to follow the lead all the way to the manufacturer. He'll call back when he has more news. Any instructions to give him?"

"No, that's okay. Tell him to keep going!"

Stutton signed off. Beffort left the radio on and got out of the car. Mie, who had heard the message, said, "Now I have a good reason for calling Inoguchi, don't I?"

"Absolutely, dear!" Smith said with enthusiasm.

But Seater objected, "Aren't you worried about compromising Ritter's investigation by informing Inoguchi?"

"Listen, Seater, we don't know if this Japanese belong to the Atomos gang or not, but one of two things will happen. Either he won't understand what Mie's talking about and we can forget about him, or he'll give us an answer and we'll cut the phone before arresting him. Warn your men at headquarters to block the telephone line if we get a positive answer. Let's go, Mie... By the way, what's this joker's number?"

Mannering gave it to him. When the Befforts went into the phone booth, Mie slipped the coins into the slot and dialed the number of Takijiro Inoguchi.

"Be careful," Smith warned, "and don't forget that you're calling from San Francisco."

Mie put her handkerchief over the mouthpiece. The phone rang several times before someone answered. In the mechanical voice of a tired operator Mie said through the microphone, "Mr. Takijiro Inoguchi?"

"Yes," a man's voice responded.

"Hold the line, I have a call from Oakland."

Mie took off the handkerchief, tapped the mouthpiece a couple of times with her wedding ring and then spoke in a distant voice. "I'm calling on behalf of Pat Ebbing. Do you know him?"

Her hesitation could have been a final precaution. He hesitated in turn before saying, "I know Ebbing."

"Who are you?" Mie asked. Smith waved to her that she was going about it all wrong, so she added, "Pat advised me to check your identity before giving you the message. You understand?"

"Speak!" the man was getting upset. "I'm Mimiko!"

In spite of her surprise, Mie did not lose her composure. "Pat's just been arrested by the FBI. He's afraid of not being able to keep silent. He wants you to make the necessary arrangements. That's all. Goodbye." She hung up and Beffort left the booth, asking Seater, "The main switchboard?"

"Got it on the radio. The line's being cut right now. The guy's going to think the Oakland operator forgot about him. A positive result?"

"And how! This Takijiro is none other than Mr. Mimiko, Mrs. Yshinari's boyfriend. Let your boys loose, Seater, we're going into action!"

In ten minutes the trucks dumped the men who were inside. At 12:45 the sector bordered by Hayes

Street, Applewood Circle and the four-story building was completely surrounded by the forces of order.

Seater received confirmation by radio. When he got off the radio, he turned to Beffort and said, "Whenever you want, Mr. Beffort."

"Okay, let's go!"

They dove into the Malibu and two cars full of federal agents followed behind. From now on it was no longer necessary to walk on tiptoes, so the three cars pulled up in front of 20 Hayes Street without worrying about slamming their doors. The G-men took up positions on the sidewalk where they kept all the windows covered with their automatic rifles and paralyzing weapons.

Smith Beffort climbed the three steps to the front door and rang the bell over and over again in vain. "GO!" he shouted. "Break down the door!"

Seater flicked his flashlight on and off. A mobile crane rolled out of the shadows and backed up. The wrecking ball, small but solid, lowered as the truck approached the door, which was gutted without a problem. When the truck cleared away from the entrance, Beffort and the G-men jumped in. Beffort turned on the lights and went through the rooms on the first floor with Mie on his heels. They went back to the entrance hall as Seater and Mannering were coming from the second floor.

"Nothing," Seater said, "and you?"

Beffort shook his head and sniffed. The air still smelled of tobacco. Mimiko could not be far.

"Upstairs," Mannering said, "three of the bedrooms are occupied. One by Mimiko and the other two by women." He opened a window, pulled the antenna out of his walkie-talkie and alerted the men outside.

"The cellar?" Mie proposed.

Beffort nodded. His wife and he had known for a long time that Madame Atomos' men moved like moles. They quickly found the entrance to the cellar, descended the dozen steps and found themselves in a completely cemented room. Crates full of bottles, two barrels, a reserve of fuel... and a big patch of fresh cement with footprints that were also fresh.

"No doubt about it," Mie commented, "Mimiko and the two women came through here."

"To forget this strip of cement they must have been in a might hurry," Beffort agreed. "They went toward this wall..."

Following the footprints, it was obvious, except the wall in question had no visible door. Beffort did not even search for a hidden opener; he ran upstairs, saying, "Follow me! I'm sure the wall is hiding a tunnel that will come out near the airport!"

Mie, Seater and Mannering climbed into the Malibu with Beffort, who peeled out, turned into Applewood and stopped near the four-story building.

From this vantage point he could clearly see the lights of the airport buildings, as well as the beacons on the two runways. Beffort leaned out and called to a policeman whose patrol had stuck him there.

"Have you seen a man and two women?"

"No, sir, nothing's budged over here."

Beffort let the Malibu cruise until it could go no farther down the dead-end road. There was a parking lot and then beyond a low wall was a field bathed in a diffused light. Very far in the distance, a Rickle was slowly towing a big airliner, but there was nothing unusual in that.

All of a sudden Mie saw three shadows pass by one of the beacon lights. It was fleeting, almost unreal, and the shadows instantly vanished in the darkness, but Mie was sure she had seen them.

"I saw three people heading for the hangars, Smith! Over there on the other side of the runway!"

They all took off at the same time, hopping over the wall and breaking into a run under the cold eye of the policeman assigned to watch the place. Mie and Seater were left behind as Beffort and Mannering ran shoulder to shoulder.

"Ridiculous!" Smith huffed. "They have too much of a head start."

With his lungs on fire, the detective did not respond. He had not run so hard since he was at college and he felt like his legs were slowly crawling up into his stomach.

"Keep up, Mannering, it's only half a mile!"

Mannering gritted his teeth and then felt a surge of energy when he saw three silhouettes around another beacon. Beffort had also seen them. He stopped Mannering. "We can stop... They're at the hangar... A plane must be waiting for them..."

He was breathing heavily and speaking in spurts, but Mannering understood and agreed. "Your walkie-talkie?" Beffort asked.

"In the car," the inspector said in anger.

"Bad luck. To get such a head start on us Mimiko and the two women must have ran off right after my wife's call, before the area was completely cordoned off. Something had alerted them, but what?"

Mannering shrugged his shoulders. The sound of an engine suddenly spluttered out of the hangar.

"Let's get back to the car," Beffort decided. They turned around and were amazed to see the Malibu racing forward with headlights beaming in the middle of the north-south runway. When the car got to them, Mie slammed on the brakes. "Get in!"

They did not have to be told twice. The Malibu shot off like a rocket. "Easy," Beffort advised, "we have to cut across the field toward that hangar."

Mie veered off and the car started jumping over the uneven terrain. Everyone watched as the hangar grew bigger. A small, red airplane was puttering out of it, but its occupants were still not visible. As the Malibu raced closer to it, the plane turned and Beffort saw that there was only one man inside, a blond man, not at all happy to have headlights shining in his eyes, and shouting inaudible insults in his cockpit.

Beffort sank a little in his seat and Mie let off the gas. In all likelihood, Mimiko, Icho Fuji and Mrs. Yshinari never had any intention of escaping on a plane.

"It was all a decoy," Mannering said. "Right now they're probably cruising safely toward some unknown destination."

And he was not wrong. Behind the hangar was a parking lot reserved for airport personnel and at least a hundred cars were parked there. Farther on at the boom gate the guard confirmed that a car had left the airport ten minutes ago. No, he had not really paid attention to the passengers. He was only there to open and close the damn machine and keep unauthorized trucks and cars from getting in.

From the Malibu Beffort sent out a search call that Ralph Stutton broadcast and Seater loosed the men who were still surrounding Hayes Street.

"Let's get back to headquarters," Beffort said.

"And Mimiko's house?" Mannering asked.

"You won't find anything there," Beffort assured him. "I wonder what could have alerted Mimiko? Mie told him the truth and made no mistake about it. Pat Ebbing really exists, seeing that Ritter arrested him. It makes no sense!"

Mie took a deep breath, parked the Malibu at the curb, and said, "Smith, it's your fault. Aren't you the one who told me not to forget that I was calling from Oakland?"

"Of course. Why?"

"At the time I didn't think about it, but everything between California and Colorado works automatically. When I opened my mouth, Mimiko knew immediately that I couldn't be calling from California. Pretending to be an operator was overdoing it, Smith!"

Beffort clenched his jaws. In his fight against Madame Atomos, this was the first time that he had made such a gross error.

Chapter X

At two o'clock in the morning Ritter had gathered enough evidence against Pat Ebbing to send him to prison for 30 years: drug trafficking, blackmail, prostitution, etc. But, and here was the rub, Ebbing denied being or ever having been in contact with the A.O.F.M.A. and Ritter could not prove otherwise. Under the blinding brightness of the iodine lights Ebbing was sweating, but he was not changing a word of his version of things.

"The guy came regularly to watch the shows twice a week. Last week he asked me if I could do him a favor. For 500 dollars he wanted someone to load some brooches and send them to Sterling. I could have done it in a car, but the guy refused. We examined the issue from every angle and in the course of our discussion I accidentally told him that I knew the daughter of Weyerhauser. He worked the whole thing out and Dani did the job. That's all I know."

It was simplistic and unlikely. Nevertheless, it certainly sounded like the truth to anyone not involved. For example a judge in Oakland. If Ebbing went before the court, the matter of the brooches would not worsen his case. They would figure that a crook like him could very well be mixed up in such a racket without knowing the ins and outs for the simple reason that his reputation predisposed him to these kinds of shady dealings.

"You know," Ebbing said, "where I'm sitting now, I would tell you everything I knew."

He was clever enough. Ritter smiled. "Tell that to the judge, not me. In reality you belong to the A.O.F.M.A. or to the Atomos gang and you're keeping your trap shut out of fear. If they find out you talked, they'd knock you off, even in state prison."

He stood up, walked to the window and without turning around said, "I'm sure you're the number one man in this affair and the guy you're hiding behind doesn't exist. You're rigging the game. So, I'm going to rig mine, too. Harker, call a press conference for nine o'clock. Our friend Pat's going to have his mug all over the papers across the USA with the caption: *Pat Ebbing, the man who was brave enough to tell the FBI the whole truth about the Atomos gang!*

Ebbing shot up. "You have no right to do that!"

A G-man pushed him back down. Ritter raised an eyebrow. "Hey, that's right. Morally I have no right to do that. Say, Pat, don't you know that we can be as crooked as you? What really counts in life is staying honest... Hey, since you don't like what I'm going to do, how about we make a deal. You confess and you have my word as a cop that no one will ever know anything. What do you say?"

Ebbing sneered. He was cornered. His eyes wandered to the window where Ritter had just pulled up the shade. They were on the fifth floor of the main police station in San Francisco so even if he dove out the window, he had no chance of surviving the fall.

"Well, Pat," Ritter said softly, "don't you want to tell me what you think? And yet the problem is simple: if you talk, I don't call the papers. If you stay quiet, everyone will know that you played ball."

"I don't know anything!"

"Of course you do, you know everything," Ritter insisted. "I bet you can tell us where the brooches were made and irradiated. It must have happened in a lab in

Oakland or somewhere around here. Come on, Pat, put a little heart into it."

Ebbing put his elbows on the table, buried his face in his hands and asked, "Let me think for a minute. It's not as simple as you think."

Ritter and Harker glanced at each other. Ebbing was starting to crack!

Around midnight the telephone jingled at Mike Sanders' place. He picked up without getting out of bed, without turning on the light, and said, "Mike here, who's there?"

"Hello, Sanders. It's Benny."

"Are you crazy? Calling me at this hour—it's midnight and I was fast asleep!"

"You're slow, Mike, it's almost one o'clock. I have a job for you from Mimiko so you'd better hop out of bed right away. Looks like that bum Pat Ebbing got himself nabbed by the FBI."

Sanders did, in fact, jump out of bed, all goggle-eyed in spite of the pink eye he suffered from. "God damn it!"

"That's right, Mike. If he talks, our goose is cooked. You've been chosen by Mimiko to shut him up before it's too late. I've been tipped off: Ebbing is being interrogated on the fifth floor of the main police station. My informant said that the building across from it has a fire escape running right down between the windows. Got it?"

"Okay, I got it."

"Work fast! Call me when it's done." Benny hung up as Sanders was already pouncing on his clothes and sniper rifle.

At two o'clock in the morning he was shimmying up the metal fire escape. Down below and to the right a policeman was walking around in front of the door of the station. It was his fault that Sanders had lost time. He had to use Indian tricks to avoid being spotted, hopping forward every time the policeman's back was turned and flattening himself in the shadows of the walls when he came back. It had taken a long time and was a pain in the neck.

When he finally got to the fifth landing, he was sweating and his hands were shaking. He leaned back against the wall and examined the administrative building across from him. On the fifth floor there were two windows still lit up and through the one on the left Sanders easily recognized Pat Ebbing. He was sitting down with a bright light shining in his face.

Sanders screwed a silencer onto his rifle, focused the scope, raised the weapon and used the stairs to steady himself. When the guy with the baby face stopped pacing in front of the window, he shot Ebbing like a sitting duck.

Ritter was standing by the window. "Well, Pat, how about this confession?"

Ebbing leaned back in the chair and said, "I can say a lot, but it'll cost you. Thanks to me you'll be able to destroy a little factory and laboratory belonging to Madame Atomos. You'll be able to arrest a dozen people from the A.O.F.M.A. and a few killers from the gang. What are you offering me in exchange?"

Ritter furrowed his brow. "I'll keep silent about your arrest and no journalist will know who you are. You'll go to prison, but my silence will end up saving your life."

He was impatient and Ebbing could feel the pressure mounting. He knew that Ritter would eventually make him talk. Giving him a dose of truth serum in a cigarette or an injection... The FBI was not lacking in resources.

"I'm 35 years old," Ebbing said, "and if I go to court they'll give me the same behind bars. Would you be happy with idea of getting out of prison at 70?"

Ritter moved away from the window to sit across from the prisoner. "You know perfectly well that you might expect a reprieve or no time at all. It all depends on how much help you give us and I..."

There was a strange little cracking sound from window and at the same time a purple spot appeared on Pat Ebbing's forehead. Ebbing opened his mouth and flapped his arms before falling over to the side. Harker and the other G-man rushed to him while Ritter jumped to the window.

"He's dead!" Harker shouted.

Ritter saw that the window had a small round hole in it. He threw it open. The building across the street had nothing but offices and no light was shining on any of the twelve stories. The fire escape was drowned in darkness, but Ritter saw something moving on the third landing.

"Harker," he yelled, "call the guard! Someone is running down the stairs across the street! We have to take him alive!"

Harker gave the alert and a dozen police men poured into the street just when Sanders landed on the sidewalk. The killer knew he was a goner, so he pulled the trigger twice and one of the cops answered him by reflex. Disheartened, Ritter watched the gunman twitch on impact and roll into the gutter. Now the trail had gone cold.

After a few hours of rest Mie and Smith Beffort went to the hospital where Akamatsu was being treated. A private room with a radio and TV.

"You're high on the hog here," Beffort said. "We brought you your suitcase."

Akamatsu was serious. "What they're saying about Icho Fuji is true, Smith?"

"Yes. But don't blame yourself, Yosho. She's a pretty girl and any normal man would have fallen for her."

"Who is she?"

Beffort sat on the edge of the bed as Mie pulled up a chair. "We haven't found out yet," Smith answered. "They don't have her fingerprints on file in Washington and no one's ever heard of her. In fact, Yosho, this false Miss Fuji couldn't be more mysterious if she came from another planet."

"And in Japan?" Akamatsu pressed.

"Unknown," Beffort shot back. "The *Tokkaka* sent us a negative report. Moreover, Mie and I had some bad luck. Because of a telephone call Mrs. Yshinari, Mimiko and Icho Fuji got away from us at the same time as Ritter's main suspect was assassinated in Riverside."

Akamatsu nodded gravely. "And where are you now?"

"Exactly where we were in Chardon," Mie answered, "except that we know Icho Fuji is Madame Atomos' right hand. And they have something else in common: both of them have the top of their right index finger amputated. Besides that, Icho Fuji, Mimiko and Mrs. Yshinari are on the run or else hiding somewhere close to us in one of the countless shelters of their sinister boss."

Akamatsu slapped the side of his head in anger. "And here I am stuck in bed!"

"Don't make a tragedy out of it," Beffort consoled him. "For the moment you wouldn't be any use. Proof is that Mie and I have time to visit you. So, how long are the doctors going to keep you here?"

Akamatsu shrugged. "It all depends on my reaction to the radiation I was hit with in Padanaram. I only got rid of that radioactive watch yesterday, but I feel better already. Smith, don't you think that Icho Fuji will try something else against us?"

Without a word Beffort went to open the door. A G-man was standing in the corridor. Beffort closed the door. "See, we've taken precautions, Yosho." Then he pointed to the window and added, "I've also taken care that they can't attack from there. Someone is keeping watch outside. As for my wife and I, that's a different story. We're in good health and really hoping that the Atomos gang takes a shot at us."

A nurse entered and said, "Sorry, but Mr. Akamatsu has to undergo treatment."

Mie and Smith got up, promised to return the next day if possible and then left the hospital. When the Malibu pulled away from the curb a big Chrysler fell in behind it, far back, being terribly cautious. Four men were inside.

When the two cars were long gone, a young woman got out of a small MG that was parked for a little while in the Shauber store lot. She was pretty and elegant, the typical American beauty that magazines like to put on their covers. In her hand she carried a square package carefully wrapped up.

She entered the hospital and went straight to the reception. "I would like to see Mr. Akamatsu," she asked kindly.

The employee looked up. "If you don't have a pass, it's not possible, Miss. You have to come back during visiting hours."

She smiled and showed her package. "I'll come back, but can you get this to him?"

The employee pressed a button with his knee and said, "Of course. Leave it here and Mr. Akamatsu will get it in less than five minutes."

She thanked him with a dazzling smile, put the package on the bench and went away. Once outside she glanced behind her, crossed the street, but instead of walking directly to her MG she entered Shauber. It was clear that this charming young lady was making sure she was not being followed but in spite of the nature of her work he could not spot the G-man who had been sent after her by the alarm at the reception desk.

In the hospital another federal agent had just taken the package. He left, slipped the package into an armored box in the trunk of his Chevrolet, climbed into his car and headed downtown. Twelve minutes later he was in the laboratory directed by Mather, who had been informed by radio. He put the package into his special chamber and a specialist started doing his job as gently as a midwife.

He very quickly blocked the system that he had just tripped. Then he turned to Mather and said, "A couple of pounds of plastic explosives. Fired electrically on opening the box. The 'recipient' would have taken a mighty hit."

The federal agent smiled, walked down one floor and called car 12 on the radio. The driver of the car in question was precisely the one following the MG. He answered the call and learned that the charming young lady was dangerous and there was every reason to believe that she was a fully-fledged member of the Atomos gang. He pushed his car a little faster to close in on the MG, which was getting ready to leave Sterling.

In the meantime, Smith and Mie Beffort were listening to Ralph Stutton's voice saying, "Witter isn't certain yet, but he thinks this Chrysler is after you. There are four men inside. Do you see it?"

Beffort eyed his rear-view mirror, but the Chrysler Stutton was talking about was not in his field of vision. "I don't see anything, Ralph. The car would have picked us up when we left the hospital, right?"

"Right. Seater is absolutely certain that the girl with the package and the four guys in the Chrysler came together. Try to wind around the streets a little so Witter can make sure."

"Okay," Beffort said, "I'll head back to the hospital."

He turned down a small street, immediately turned again, went around the block and back to the street he had just left. During the whole route he had kept an eye on the rear-view mirror, but the Chrysler remained out of sight. If it really was a tail, it was being done by men who knew all the tricks of their job.

A couple of minutes went by before Stutton announced, "No doubt about it! You're being followed! Witter is on your street. The Chrysler is behind the green Norton delivery truck."

Beffort pulled out, changed lanes and finally saw the Chrysler and then farther back Witter's black Chevrolet.

"It's okay, Stutton," he said into the mic, "you can tell Witter to drop it."

"What are you going to do?"

"First of all tell me if car 12 is still with the MG."

"Absolutely. I can even tell you that the MG just turned up a driveway in Willard, a small town about 12 miles out of Sterling."

"In that case," Beffort smiled, "our trail is back and these four guys can't tell us anything new. I'm going to take them out to the country and see what they've got under the hood. If they don't know the Malibu, they're going to be in for a surprise. Talk to you later, Ralph."

Chapter XI

The Malibu cruised lazily through Sterling before driving south on Highway 6. Then Beffort switched over toward Atwood and headed the Malibu for Willard. Next to him Mie was smoking quietly, no questions asked. She knew what the Malibu was capable of and in spite of the big Chrysler still following them she was as calm as if nothing were happening.

Right after Atwood a voice came over the radio. "6289 here," Ralph Stutton said worriedly. "Do you hear me, Yellow Mask?"

Mie picked up and said, "We hear you, Ralph. What is it?"

"Your position?"

"Somewhere between Atwood and Willard," Mie sounded bored. "We're waiting for the Chrysler to make a move. It can't follow us forever, right?"

"I have a message from car 12," Stutton said. "It seems that the property where the MG disappeared is a real fortress. From the top of the surrounding wall 12 saw a field of barbed wire. With his binoculars he could spot the lookouts on the terrace of the house as well as a 50-caliber machine gun. He also said that a helicopter is sitting behind the house. Besides all this 12 thinks the entrance is riddled with cameras and mics and that it's impossible to get in without being instantly detected."

Beffort said, "If I understand you, Ralph, 12 has just found the headquarters of the Atomos gang."

"Probably. The property is isolated and looks like a twin of the one Mrs. Beffort found outside Cincinnati. You don't have to be a psychic to know that the house has a basement where a bunch of tunnels run out of to end up near Willard, right?"

"Undoubtedly," Beffort agreed. "This kind of refuge dates back to the Atomos peak period. The United States still has a slew of these all over in spite of our searches. Tell 12 not to show them a hair on his head. He has to wait for us to get there. When the time comes, I'll ask you for the exact location of the property. Over and out, Ralph."

"Over and out, boss. Watch yourself."

When the radio was silent, Beffort looked back in the rear-view mirror. The Chrysler was no longer visible because of the curves in the winding road, but it could not have been far behind. It was an ideal place to tail a car. Curves, trees, undulating terrain...

"Smith!"

Beffort looked ahead and clenched his jaws. At the end of a long, straight stretch of road, the Atomos gang had set up its ambush, which had obviously been made in haste, ordered by radio from the Chrysler, but it was clear that they had neglected nothing. Two huge trucks blocked the road and several machine guns were nesting on the side of the road. Trucks and machine guns did not bother Beffort. However, the radio-controlled machine rolling down the road toward them looked much more menacing.

"What's that, Smith?"

"A small tank full of explosives," Beffort answered as he feathered the brakes. "If it reaches us, the Malibu's armor won't hold up. We have to get away from here, Mie."

He turned the car around quickly, thanks to its extraordinary handling, and sped up. He was expecting to meet the Chrysler head on, but it was nowhere in sight.

However, its occupants had cut down two trees across the road and they had done it in less than five minutes, that is to say too fast to be a split second decision. In any case, the road was blocked and in his rear-view mirror Beffort could see the tiny tank moving forward. It was still 300 yards away, advancing slowly but surely.

"What are we going to do, Smith?"

"I don't know. If we get out of the car, the gang will bring out the machine guns. If we stay in the car, we'll blow up with it. Have you noticed how the gang hasn't fired a single shot at us?"

"That means these men know that the Malibu is armored. Smith, I think the girl in the hospital was only used to lure us into this trap. The gang knew that the package would be intercepted, that the girl would be followed by one of our men and that we would decide to go to Willard and get rid of the Chrysler on the way. Everything's been prepared with meticulous care. The two trees were only being held up by a rope and this long, straight road had been chosen so that we wouldn't be able to use our paralyzing cannon, which is useless beyond 500 yards."

It was a long-winded tirade, but Mie had just very clearly explained their situation.

"We have to stop that tank," Beffort grumbled, "or else we won't get out of this alive."

He swung the Malibu around again and saw that the tank as well as the two trucks were much closer. Obviously they were trying to minimize the Malibu's field of action. Once caught between the trees and the tank, it would become easy prey.

"Less than 250 yards," Mie said.

Beffort stopped the car, targeted the tank in the dashboard sights and fired the two front machine guns.

All the bullets hit the bull's eye, but the tank kept crawling forward. Beffort let loose two more rounds without any result as he watched the sparks ricochet off the machine without even scratching the armor.

He dropped it and backed the Malibu all the way up to the thick tree trunks lying hopelessly across the road. Mie, a little pale, turned and stared at him. Beffort looked away. In the rear-view mirror he saw the four men from the Chrysler. They were hunkered down at the curve, beyond the line of fire of the Malibu's rear guns, ready to shoot if the Befforts tried to get out of the car.

In front, the small tank and the two trucks were no more than 200 yards away. Beffort winced. Why did the trucks need to stay less than 50 yards from the tank? If the machine was radio-controlled, it could be maneuvered from a distance.

"Give me the binoculars, Mie."

The young lady searched in the glove compartment and found what her husband had asked for. Beffort focused and got a remarkable close-up of the tank. He could not help but smile when he saw the wire snaking over the ground.

He gave the binoculars back to his wife and said, "Look, Mie. The Atomos Organization is not what it used to be. Once upon a time we would have had no chance at all of getting out of this because the tank would have been guided from a hill by an unseen hand. Today we just have to get rid of the men in the trucks with our paralyzing ray."

With the binoculars to her eyes Mie shook her head. It won't do any good, Smith. The trucks are radio-controlled, too."

Beffort swore as he grabbed the binoculars. Between the two wheels of the two vehicles, under the chassis, he could see the two other wires.

Mie warned him, "Less than 150 yards."

Beffort tossed the binoculars in the back seat, adjusted the sights on the truck tires and pushed the button. The machine guns fired; the tracers bore witness to the competence of the electronic gun sight. The tires were literally torn apart and the heavy vehicles started veering off from each other. The controller must have been fighting like mad to keep the trucks in a straight line.

Everything seemed to stop for a moment before one of the trucks went off the road. Its wheels turned sharply, slipped out of control, and then dove into a ditch. The other truck made a slow, arching turn and then bounced across the ditch before coming to a stop between two trees.

And yet, unexpectedly, the tank kept coming down the middle of the road.

"The trucks are out of the race," Beffort said, "but they're still hooked up. If the wire doesn't break, we're goners."

In the enemy camp they had also seen the danger because a dozen men had just poured out of their hole. They were trying not to be seen, but Beffort now had a clear view of the practically empty road. If it was not for the damn miniature tank, the Malibu could go on its way to Willard.

"We have to cut the wire with the machine guns, Smith!"

"Easier said than done. If not impossible... But look, it's tightening up!"

With its limited length, the wire was, in fact, reaching the end now that the trucks were not following it.

This was the reason for the flurry of activity of the gang members. They were probably going to try to free up one of the trucks so that the tank could reach the Malibu.

It was a matter of seconds. Beffort gave it all he had, showering the road with the paralyzing cannon and the machine gun. A few men dropped. The others dove into the ditch and opened fire on the Malibu, which was hit hard but showed no trace of it.

The shooting got heavier on both sides and then the wire connecting the tank to the trucks snapped after forming a V and the tank suddenly stopped moving. Now it was nothing but an inanimate hunk of metal.

Beffort floored the accelerator, swerved around the tank, passed by the trucks and sped down the road without meeting the least resistance—the men of the Atomos gang were still hunkered down in the ditch. They would soon flee across the woods, leaving their dead and the useless material behind.

At the end of the straightaway Beffort called 555-6289. "Yellow Mask here, Ralph. We just got out of a hard scrape and didn't have time to clean up. Send the police around five miles down the road from Atwood to Willard. There are two trucks and a miniature tank full of explosives. As for the men, they'll have to hunt them in the woods. Any news from car 12?"

"He's still waiting for you," Stutton replied. "Nothing's moved on the property since the MG got there."

"Tell him that we'll be there in 15 minutes. Where's it at?"

"Go all the way to Willard, through town and a little over a mile beyond town you'll find a dirt road that leads into the forest. It'll take you to the property and 12 will signal you."

"Got it."

Beffort hung the mic up and turned to Mie. "If 12 says that nothing's moved on the property, where did the two trucks and all the men come from?"

"They left before the MG got there."

"In that case 12 would have crossed the trucks. It's weird that he didn't tell Stutton about it. Besides, it doesn't add up chronologically. Don't forget that we were still in Sterling when the MG arrived at the property. At the time no one could have guessed that we would go to Willard too… No, it doesn't stick. Your theory of the girl leaving the package in the hospital to make us fall into a trap is not right, Mie. I prefer to think that the Chrysler knew where we were going only when we turned at Atwood. It wouldn't take a genius because the road only goes to Willard."

Now Mie's face showed signs of uncertainty.

"And then," Smith added, "if the girl in the MG knew that we were following her, do you think she would have so kindly led 12 to the gang's hideout?"

Mie put her hand on his arm and smiled. "We each have our version, Smith, but maybe there's a third explanation that we haven't thought of yet."

"For example?"

"Underground tunnels. If one was big enough to drive a truck through…"

"I don't think so, Mie. In my opinion the girl in the MG and the commando team that attacked us were on two different missions without anything in common. Otherwise 12 would have been killed a long time ago."

The Malibu reached Willard and the conversation died for lack of new arguments. Moreover, Beffort knew they were talking just to talk. Madame Atomos' actions were always deadly, but it was hard to see the start even when the final goal was obvious.

In any case, no one could deny that Madame Atomos had been following the same course of action for months and that she had expertly forbidden her enemies from looking too hard for the location of her new laboratory. In Oakland when there had been an alert, the sinister woman had done what was necessary to give Beffort other fish to fry. Otherwise most of the anti-Atomos troops would have concentrated their efforts on California.

The Malibu cruised through town and got on the highway that Ralph Stutton had mentioned. A little over a mile out of town Smith spotted the dirt road. He turned and drove into the trees. The path was so narrow that no truck or any other heavy vehicle could have taken it; the Malibu only barely made it.

After another half-mile in the middle of the forest, a man suddenly jumped out of the brush, waving a friendly hand.

"Charlie Hyde!" Mie shouted. "Stutton should have told us he was 12!"

Beffort braked and Charles Hyde said, "Glad to see you, but let's keep our greetings for later. You can hide your monster over here."

"Is it dangerous?" Smith asked.

"Not for the moment, but there's some activity on the property. It's best to clear off the road fast."

Beffort drove into the clearing Hyde pointed out, turned to the right and parked next to the G-man's Chevrolet under the cover of trees and brush. The place was so well chosen that not a trace of the two vehicles could be seen from the road.

Smith and his wife exchanged firm handshakes with Hyde before Smith asked, "When did you arrive in Sterling?"

"Last night. J.E.E. figured that my work in Ohio was finished. As for Miss Icho Fuji, I can confirm that she's never lived in New York or…"

"We've got the picture," Beffort interrupted, "tell us instead about the girl in the MG."

Hyde moved a dozen steps away and said, "From here you can see the outer wall. If you lean over a little you can make out the corner of the terrace. But watch out! There are guards up there with binoculars. As for the girl in the MG, I can't say anything about her. I tailed her from the hospital. She tried to lose me by going into Shauber, but she couldn't do it. Afterward I just followed from a distance and we came here with no problems. Dead calm."

"This activity you were talking about?"

"It just started. In fact, it's only a few guys transporting wounded men on stretchers. I thought they were going to load them into a car to take them somewhere, but they just disappeared into the house."

Smith and Mie glanced at each other. It seemed unlikely, but they were both thinking that the wounded men belonged to the commando team that had attacked them.

'What's wrong?" Hyde asked. "Did I say a whopper?"

"No," Beffort assured him, "but did you wonder how these guys got hurt?"

"Sure, and I'm still waiting for an answer. Especially since the group popped up out of nowhere, as if they'd come straight out of the ground."

At that moment 6289 called. Beffort went back to the Malibu, signed in and Ralph Stutton said, "I have some weird news for you, boss. Except for two trees lying across the road, the police didn't find anything at the battle site. You did say two trucks and a miniature tank?"

"And the four men from the Chrysler?"

"Nada! No Chrysler, no trucks, no tank and not a single corpse on the asphalt. If the ground wasn't riddled with machine gun cartridges, you'd think the trees just fell by themselves."

"Great, Ralph, I think I understand. Tell the police to keep searching. Objective: an entrance to an underground tunnel."

Stutton whistled. "Got it! Should have thought of that. Over and out?"

"Over and out, but stay on the air. In a little while we might be calling in the air force. I'll be back in a minute."

Beffort turned to Mie and Hyde. "I guess you got that?"

"I'm not surprised," Mie said. "That was one of my hypotheses, wasn't it?"

Hyde kept silent. He did not understand her reference.

"I'll explain later," Beffort promised. "For now let's go see what's cooking behind this wall."

Chapter XII

Using some big stones, Charles Hyde had built a platform high enough to survey the property with ease. Beffort climbed up and cautiously peeked over the wall. Just as Hyde had said, there was a web of barbed wire and armed men were on the terrace. Through an opening he could see a helicopter and a plain building without a window or chimney anywhere. Between the surrounding wall and the barbed wire they had let nature run its course and the strip of land was thick with vegetation.

Hyde scrambled up next to Beffort and said, "I had to search a long time to find this lookout. From here it looks like the property is out in the open, but in fact it's really well hidden by the trees. From the road you can't see anything and since the gate is wide open no one would imagine that the people here have anything to hide. As camouflage it's impressive work."

He was whispering and keeping his eyes just over the wall. Being an old hand in the anti-Atomos fight, Charles Hyde had learned to watch out for microphones and cameras.

"Where did you see the group of men carrying the stretchers?" Beffort asked.

"They came out from behind the building that looks like a little hangar."

"That's the right word, Hyde. It's nothing but walls and a roof. But I bet it's tall enough and wide enough to let a truck through. The door must be on the other side and the ramp to the underground passage, too."

"Not just an underground passage but a tunnel."

"Right. A tunnel with a road and maybe tracks for a train."

Charles Hyde stared at Beffort. "Do you have second sight?"

"Simple logic. The men were wounded in an attack against us. After the fight these guys were stuck in a ditch. We came here directly in the Malibu, and fast, and yet the commando team was faster than us even though their trucks were out of commission. What a feat! I mean, before starting back, the men in good condition had to pick up the dead and wounded and make the trucks and tank disappear."

Hyde scratched his nose. "If this group consisted of the men who attacked you, they didn't come back in a train but in a rocket ship."

"With Akamatsu I had the chance to use an Atomos train outside of Bishop[11]," Beffort said, "and you're not exaggerating when you compare it to a rocket. And there could be two or three tunnels like that. The one here must be almost four miles long if we figure that it comes out where we got ambushed. Why wouldn't the others be just as long? In that case the Atomos gang won't wait for us to surround the property to escape."

Mie hoisted herself up next to him. "Before trying anything we should first make sure that Mimiko, Mrs. Yshinari and Icho Fuji are hiding here. Otherwise we'll just be capturing the small fry and we'll have to start all over again."

Beffort said, "We have plenty of time." He surveyed the property and added, "Hyde, was it as calm when you arrived?"

"Yes. Why?"

---

[11] See *Madame Atomos Spits Fire* in *The Monsters of Madame Atomos.*

Beffort looked at his watch. "It's been over 30 minutes since we escaped the ambush. The commando team saw us take the road to Willard and therefore to this property. Why isn't anyone trying to figure out what happened to us?"

Mie and Charles Hyde were struck by Smith's reasoning. The gang's lack of reaction was surprising. When you see an enemy head for the opposite camp, you know that he is going to attack and you prepare yourself either by fleeing or giving him a warm unwelcome. Here the gang seemed to be completely neglecting its security, contrary to the methods of the ex-Atomos Organization that worked in the shadows without ever offering a foothold to the forces of order.

"If it's a trap," Mie concluded, "it makes no sense. Don't you think it'd be good to inform Stutton, Smith?"

Beffort nodded, climbed down from the platform and walked to the Malibu. He reached for the controls and called 555-6289. His first call did nothing. Every time he tried to listen, the speaker sent out nothing but loud crackling and sizzling.

"Broken?" Charles Hyde inquired.

"Probably. You want to try your radio?"

Hyde got in his car and tried to call dispatch under Beffort's watchful eye, but his results were no better.

Beffort said, "Jammed. Now that's more like it. Madame Atomos' people know that we're here and would rather isolate us than attack."

Hyde grimaced. "We're in a tight spot. The road going back to the highway can be easily blocked and we..."

Two nearby explosions interrupted him. They came from the other side of the property, that is from the Willard road, and even though very small, the two detonations obviously marked the start of a large-scale offensive. Beffort gestured to Mie and Hyde to stay put and then snuck over to the edge of the road. 200 yards away there was now a big crater in the middle of it. Dust was still settling in the air and tree branches were strewn over the ground, but no human being was anywhere to be seen.

Beffort went back and said, "It was a trap, Mie. The road must have been mined, which explains why the explosions sounded weak and now our cars can't get through. From here on out we can only escape through the woods if things turn really ugly."

He was worried and did not try to hide it. Hyde said, "Stutton knows our position. He'll give the alarm when we don't answer his calls."

"I don't know," Beffort said. "He'll think his own transmitter is broken and first try to pinpoint the interference. Before he figures it out, the gang will take advantage of the delay..."

The calm and silence surrounding them seemed to belie his words, but since the explosions it felt as if the ambiance had become noticeably, unexplainably heavier. The threat was vague, but the Befforts and Hyde felt it looming over them like a deadly mantle.

"They won't attack us head-on," Smith whispered, "because we have the Malibu and our paralyzing pistols. I wonder how they're going to do it."

Hyde climbed up on his pile of stones, glanced over the beveled top of the wall and said, "Nothing's moving. You'd think the property was empty. Even the guys on the roof look like scarecrows."

Beffort took a look. On the terrace the lookouts were not moving an inch and no one was walking around by the house.

Hyde commented, "If things are going to heat up, it won't be anytime soon."

"Not in your opinion," Beffort grumbled. "This is the calm before the storm. I don't like waiting for them to bombard us, Hyde. Let's get in the Malibu. A little reconnaissance is called for."

They got in the car and backed up onto the road before heading toward the entrance to the property. While driving alongside the wall, Beffort tried to contact Stutton again, but the interference was still jamming the signal.

Hyde asked, "Do you plan to go all the way to the gate?"

"As long as we're here," Beffort responded coldly, "why not go all the way to the house? At least we'll have a clear conscience then."

Hyde took his paralyzing pistol out of his holster while Mie worked the electronic sights. The Malibu reached the gate, swung through and sped down the gravel driveway. After two sharp turns the car came out on a strip of land big enough to be a runway for a small private plane. The house was across from them, standing squarely and imposing with its shutters closed. The hangar was on their left and they could make out the nose of the helicopter. Because of their position they could not see the lookouts on the terrace. Nevertheless, Beffort could see the barrel of the 50-caliber machine gun uselessly aimed at the horizon.

"I told you," Hyde spoke with worry in his voice. "It's dead calm here."

Beffort continued driving all the way to the hangar, stopping a few yards from the helicopter, but leaving the engine running. Hyde put his hand on the door handle.

"Don't move!" Beffort ordered. "They're just waiting for that to pick us off."

Hyde let go of the handle. "Do you really think there's still anyone in this shack?"

Beffort did not have time to answer. A tiny tank had just appeared in his rear-view mirror. It was the same type as the one on the Atwood-Willard road with one difference: there was no wire dragging behind it so it looked like it was much faster.

Beffort said, "Look back there, Hyde. That should answer your question."

When the G-man turned around, a second tank showed up on the strip of land, right in front of the driveway leading to the gate. The two tanks must have been controlled from the house or the terrace.

"We're victims of the Malibu's reputation," Mie spoke calmly. "No one will come out as long as we're in it. But if we don't get out, the little tanks will blow us to smithereens. Nice choice, isn't it?"

Smith drove around the hangar and took up position across from the house and the tank that had just turned around. It must have been going more than 30 miles an hour and it obviously handled very well.

"They won't get us too easily," Hyde said. "That strip of land is wide enough for our car to play bullfighter, but only as long as we've got gas."

Beffort had not thought of that. He looked at the gauge and saw that the tank was half full. "Still 10 gallons and change. That's plenty."

However, the tank had reached the end of the hangar. Beffort let it come on and threw the Malibu in the opposite direction, speeding off to the end of the land strip. Then the tiny tank came back toward the house, heavy but steadfast, kicking up gravel under its narrow tracks. In the middle of the driveway, the other tank guarded the driveway vigilantly.

Two minutes passed before the Malibu was forced to escape again. Beffort steered toward the hangar, stopped around the door and saw the tank swinging around and charging back. Whoever was controlling it was not trying to catch the Malibu, but forcing it to keep driving around. Apparently they were counting on it running out of gas.

"The radio?" Mie proposed.

Smith tried to contact 6289 again, but without success. The interference was total now; no sound came through the speakers. Beffort watched the tank arrive. This silent battle against a machine was kind of eerie.

"It'll take their time," Mie said, "but we'll end up running out of gas. Then we'll be forced to get out and they'll open fire."

Beffort was starting to think that Mie was right. If this little game lasted all day—and there was no chance of stopping it—the Malibu would inevitably run dry. Just to see what would happen, he opened his door and pretended to get out. Gunfire instantly burst out from the terrace and a few projectiles smashed into the car. Beffort slammed the door shut and shot off, making a wide turn to avoid the tank, before letting off the gas when he figured they were far enough away.

"Hyde," he said, "you're going to take my place. Mie, take the wheel and keep your foot on the gas while we switch."

Mie drove the car without moving from her seat and the two men climbed over the seat to change places. Hyde took the wheel and asked, "What now?"

Beffort checked that his paralyzing pistol was all ready and said, "I think our enemies won't see that I'm missing. They have a bird's eye view of the car and are probably only watching the doors. On our next pass, shoot by the front and I'll jump out."

Mie turned around. "That's taking a big risk, Smith," her voice was suddenly hoarse. "What are you going to do?"

Beffort slipped his weapon into his belt. "I'm going to have a little chat with the boys on the roof. At the same time I'll try to put this jamming mechanism out of order. Watch out, Hyde! Here comes that damn machine."

The G-man cranked the wheel and swerved around the tank, heading straight for the front of the house.

"Okay," Beffort said, "slow it down."

Hyde lifted his foot and Beffort jumped out, rolled over the ground and popped up next to the wall. If the gang noticed that the car had only two passengers, it would react immediately. But no shutter opened and the mini-tank cruised past Beffort without changing its course.

Smith advanced slowly, searching for the door to get into the dwelling and keeping a close eye on the first floor windows where death could spring out at any second. He found the door on the left side of this kind of fortress, but he knew that he would never be able to break it down without attracting attention. However, he spotted a small cellar window farther on that amazingly had no bars. It was odd, maybe even a trap, but Smith was in no mood to pay attention to minor details.

He used his coat to cushion the butt of his weapon so the window broke almost without a noise at the very moment when the Malibu was sliding over the landing strip, spraying gravel everywhere. Then all he had to do was unbolt the window and slip down a pile of coal.

The light was scanty in the cellar. Smith thought the space was too cramped for such a big house. He struck his lighter, rummaged around, but found nothing of interest except the stairs, which were not too steep and led up to a landing on the ground floor. Here, however, he came up against a heavy, metal door fitted with a slot that was unfortunately blocked by a grill. He feared it would be an insurmountable obstacle, but the handle turned on his first try and the door opened into a cold hallway the stank of mildew and clogged with cobwebs. Huge, hairy garden spiders, as calm as beachcombers, shimmied up their long threads when the light hit their eyes.

Beffort swept away the cobwebs with a sickened hand and skirted around the bug ballet. He turned a corner and finally saw a light shining under another iron door with a massive lock. This was the barrier, the border between what was alive and what was left to die. Of course the door did not give in. Beffort swore quietly, felt the lock and then smiled when his pinky finger went through. Big lock but no security.

Beffort bent a rusty nail that he found lying on the ground and twisted it inside the lock until it made a dull click. The hinges creaked like mad. They were covered in rust and to Smith's ears they sounded like a grenade exploding over the staccato fire of machine guns.

When the door was open wide enough, he slipped though and found himself in an extension of the hallway. Farther down was the entrance hall. The front door was to the left. To the right were stairs that thankfully went up...

Beffort grabbed the butt of his paralyzing pistol and put his foot on the first step. Outside the Malibu was continuing to play hide and seek with the tiny tank.

Chapter XIII

Long ago, undoubtedly, the house had been built for luxury and well maintained by a big landowner, but that was all in the past. Today the paint was peeling from the humidity and the ceiling was stained with circles where the rain leaked through. The roof terrace must have been cracked and water dripped down through the floors to puddle in the basement. The shutters were closed because the windows had no more glass and the bronze banister was covered in verdigris.

Without making a sound Beffort climbed the broken stairs, which were so water-soaked they did not creak, until he stepped onto the second floor landing. Marble tiles, wallpaper falling off, the bottom of the doors gnawed away by rats. The desolation of a circular hallway drowned in darkness. For some reason Beffort's shoes started squeaking. He took them off, tied the laces together and hung them from his belt.

The sounds of skidding and flying gravel came in from the outside. Beffort cautiously cracked open a shudder to see the small tank pass by. From above it looked like a fat, clumsy turtle, but terribly powerful. The Malibu pulled a U-turn and was heading for the hangar. The tank followed, passed by Beffort's window again and hissed away.

Up above Beffort heard muffled footsteps, walking with the tank. Listening carefully Beffort followed the footsteps to the angle of the circular hallway and then back again. The guy on the third floor was following the tank.

Beffort counted the seconds, flew up the stairs when the radio-controller, the tank and the Malibu were on the right side of the house, and then hid on the third floor landing. He peeked out and saw Mr. Mimiko striding calmly along the hallway, holding a radio transmitter in his hands so he could control the tank without being seen. Around his shoulder he had another transmitter, probably for the machine that was blocking the driveway.

Mr. Mimiko was somewhat fatter than in his photo, but he looked just as seedy and unpleasant as ever. Beffort let him complete his round trip and then smacked him on the head with the butt of his pistol, catching him as he fell and stopping the transmission. Then he headed for the terrace. Now he had to act quickly. The lookouts would notice that the tank had stopped and know that something must have happened.

In his socks Beffort moved like a shadow. He hopped onto the last landing, saw ten stone steps and a big rectangle of sun that a thin silhouette kept passing by like a windshield wiper in the rain. Beffort snuck up the steps and popped his head into the light along with his paralyzing pistol. He found himself face to face with a guy who looked like Scarlett and whose jaw dropped to let out a war cry.

Beffort shot him with his ray and Scarlett collapsed, his mouth still open and with a stupid look in his eyes. When he wakes up in an hour, it will be hard for him to close his mouth again.

Beffort came all the way out and saw two men. Their backs were turned as they were hunched down behind the 50-caliber machine gun whose barrel faithfully imitated the Malibu's movements. Right now the barrel was still motionless. One of the two stood up. "Is Mimiko sleeping or what?"

Beffort pushed the trigger button of his weapon and the two men were instantly plunged into a fitful nap. After that Beffort showed himself to Mie and Hyde, waved that everything was all right, but also motioned that the Malibu should continue roaming around. Hyde nodded and the car took off.

Beffort found an antenna and traced its cable to a transom through which he saw a radio operator with headphones on, smoking a cigarette, very relaxed, his legs up on a desk. Beffort made him even more relaxed with a shot from his pistol, climbed down into the room and cut off the power. Now there would be no more interference and Mie could contact 6289.

Beffort left the room and was back in the circular hallway. He got back down to the second floor just when Mimiko was starting to come around. A few slaps helped the process. He opened his eyes.

"No yelling," Beffort advised. "Or else I'll put you down for the count."

He had spared him the paralyzing ray so that he would not have to wait an hour to interrogate him. Mimiko was sitting against the wall, rubbing his neck and touching the huge bump on his head. He grimaced, making his already ugly face look completely hideous.

"Where's Madame Atomos?" Beffort asked like he was asking for the nearest subway station.

Mimiko shrugged his shoulders, shut up in a hostile and scornful silence. Beffort smiled, pocketed his pistol and pulled his prisoner up with one hand, saying, "If you don't talk, I'm going to hurt you."

He was being straightforward; the kind of typically American naïveté that was so foreign to Asians. Mimiko attacked silently, like a reptile, body to body, and sent Smith flying with his shoulder. Mimiko went after him trying to immobilize him in a stranglehold. Beffort swore to himself and put all his weight behind a right hook to the liver. Mimiko let out an "oof" and dropped like an empty sack. Judo against boxing—it was a sure loser.

Beffort picked up his pistol and shoes, put the first in his belt and the other on his feet before dragging Mimiko into an empty room. The short fight had not made much noise and the Malibu was still circling around outside.

Beffort paralyzed Mimiko and went back into the hallway. He was not quite sure what to do. The house had a lot of rooms and other cellars where several underground passages might be located. If Mimiko and Scarlett were here, it was likely that Mrs. Yshinari and Icho Fuji were here too. As for Madame Atomos, that was another story.

Beffort went down the hallway and then down the stairs to the first floor without worrying about making noise. He heard a door close and then a rapid hammering. Guided by the sound he came to another metal door, the same as in the cellar except that there was no visible lock. To all appearances, his prey was scampering off through the basement.

Beffort ran back, unlocked the front door and raised his arm to stop the Malibu. The radio was working and Charles Hyde was feeding information to 6289. Beffort interrupted him. "Stutton!" he shouted into the mic, "Send some people here to pick up Mimiko, Scarlett and two other guys sleeping in the house."

"Paralyzer?"

"Yes, about 15 minutes ago. Let Witter take charge of it. When he gets here, tell him to go into the kitchen where a door will be open. I think it leads to an underground passage that Hyde, my wife and I are going to follow. You got the rundown, Ralph?"

"Okay. Witter will come on the double. I'll get word to him."

"That's it, Ralph. Also pick up the Malibu. I'll keep in touch by walkie-talkie on 27 megahertz whenever I can. I'm gone!"

He did what he said, grabbed a machine gun and waved to Hyde and Mie to follow him. In the kitchen the machine gun hacked away at the door until the invisible mechanism opened up. On the other side, just as Smith had figured, was a stairway down to a cellar. It was well kept, without humidity, and seemed to go on forever.

Hyde counted the steps, "52, 53…"

The flashlights shined on cement wall, but their weak light did not do much to dissipate the dark void that engulfed the stairs. It was undeniably a construction from the grand Atomos era.

At the 78th step the stairway ended. A narrow underground passage led westward with a bare light bulb shining every 50 yards. No road or railway, but a simple pathway where two people could barely walk side by side.

Beffort took the lead and Hyde brought up the rear. After a little more than half a mile Beffort saw a body lying on the ground. It was Mrs. Yshinari. They had shot her through the heart, at point blank range, and certainly by surprise since the face of the Japanese woman looked strangely relaxed. Blood was still bubbling out of the wound.

"She hasn't been dead long," Mie assessed. "We should have heard the shot."

"Silencer," Smith said coldly.

Charles Hyde knelt down to search her clothes and the black leather handbag: handkerchief, comb, a roll of bills, identity card and a car key numbered 02752B. "If the members of the gang," he said, "all kill each other, what are we going to do?"

"Come on," Smith ordered, "the corpse is here only to slow us down. A crime signed Madame Atomos."

He strode down the passage. Mie had a hard time keeping up with him. Hyde picked up the handbag and followed suit. After a few more minutes the underground passage gradually rose up and came to a sudden stop before a new set of stairs. 40 steps brought them to a trap door that Beffort forced open with his shoulder. They clambered into a strange living room smelling of wax polish.

The sun filtered through the windows; the furniture sparkled; and an old man was lying in front of the door in a puddle of fresh blood. He, too, had not been dead long and they had shot him just like Mrs. Yshinari. Through the window Beffort could see a road, an intersection and a sign post marked: Willard 3, Sterling 12, Stoneham 5. A sandy walkway led from the house to the road and when Beffort walked out he smelled the faint odor of burnt gasoline in the air. Then he saw the 32 automatic with a silencer thrown against the wall. He picked it up, sniffed the powder and checked the two bullets missing from its cartridge.

"Now," Charles Hyde said, "it's clear. The woman we're chasing skedaddled in a car after killing the old man to keep him from talking."

Smith had already pulled out the antenna of his walkie-talkie. He pressed the talk button and said, "Yellow Mask here calling 6289."

"Okay," Stutton answered, "go ahead."

Beffort gave his approximate position and told him to set up roadblocks right away on Highway 14 between Willard, Sterling and Stoneham.

"It's done," Stutton replied. "And the identity of the suspect, the make and license plate of the car?"

"I don't know," Beffort confessed. "The police have to check everyone and feel it out... From here on out we're in the dark. And Witter?"

"He just arrived on the property. The dirt road that was blown up by the mines now has a wooden bridge."

"Tell him to pick me up in the Malibu at the intersection of Highways 14 and 11. And send some men into the underground. They'll find the body of Mrs. Yshinari. Keep going and they'll end up in a house with another corpse. I'll wait for Witter in the house—he can't miss it. It's right at the intersection."

"Got it," Stutton said.

Beffort signed out and they went back up the path. Hyde remarked, "Do you notice how there's no tire tracks?"

Smith jumped. The driveway was indeed as smooth as the silk. "Damn!" he swore. "We have to search the house right now. First the garage..."

The garage door opened smoothly revealing a big, sky blue Cadillac. Beffort turned the ignition to make sure that it was working, saw that the gas tank was full and looked questioningly at Mie. "I don't understand," he said. "Nothing would be easier than to climb into this car and take off."

He unconsciously turned the wheel and felt a strange resistance. When he looked down, he saw that the Cadillac was equipped with a new anti-theft device. The steering was blocked even though the engine worked. With his flashlight he examined the device and made out the number 02752B.

"Unbelievable! Mrs. Yshinari tricked her killer without even meaning to. They had the ignition key but didn't know that..."

A dull banging from the trunk cut him short. Charles Hyde approached, pistol in hand, opened the trunk and stood staring at Icho Fuji, who said in a frightened voice, "Please, don't shoot!"

Mie and Smith ran back. "What are you doing here?" Mie asked.

Icho Fuji opened her eyes wide and shook her head. "I don't know... I can't say... Someone locked me in here and then the motor started, but it stopped and they tried to open the trunk but I held it shut and the woman swore and left."

"The woman?" Beffort said suspiciously.

Icho Fuji looked at him, furrowing her brow. She was clearly trying to remember. Finally she said, "It was an older Japanese woman with a diabolical face... Say, who are you?"

There was a short silence. Beffort leaned over. "Smith Beffort, Yosho Akamatsu, the Statler Hotel, remember?"

"Not at all. What are you talking about? All I know is that my husband and daughter are going to be worried. I went out to buy some milk..."

"What's your name?" Beffort clenched his jaws, feeling anger rise up.

"My name is Inoki Yosoto," the scared woman said.

"And you have a husband and daughter? Where do they live?"

"In Philadelphia, not far from here. Please be kind enough to tell me what I'm doing in this car and how I got here... I feel like I'm going crazy."

The Befforts and Charles Hyde were like statues. Privately Madame Atomos, aka Icho Fuji, aka Inoki Yosoto was jubilant... and breathing more easily. At the start, when the Befforts and Hyde had barged into the property, she thought she was finally going to be able to fulfill her vengeance. Then Beffort had taken out Mimiko, Scarlett and the two machine gunners so that Madame Atomos could not put up a fight without putting herself in extreme danger. Then there was the flight with Mrs. Yshinari whom she had to kill to gain a little time. In the house the old man, a contact of the A.O.F.M.A. might have turned into a lethal witness. She killed him in cold blood then ran to Yshinari's Cadillac. The steering was blocked and all escape impossible! Madame Atomos could see the barricaded roads and the identity checks, so she decided to put her plan B into action.

Now with her big eyes she was staring at Beffort and Mie who did not know what to believe and would obviously have to investigate. She had to force herself not to smile. Almost anything could happen to a victim of Madame Atomos...

In the first place when he got back to headquarters in Sterling, Smith Beffort got a hold of a Philadelphia phone book and looked up the number of Miko Yosoto. He found it quickly and it corresponded with the one Inoki Yosoto had given, as well as the address.

Grinding his teeth Beffort called the chief of police in Philadelphia and was told all about Inoki Yosoto's disappearance being reported by her husband at the beginning of May. It coincided almost to the day of Icho Fuji's appearance in Padanaram.

Then Beffort called Miko Yosoto, the husband, and was lucky enough to get him on the phone right away. He said, "This is the FBI, Mr. Yosoto, it's about your wife."

"Have you found her?" the man asked anxiously.

"We've found a woman who looks like her. Could you tell me if Mrs. Yosoto has a scar on her right cheek?"

"No! I already told the police that my wife had her index finger amputated! I never said anything about her cheek!"

Furious, the man hung up. Beffort did the same and turned to Mie and Hyde who had heard the conversation through a speaker.

"Well?" he said, "What do you think?"

Hyde said, "No doubt about it. Madame Atomos kidnapped the young lady and turned her into a servant under hypnotism or something of that sort. It's not the first time it's happened, right?"

Mie did not say a word, but Beffort and she were on the same wavelength. Before clearing Inoki Yosoto, they had to make sure.

Chapter XIV

After such an adventure, just to appear "real", Madame Atomos-Fuji-Yosoto had to play her nervous breakdown card. Indirectly it backfired in that Smith Beffort was kind enough to admit her to a mental hospital. Moreover, to prevent Madame Atomos from attacking her again, two G-men were stationed there for her protection.

Madame Atomos could have fought back and demanded that they release her immediately since there was no evidence to keep her locked up, but she did nothing. She was simply hoping that she had taken all precautions.

Just as she suspected, the Befforts went to Philadelphia, literally "the city of brotherly love", rented a room at the Franklin Motor Inn and took a short tour of Marker Street where Miko Yosoto had a store that was pompously called The King of Shirts, but was not much bigger than a bread box.

No clerk, but shirts everywhere and a short, sad Asian man slouching behind his cash register. His thick glasses did a poor job hiding the melancholy in his eyes and even worse the panic when Beffort showed him his FBI badge.

"Mr. Yosoto?"

"That's me." His voice sounded hollow. Beffort thought that he had never seen such a terrorized man. Really. Yosoto looked like he had been sitting in an electric chair for months.

"We know where your wife is."

Yosoto turned gray, tried to smile, managed to grimace like a squeezed orange, and said, "It can't be! Are you sure?"

The worst actor in the Ziegfeld Theater could do better.

"No," Beffort said, "and that's exactly why we came to see you. Do you have a recent photograph of Mrs. Yosoto?"

The man nodded as he got up. He was very short and bow-legged with a belly like a football. While he rummaged through a cupboard Smith and Mie exchanged glances. The man did not fit at all with the ravishing Inoki Yosoto. It was blatant. So blatant that it could not be a set-up.

"Here you go," Yosoto put a photograph on the counter.

The Befforts leaned over. The ex-Icho Fuji was there with Miko and a little girl around five or six years old, smiling.

"Your daughter?" Beffort asked.

Miko's eyes blinked behind his glasses. "Yes. She was six two weeks ago. Do you recognize my wife?"

"There's a resemblance," Beffort said cautiously. "Tell me, Mr. Yosoto, how long have you been married?"

The Japanese tilted his head, thought for a minute, then said, "Eight years now."

So far everything he said corroborated Inoki's statement. But the Befforts were determined to dig deeper. To put their minds at rest they had to sweep away the slightest doubt.

"I would love to talk to your daughter," Smith said.

Yosoto was suffering. "You can't. She's in school."

"Which school?"

"She's there all day," Yosoto avoided the question. "If you really want to see her, you'll have to come back tonight at 7 p.m."

Beffort smiled. "It's not very important," he lied. "So, Mrs. Yosoto disappeared at the beginning of May?"

The Japanese was suddenly calm. "Yes. At the beginning of the month of May, a Tuesday, if I remember... She had gone out for five minutes. There was no milk. The store is just on the corner and you can get there and back in no time..." He told how he had worried and finally decided to go to the police, etc. But while he was babbling, Smith and Mie felt like they were listening to a recording or a lesson learned by heart. And Miko Yosoto was shaking. He shook constantly, unhealthily, with nervous tics, blinking, his skinny shoulders twitching.

Beffort let him said everything he had to say. When it was over he asked, "If you've been married for eight years, you should have other photos of her. A kind of family album?"

Miko sat on his stool and buried his face in his hands. "Ah! Soon after my wife disappeared, there was a short circuit in my house and the chest where I kept all my papers was completely destroyed."

"The family photo album, too, I guess? So now you don't have any other photo of your wife? That's really too bad, Mr. Yosoto."

"I know. The police already told me. But you can go upstairs. You can still see traces of the fire and here's my insurance declaration."

The paper was in order, saying that a short-circuit had clearly started a fire at Mr. Miko Yosoto's residence on May 6 and a chest had suffered serious damage along with the ceiling, floor and wall separating the bedroom and the dining room.

"Go on up, go on," Yosoto said almost aggressively. "You'll see I'm not lying!"

Customs officers often will not examine a suitcase if you open it without them asking. Beffort thought that Yosoto might be offering a look because he was concealing something. The tree hiding the forest.

"Okay," he said, "I'll go up."

Yosoto bowed his head and pointed. "The stairs are there. Excuse me if I don't go with you, but I wouldn't want to miss a customer. Business is so bad nowadays."

Mie and Smith climbed the spiral staircase and stepped directly into the dining room. Linoleum, bright green wallpaper, cheap furniture. Mie went into the bedroom and saw the ceiling, wall and floor were cracked and blackened.

"Weird guy," Smith mumbled. "It's like he's trying to hide something. And the fact that we found his wife doesn't seem to fill him with joy."

Mie opened a door to reveal a closet. It contained three suits obviously belonging to Miko Yosoto and a dozen old dresses. In a drawer Mie found two, small cup bras, a girdle and thick, everyday stockings.

"Icho Fuji cannot be Inoki Yosoto, Smith. Her breasts are too big to fit in these bras and she doesn't wear a girdle!"

Smith was picturing her see-through underwear, her tiny panties and sheer stockings. "There's something fishy going on here," he whispered. "I want to believe that Madame Atomos got Inoki under her control, forced her to dress more fashionably, but a breast size can't change. Come on, let's go back downstairs."

They were in the middle of stairway when they heard the brief sound of a bell, like when you hang up a phone. Smith jumped down the final steps, but Miko Yosoto was far from the phone, his hands behind his back, watching for potential customers through the window. When he heard Beffort, he turned around and smiled. "Did you see?"

"I saw. Tell me, those bras, are they your wife's?"

Miko turned red and shifted from one foot to the other. "Yes," he said shyly. "But they're very old. Inoki couldn't wear them after she had a child. You know, I think you're making things very complicated."

While the Befforts were upstairs, he must have had time to reflect. He showed an identity card and said, "Inoki's photo and fingerprints are on here and under distinguishing marks you can see the tip of her right index finger missing. If the woman you found..."

"I know," Smith cut him off. "I already have all this information." He threw a bra on the counter and added, "Where did you say your daughter went to school?"

"At Saint John's on Stenton Avenue on the other side of the city."

"Why so far? There are schools in this neighborhood."

"It was my wife's idea," Miko looked embarrassed. "Saint John's is a private school and..."

"Thanks," Beffort did not let him finish. He was in a bad mood. "I'll come back tonight to talk to your daughter. At least you could tell me what really happened to your wife?"

Miko turned white. It was amazing how quickly he could change colors. They guy must have been under so much pressure for so many months that his skin had become extremely sensitive. "I told you everything I know," he mumbled.

Beffort took his wife's arm and left the store without saying a word. On the corner he hailed a taxi. "Saint John's school on Stenton Avenue."

The taxi took off and Beffort leaned back in the seat. He was thinking hard and Mie respected his silence. Finally around Hunting Park Smith said, "Miko Yosoto is scared. Terribly scared. Like people who aren't directly threatened feel."

"What?"

"His daughter, the A.O.F.M.A." Smith recited like a telegraph.

Mie frowned, "He wouldn't have given the address of the school."

They were whispering, which strongly interested the cab driver who kept an eye on his rear-view mirror. The initials A.O.F.M.A. had pricked up his ears. Smith advised him, "Watch the road, pal, we're still too young to die." Caught red-handed eavesdropping, the driver hunched over in the front seat.

Saint John's school had the charming ugliness of a British institution. Brick walls, gold-tipped bars on the gate, a mowed lawn with rotating sprinklers. The hallway was waxed like a dance floor and furnished with uncomfortable benches, secret doors and lots of stained glass. After being informed by the concierge, a thin, severe woman dressed in black came striding down the hallway with her nose held high. Her eyes were two tiny, lifeless marbles, her mouth a hyphen in her face. She sized up the Befforts like they were naughty children.

"What is it?" said the old headmistress with a superiority complex.

Beffort flashed his badge to shake her up a little. "I want to speak with the Yosoto girl. Now."

She was dying of curiosity. The FBI? Her eyes rolled around for a moment before settling down. "Her father just called," she screeched. "What happened?"

Beffort wanted to be rude. "It's none of your business. Go get the girl."

"May is in class. Just now she couldn't stop crying. I…"

Mie pushed her gently along. "Go and look for her now, okay?"

The headmistress yielded to the soft voice and gentle contact on her arm. She thought she had seen Mie before in the papers or on TV, remembering something connected to the Atomos affair.

Two minutes later she returned with May Yosoto. First name American, last name Japanese, and not the slightest resemblance to Icho-Fuji-Inoki Yosoto. Her eyes were still red and she was holding a rolled up, wet handkerchief in her tight fist.

"Thanks," Beffort said to the headmistress. "You can go."

He was a sharp with her because he was on edge, but the woman in black went away without saying a word. The little girl standing in front of the Befforts was a block of marble.

Mie crouched down to her level, smiled gently and whispered, "You see, I'm from you country."

The little girl shot her a mean look. How do you negotiate with a six-year old? Smith, at least, had no idea. Mie's smile became even gentler. "In Japan I was in the same class with your mom…"

She was trying to hit a sensitive chord, so she left her sentences hanging. A tear beaded and rolled down the little girl's cheek, who was standing very straight, frozen in tragic dignity. Her hands had patches of modeling clay and a button on her dark blue apron was hanging on by only a thread.

Foolishly Mie felt herself crumble. She was thinking of her dead son, telling herself that he could have been like May Yosoto with modeling clay all over his hands... Her eyes clouded over and she hugged the little girl. A moment passed before May Yosoto started crying her heart out without a word being said.

Smith felt embarrassed so he stepped back and sat on an uncomfortable bench. Something was going on between Mie and this child that he did not understand. Mie was whispering in the little girl's ear, but he could not pick up most of it.

"I know your mommy... she's fine... if you want her to come back... your daddy called to tell you not to say anything, but he's wrong..."

It lasted a long time, then the little girl nodded yes between two sobs. Mie held out her hand to Smith. "The photo?"

Beffort looked in his briefcase and handed her the photograph that May's father had given him. Mie showed it to the girl, speaking softly in Japanese. Then it was like the dam broke. May started chattering, still hugging Mie, her tears suddenly dried up.

Beffort sighed. He did not understand Japanese and could only see by the expression on Mie's face that she did not understand the girl's explanation. At the end of the hallway the black form of the headmistress was getting impatient.

Finally, Mie stood up, caressed the child's cheek and waved the headmistress over. When she arrived, she asked no questions, just took a smiling May Yosoto away with her as she left.

In another taxi Mie explained. "The woman in the photo is not her mother. In fact, she only saw her once, on the day this photograph was taken, but her mom had already been gone a long time. She couldn't say exactly how long ago, but remembered that it was in the evening. Her mother did go out to get milk... I think Miko Yosoto hid the truth from his daughter and made her lie because Inoki really did disappear."

"The index finger?"

"No. May said that her mother had all her fingers."

The taxi stopped on Market Street. Miko Yosoto was still behind his cash register, a little whiter, a little shakier, smiling sadly at nothing, like a drunk. Beffort walked around the counter and went straight up to him. "We're coming back from Saint John's. May told us everything."

With Beffort hovering over him, Miko looked crushed and shrank down. Beffort brought out the photo. "Your daughter knows that this woman isn't her mother... I'm listening."

Totally pale, Miki said, "It was bound to happen, but now they're going to kill her." He was trembling like a leaf.

"Who's this 'they'?" Beffort asked.

"I don't know. Inoki was kidnapped, then a man came. A stocky, fat Japanese man. He told me no harm would come to Inoki if I did exactly what he said. I had to go to the police, show these papers with my wife's name but the picture of the other woman... a pretty woman with her finger missing."

"Okay, I get it. The fire to destroy the chest and the family photos and your daughter in a school far away to keep her quiet. How can you be sure that your wife is still alive?"

Miko straightened up and his gloomy eyes sparkled. "She calls me every week to tell me that she's okay, but they must stay with her because she never says anything else and doesn't answer my questions."

From his briefcase Beffort took out the photo of Mimiko. "Was this your visitor?"

"That's him!" Yosoto got choked up. "How…"

"Stay calm. Right now he's behind bars and we're going to force a confession out of him."

Without asking permission Beffort picked up the phone and asked for an urgent connection with the FBI headquarters in Sterling. After seven minutes he was on the line with Seater. He told him to rake Mimiko over the coals and double the guard around Icho Fuji. The first had to confess where the real Inoki Yosoto was being held prisoner. The second was under heavy suspicion.

"Okay," Seater said, "I'll take care of it."

"But watch out," Beffort warned, "Madame Atomos won't hesitate to kill anyone who she can't use anymore. Yshinari is a perfect example."

"You can count on me. When are you coming back?"

"On the next plane. I'll be in Sterling this afternoon. Don't forget, Seater, keep your eyes open."

An hour later the Befforts were boarding a jet. In his pocket Smith had the picture of Inoki Yosoto. A small woman, pleasantly ugly, as flat as a board who would fit perfectly into the bras from the drawer.

Chapter XV

In Sterling Seater followed Beffort's orders to the letter. They took Mimiko and stuck him in a chair so that four G-men could take turns interrogating him. He held out for a certain time, but in the end they shot him with a truth serum and he told everything.

Likewise they started interrogating Scarlett and the wounded men whom the police had found in the house. Furthermore, two more federal agents were sent over to guard Icho Fuji.

This haul was important. The Atomos gang had one of its tentacles cut off. Seater was feeling good but was wrong to be satisfied with winning a battle when with a little imagination and initiative he could have won the war. In fact, where things stood, nothing was keeping them from arresting Icho Fuji outright. Except Seater did not have the guts; he did not know how to interpret Beffort's brief telephone message, who was too pressed for time to be more precise.

At 1:30 p.m. Madame Atomos-Icho Fuji left the cafeteria of the Lobatos hospital and under the watch of her FBI guardian angels went back up to her room on the fourth and top floor of the building. The two G-men stayed in the corridor. The woman whom they were "protecting" was a picture of docility and their two colleagues were stationed down under the window of Icho Fuji, aka who knows what.

Madame Atomos locked her door, lay on the bed and did not move. The results of her last operation looked disastrous. However, it was not really important as long as the laboratory kept being built and Madame Atomos remained free. Now, although the first of these necessities was being met, the second was less encouraging. In fact, the terrible woman was not fooling herself: the situation could become critical if Miko Yosoto in Philadelphia suddenly cracked. It was an intolerable uncertainty.

At 2 p.m. Madame Atomos got up, slowly opened the window and climbed up on a chair to look over the treetops. The A.O.F.M.A. knew about her being in this place, of course, and since Icho Fuji was the protégé of Madame Atomos, it would inevitably rush to help her if the danger became too imminent.

Nothing happened for more than ten minutes and then a little light started blinking on the eighth floor of a nearby building. Morse code: dash, dot, dash, dot, dash. Start. Madame Atomos grabbed paper and pencil, climbed back up on the chair and got ready to write. She had no way to respond, but she figured that they were spying on her movements through powerful binoculars. As if to confirm her supposition, the light said, "A.O.F.M.A. here. If you read us, raise your hand."

Madame Atomos raised her hand. Right away they repeated Start and then the message followed, which she jotted down on the paper: *Smith Beffort knows you are not Inoki Yosoto. He doesn't yet know your exact role but won't take long to suspect. Prepare to escape. Here's what we'll do it...*

At 2:40 Mimiko started talking like a magpie under the effect of a massive dose of scopochloralose. He told them that Inoki Yosoto was being held in a house on Cortez Street in Sterling and that she was being watched by a guy named Robson, Scarlett's sidekick. Seater got the exact address out of him before asking, "What do you know about the brunette driving an MG?"

303

She had escaped the FBI raid. In fact, Hyde was the last one to see her when she drove onto the property. Since then, even though they had found her car, no one knew what had become of her.

In his drug-induced monotone, Mimiko said, "Her name's Ida Brown. She belongs to the A.O.F.M.A. and Miss Fuji sent her on a mission when she got back to the property."

"What mission?"

"I don't know."

"Who is Miss Fuji?" Seater asked.

"Miss Fuji is Madame Atomos' replacement," Mimiko recited, "and we have to obey her orders without discussion."

Seater's heart skipped. "Is Miss Fuji acting against her will?"

"No. She's completely rational. Mrs. Yshinari thought she was Madame Atomos' daughter. It could be since Madame Atomos gave her full powers during her absence. Plus, Miss Fuji is directly supervising the construction of the laboratory in Oakland."

At that moment Seater should have jumped on the telephone and arrested Icho Fuji immediately. He did not do it because he trusted the vigilance of the men guarding her and also because he was captivated by Mimiko. Carried away on this river of confessions, he could tell them all kinds of things.

"Where is this laboratory?"

"I don't know," Mimiko said.

Seater thought that the effect of the scopochloralose was wearing off and that Mimiko was starting to fight against the interrogation. Because the location of the laboratory was of prime importance among the information that Smith Beffort wanted, Seater stood up and ordered, "Another dose. This man has to tell us everything."

The doctor nodded and was preparing a syringe just when the police were gunning down Robson and pouring into the house on Cortez Street. Sergeant Walsh broke down a door and found Inoki Yosoto hook to a chain on the wall but in good health and in relatively good spirits. She said that she had been well treated and got regular news about Miko and May and that Miss Fuji had even visited her a couple of times.

Walsh asked her, "What do you think of Madame Atomos?"

"She's not an evil woman," Inoki answered irresponsibly.

"She's killed thousands of innocent people!"

The woman smiled and corrected him, "Americans, not Japanese."

Walsh took note of that. Inoki Yosoto had been masterfully brainwashed. If freed, she might go and volunteer for the A.O.F.M.A. The FBI in Philadelphia would do well to keep a close watch on her.

In Oakland Ritter's patience and nerves were exhausted in his desperate search for the famous laboratory they suspected was in the area. He and his team rapidly went through the sector with a fine-toothed comb. Factories, workshops and isolated houses were searched meticulously, but to no avail. Now they were looking at businesses that did work recently, of any kind, but the situation was not developing positively. In his office Ritter was on pins and needles when a call from Sterling shook him out of his gloomy thoughts. He picked up and heard Seater's voice on the other end of the line.

"I can guarantee that the laboratory really is in your sector."

"I already knew that," Ritter grumbled. "Will you be kind enough just to give me the address?"

That Seater could not, so the FBI found itself looking for a needle in a haystack. It might take months, even years.

On the fourth floor of the Lobatos hospital a door opened and the G-men saw Icho Fuji appear in the doorway. She was still ravishing but her face looked tired and her eyes looked like they could barely stay open.

"Sorry to disturb you, gentlemen," she said with a humble smile, "but I have to use the bathroom."

Seater had given no strict instructions about her so the G-men looked at each other and one of them stood up. "Let's go, Miss."

The bathroom was at the end of the corridor. The G-man entered first to examine the narrow window. Icho Fuji was thin enough to squeeze through, but the wall outside was smooth down to the ground. He thought for a second of sending his colleague downstairs to keep an eye on the window while Icho Fuji was inside, but he did not bother. To jump from the fourth floor would be suicide.

"I'll be right out here," he said. "If you need anything, just call." He had just remembered that he was supposed to be protecting her.

The young lady smiled. "Be patient, okay? I'm really not feeling well."

He nodded as she closed the door and turned the lock. A few seconds went by and just as she had expected, the G-man stepped away politely. Thus Madame Atomos could swing open the small window and wave her hand outside. Immediately an object scraped against the wall and a rope ladder rolled down from on high. She slipped out the window, balanced the ladder and stepped on. Down below was the yard, but it was on the side of the hospital not being watched.

Madame Atomos shimmied up to the gutter, hopped onto the slightly sloping roof and saw Ida Brown's head pop out of a skylight and signaling to her to hurry up. Madame Atomos had no problem scurrying over the roof to the window and following Ida Brown down another ladder that brought them to the attic floor.

"We have to act fast," the brunette said. "It's visiting hours so we can leave without being noticed if your guards don't sound the alarm. Put on this raincoat and hat and pull down the veil. I'll get the rope ladder."

Madame Atomos was ready in a few seconds. Ida Brown threw the ladder in the corner and said, "Perfect. Hunch over a little and keep your head down, you'll look like an old lady. Take my arm and if they stop us, let me do the talking."

Madame Atomos nodded. She was worried. In her already long career, this was the first time that she had to flee under such hazardous conditions.

Ida Brown led her to a dark stairwell. They descended until they came to a door. "Watch out," Ida Brown whispered, "This is the most dangerous point for our team. This door opens directly onto the treatment room in the front of the building and we can't do anything."

Madame Atomos looked at her watch. Six minutes had passed since she entered the toilet. Very soon the federal agent was going to think it was a long time... The two women crossed the room, passed through the swinging door and went down a deserted fourth floor hallway.

"Lean on me," Ida Brown said. They were across from the bathroom and there was little chance that a G-man would be hanging around there, but only the angle of the building forming a bend screened them and the smallest thing could turn this escape into a total disaster. Madame Atomos hunched her shoulders and dragged her feet. The two women stopped in front of the elevator and waited as an orderly arrived pushing a cart.

"Are you looking for a room?" he asked.

"No," Ida Brown said. "We just got the wrong floor."

Another orderly came up with a pile of sheets under his arm. "Who did you come to see?" he asked.

Madame Atomos felt her companion tense up and then heard the swish of the elevator arriving. The operation had been launched so quickly that the A.O.F.M.A. did not have time to take all precautions. So, Ida Brown could not give a name for the simple reason that she did not know one.

She sidestepped the question and answered, "We're going to room 22."

She spoke off the cuff and bit her lip when the orderly pointed to a door at the end of the corridor. "There you go. The patient is Drummond, right?"

The silence was broken by a distant crash. The federal agents had just broken down the bathroom door. Madame Atomos opened the door of the elevator and said, "We'll come back later, dear, I'm tired."

She pulled Ida Brown inside, closed the door and pressed the button for the first floor under the stunned gaze of the orderlies.

"Idiot! Why didn't you say we were just finishing a visit?"

Ida Brown calmed her trembling body. "I didn't think of that," she admitted.

The elevator stopped. With their backs straight the two women crossed the lobby, went down the front steps and were on the sidewalk where Ida Brown broke into a run to get to the car. Madame Atomos followed her and climbed into the backseat as the driver sped off. When they were some distance away Madame Atomos turned around to see that the street was deserted—no one was onto them.

Once again the sinister woman had escaped from justice, but now her new appearance was "blown". In the future they would be looking for Icho Fuji with the same energy as they were looking for Madame Atomos!

Dejected, Madame Atomos slumped down in her seat. She was thinking that before she reappeared, she would have to rebuild her power in her new laboratory. And it would take at least a year to make things perfect...

Five days later Smith and Mie Beffort knew that Icho Fuji and Ida Brown had definitely escaped from the team sent after them. They decided to visit Yosho Akamatsu and tell him the bad news. The Japanese special agent was slowly recovering his health and little else mattered to him. He had to force himself to listen to what Smith was saying. His lack of interest was so glaring that Smith lost his temper.

"Come on, Yosho! Don't tell me that you don't care about Madame Atomos anymore!"

Akamatsu smiled. "That's right, Smith, exactly right. But I'm all worked up about the charming Icho

Fuji. You see, I've just been lying here and I've had a lot of time to think. It's a good thing to do and even in good health we should do more of it."

Beffort snarled, "You've been thinking?"

Akamatsu nodded solemnly. "Yes. And I've come to a very simple conclusion that's been right in front of our noses."

Beffort laughed and leaned forward. "Do tell, Yosho, I'm hanging on every word."

"Me, too," Mie assured him.

Akamatsu sat up and adjusted his pillows. "Madame Atomos is dead. At least since Icho Fuji showed up, but no one, including the A.O.F.M.A., knows about it. Therefore, in order to destroy the Atomos forces for good, all we have to do is make it known that our sinister enemy is dead."

Beffort shrugged his shoulders. "Ridiculous! No one can be so crazy as to take over the projects of Madame Atomos!"

"Icho Fuji did it," Mie reminded him.

"No! I still believe that she's acting under duress," Beffort said.

"I don't agree," Akamatsu declared. "Icho Fuji is the direct successor of Madame Atomos. See, Smith, when she came to Padanaram..."

They discussed it for a long time without coming up with a rational explanation and when they separated, the Atomos mystery was more puzzling than ever. Except now the FBI had a file with the name of Icho Fuji, but with the fingerprints of Madame Atomos. In the future this would surely change the form and feel of the battle against the sinister woman.

François Darnaudet & J.-M. Lofficier:
Au Vent Mauvais...

Somewhere in the U.S.A.., July 1969

> *Et je m'en vais / Au vent mauvais*
> *Qui m'emporte / Deçà, delà,*
> *Pareil à la / Feuille morte.*
> Verlaine
> *Chanson d'Automne.*

The light of the television screen lit the entire room.

The location did not matter. It was an anonymous meeting room of a type found in millions of office buildings throughout the United States. There was a conference table, half-a-dozen leather chairs and four trite seascape paintings on the fake wood-paneled walls.

The television set had been tuned to CBS, where Walter Cronkite had been entertaining viewers with models of the LEM and conversations with Arthur C. Clarke and Robert Heinlein.

It had been a hot day, but now it was night; a rather hot night. The crescent Moon was tantalizingly high in the west. The Moon landing had successfully occurred some six-and-a-half hours earlier. Now they were waiting for the first man to walk on another world.

On the table, quite appropriately, were a bucket of ice with a bottle of champagne and two glasses made of the purest *cristal d'arques*.

There were three people in the room, a man and a woman, sitting across the table, riveted by what was happening on the television screen, and a tall Japanese man in a chauffeur uniform who stood rigidly next to the door.

"Ozu, you may open the bottle of champagne now," said Madame Atomos. Few would have recognized the sworn enemy of America in this stunning young Oriental woman dressed in the latest Fifth Avenue fashion.

Her companion was a dark-haired man, handsome in a way that could only be described as "dangerous." His attire was European in style and he could easily have been taken for one of those European playboys who spent their lives jet setting from Saint-Tropez to Saint-Moritz.

"You will toast with me, *n'est-ce-pas*, Monsieur Zemba?" asked Madame Atomos.

"Naturally, my dear," replied the man, with barely a hint of French accent.

"I believe that, this time, you have outdone your notorious grandfather."

The Frenchman could not keep himself from casting a covetous glance at Madame Atomos' long, shapely legs, alluringly covered by black silk tights, and which she crossed and uncrossed with consummate skill.

Zemba III, or Zemba The Third, as he liked to be called, smiled in self-satisfaction. Yet despite his outward calm, he was actually quite uncomfortable. He had heard of Madame Atomos; her sinister reputation, her obsessive ruthlessness and hatred for all things American had spread far and wide, even amongst the European Underworld.

She had been trying to hire a master-thief, and many in the game had turned her down, despite the truly staggering fortune she had offered.

More than the money, it was the nature of the assignment that had made Zemba III agree to take it. If he succeeded, his reputation would be made. He would no longer be a joke, a comical version of his prestigious grandfather, Gaspard Zemba, who had once been called the Master Criminal of Paris.

Ozu had opened the magnum of champagne in a manner that would not have shamed a sommelier at Maxim's; he was now carefully filling the two glasses.

On the television screen, Cronkite was becoming increasingly emotional. Understandably so, since he had been on the air 27 of the 30 hours it had taken the spacecraft to reach the Sea of Tranquility. The great moment had arrived. Soon, very soon, Neil Armstrong would step out of the LEM and would become the first human to walk on the Moon.

Madame Atomos and Zemba III grabbed their glasses.

"Look! It's happening!" he said.

"That's one small step for a man, one giant leap for mankind."

Armstrong had finally stepped off the lander's ladder. The reception was particularly good and the sound crackled, but it was spectacular nevertheless. Cronkite shed a tear.

"Americans are such children," said Madame Atomos contemptuously.

Zemba III said nothing. He didn't share Madame Atomos' obsession. On the contrary, he was somehow moved by the astounding venture.

"We still have a couple of hours to go, " he observed meekly. "Let us drink to the success of your enterprise."

"It has made you a very rich man," said Madame Atomos.

"For that, too, I am grateful, but now I can tell you: I would have done it for free."

Two hours went by. On the Moon, Buzz Aldrin and Armstrong were drilling core samples, photographing what they saw and collecting rocks. But finally, the moment they had been waiting for came: the planting of the American flag.

"Here it comes," said Zemba III.

Madame Atomos leaned forward to not miss a second of this historical event.

The House and Senate of the United States had stated, "This act was intended as a symbolic gesture of national pride in achievement and was not to be construed as a declaration of national appropriation by claim of sovereignty."

Armstrong grabbed the flag that had been mounted on the left-hand side of the LEM's ladder to make it more easily accessible. To protect it from the temperatures of up to 2,000 F during the 13 seconds of the touchdown, it had been wrapped in an insulating shroud consisting of three layers of stainless steel, Thermoflex and aluminum.

Armstrong began to unfurl the flag by extending the telescoping crossbar and raising it to a position just above 90 degrees. He then lowered it to a position perpendicular to the pole, where a catch prevented the hinge from moving. The upper portion then slipped into the base portion of the flagpole, which had been driven into the ground using a geological hammer.

It was an ordinary 3 x 5 foot nylon flag, which weighed only 9 pounds and 7 ounces.

"It's strange, it looks like it's flying in the breeze," said Zemba III, watching Armstrong salute the Stars and

Stripes. "You don't think this is all a hoax staged some-where in Nevada?"

"No," replied Madame Atomos. "They sew a hem along the top of the flag. A horizontal crossbar gives the illusion that it's flying."

A NASA secretary who had gone to the local Sears department store during her lunch hour purchased the flag for $5.50. Ironically, its insulating shroud cost several thousands of dollars.

"How did you ever manage to steal their flag and replace it with the one I provided?" asked Madame Atomos.

"Like you, I have my secrets," smiled Zemba III. "But if you must know, dear Madame, demonstration tests were performed to make sure that the flag would operate properly. Suffice it to say that the Jack Kinzler, the Chief of Technical Services Division who flew to Kennedy Space Center on June 25 to participate in a mock review of the lunar flag assembly may not have been who everyone else thought he was."

"I see. Very clever indeed."

"Thank you."

The bottle of champagne was now empty, as Zemba III found when he tried to refill his glass one last time.

"I drink to your victory, Madame Atomos. When will the flag now turn into your flag? The Stars & Stripes replaced by 'Hiroshima. Nagasaki. With the compliments of Madame Atomos.' I can't wait to see their faces!"

"It's not going to. Why would I want to do such a silly thing? I am above such petty vanities."

"But when you hired me, you said..."

"I lied. I told you what I thought a Frenchman like yourself would most likely believe."

"But then, why...?"

Zemba III never uttered another word. He collapsed on the table, dead.

"Make sure you remove the bottle and the glasses," instructed Madame Atomos. "The poison I use leaves no trace, but there is no reason to give the FBI any more clues than we have to."

The Frenchman had been right, thought Madame Atomos. It had been a most successful enterprise. She wasn't fooled by Congress' proclamation. Someday, America would colonize the Moon; the Imperialists wouldn't be able to help it. They would go there, build a domed city, a shrine for the site of their first landing, a memorial around their flag so conveniently abandoned on the surface.

And then that flag, in reality *her* flag, would spawn its deadly children and the first colonists would die in excruciating agony,

She had sown the first seeds of her hatred in the cosmos and an ill wind was now waiting amongst the stars.

SF & FANTASY

Henri Allorge. *The Great Cataclysm*
Guy d'Armen. *Doc Ardan: The City of Gold and Lepers*
G.-J. Arnaud. *The Ice Company*
Charles Asselineau. *The Double Life*
Cyprien Bérard. *The Vampire Lord Ruthwen*
Aloysius Bertrand. *Gaspard de la Nuit*
Richard Bessière. *The Gardens of the Apocalypse*
Albert Bleunard. *Ever Smaller*
Félix Bodin. *The Novel of the Future*
Alphonse Brown. *City of Glass; The Conquest of the Air*
André Caroff. *The Terror of Madame Atomos; Miss Atomos; The Return of Madame Atomos; The Mistake of Madame Atomos; The Monsters of Madame Atomos; The Revenge of Madame Atomos; The Resurrection of Madame Atomos*
Louis Boussenard. *The Secrets of Mr. Synthesis*
Félicien Champsaur. *The Human Arrow; Ouha, King of the Apes; Pharaoh's Wife*
Didier de Chousy. *Ignis*
Captain Danrit. *Undersea Odyssey*
C. I. Defontenay. *Star (Psi Cassiopeia)*
Charles Derennes. *The People of the Pole*
Georges Dodds (anthologist). *The Missing Link*
Harry Dickson. *The Heir of Dracula*
Jules Dornay. *Lord Ruthven Begins*
Alfred Driou. *The Adventures of a Parisian Aeronaut*
Sâr Dubnotal *vs. Jack the Ripper*
Alexandre Dumas. *The Return of Lord Ruthven*
Renée Dunan. *Baal*
J.-C. Dunyach. *The Night Orchid; The Thieves of Silence*
Henri Duvernois. *The Man Who Found Himself*
Achille Eyraud. *Voyage to Venus*
Henri Falk. *The Age of Lead*
Paul Féval. *Anne of the Isles; Knightshade; Revenants; Vampire City; The Vampire Countess; The Wandering Jew's Daughter*
Paul Féval, *fils. Felifax, the Tiger-Man*
Charles de Fieux. *Lamékis*
Arnould Galopin. *Doctor Omega; Doctor Omega and the Shadowmen*

Judith Gautier. *Isoline and the Serpent-Flower*
Léon Gozlan. *The Vampire of the Val-de-Grâce*
G.L. Gick. *Harry Dickson and the Werewolf of Rutherford Grange*
Edmond Haraucourt. *Illusions of Immortality*
Nathalie Henneberg. *The Green Gods*
V. Hugo, P. Foucher & P. Meurice. *The Hunchback of Notre-Dame*
Romain d'Huissier. *Hexagon: Dark Matter*
Michel Jeury. *Chronolysis*
Gustave Kahn. *The Tale of Gold and Silence*
Gérard Klein. *The Mote in Time's Eye*
Fernand Kolney. *Love in 5000 Years*
Louis-Guillaume de La Follie. *The Unpretentious Philosopher*
Jean de La Hire. *Enter the Nyctalope; The Nyctalope on Mars; The Nyctalope vs. Lucifer; The Nyctalope Steps In; Night of the Nyctalope*
Etienne-Léon de Lamothe-Langon. *The Virgin Vampire*
André Laurie. *Spiridon*
Gabriel de Lautrec. *The Vengeance of the Oval Portrait*
Alain le Drimeur. *The Future City*
Georges Le Faure & Henri de Graffigny. *The Extraordinary Adventures of a Russian Scientist Across the Solar System* (2 vols.)
Gustave Le Rouge. *The Vampires of Mars; The Dominion of the World* (w/Gustave Guitton) (4 vols.)
Jules Lermina. *Mysteryville; Panic in Paris; To-Ho and the Gold Destroyers; The Secret of Zippelius*
André Lichtenberger. *The Centaurs*
Jean-Marc & Randy Lofficier. *Edgar Allan Poe on Mars; The Katrina Protocol; Pacifica; Robonocchio; Tales of the Shadowmen 1-9*
Xavier Mauméjean. *The League of Heroes*
Joseph Méry. *The Tower of Destiny*
Hippolyte Mettais. *The Year 5865*
Louise Michel. *The Human Microbes; The New World*
Tony Moilin. *Paris in the Year 2000*
José Moselli. *Illa's End*
John-Antoine Nau. *Enemy Force*
Marie Nizet. *Captain Vampire*
C. Nodier, A. Beraud & Toussaint-Merle. *Frankenstein*
Henri de Parville. *An Inhabitant of the Planet Mars*
Gaston de Pawlowski. *Journey to the Land of the 4th Dimension*
Georges Pellerin. *The World in 2000 Years*
Ernest Pérochon. *The Frenetic People*
Pierre Pelot. *The Child Who Walked on the Sky*

J. Polidori, C. Nodier, E. Scribe. *Lord Ruthven the Vampire*
P.-A. Ponson du Terrail. *The Vampire and the Devil's Son; Immortal Woman*
Henri de Régnier. *A Surfeit of Mirrors*
Maurice Renard. *The Blue Peril; Doctor Lerne; The Doctored Man; A Man Among the Microbes; The Master of Light*
Jean Richepin. *The Wing; The Crazy Corner*
Albert Robida. *The Adventures of Saturnin Farandoul; The Clock of the Centuries; Chalet in the Sky*
J.-H. Rosny Aîné. *Helgvor of the Blue River; The Givreuse Enigma; The Mysterious Force; The Navigators of Space; Vamireh; The World of the Variants; The Young Vampire*
Marcel Rouff. *Journey to the Inverted World*
Han Ryner. *The Superhumans*
Brian Stableford. *The New Faust at the Tragicomique;The Empire of the Necromancers (The Shadow of Frankenstein; Frankenstein and the Vampire Countess; Frankenstein in London); Sherlock Holmes & The Vampires of Eternity; The Stones of Camelot; The Wayward Muse.* (anthologist) *The Germans on Venus; News from the Moon; The Supreme Progress; The World Above the World; Nemoville; Investigations of the Future*
Jacques Spitz. *The Eye of Purgatory*
Kurt Steiner. *Ortog*
Eugène Thébault. *Radio-Terror*
C.-F. Tiphaigne de La Roche. *Amilec*
Théo Varlet. *The Golden Rock. The Xenobiotic Invasion; Timeslip Troopers* (w/André Blandin); *The Martian Epic* (w/Octave Joncquel)
Paul Vibert. *The Mysterious Fluid*
Villiers de l'Isle-Adam. *The Scaffold; The Vampire Soul*
Philippe Ward. *Artahe*
Philippe Ward & Sylvie Miller. *The Song of Montségur*

www.ingramcontent.com/pod-product-compliance
Lightning Source LLC
Chambersburg PA
CBHW030245030726
47493CB00023B/592